A SOFT PLACE TO FALL

Tanya Christenson

Red Deer Press

Published in Canada by Red Deer Press, 195 Allstate Parkway, Markham, ON L3R 4T8
Published in the United States by Red Deer Press, 311 Washington Street, Brighton, MA 02135

Red Deer Press acknowledges with thanks the Canada Council for the Arts and the Ontario Arts Council for
their support of our publishing program. We acknowledge the financial support of the
Government of Canada through the Canada Book Fund (CBF) for our publishing activities.

ONTARIO ARTS COUNCIL
CONSEIL DES ARTS DE L'ONTARIO
an Ontario government agency
un organisme du gouvernement de l'Ontario

Canada Council   Conseil des arts
for the Arts   du Canada

Edited for the Press by Peter Carver
Text and cover design by Tanya Montini
Proudly printed in Canada by Avant Imaging & Integrated Media

Library and Archives Canada Cataloguing in Publication
Title: A soft place to fall / Tanya Christenson.
Names: Christenson, Tanya, author.
Identifiers: Canadiana 20210209771 | ISBN 9780889956384 (softcover)
Classification: LCC PS8605.H739 S64 2021 | DDC jC813/.6—dc23

Publisher Cataloging-in-Publication Data (U.S.)
Names: Christenson, Tanya, author.
Title: A Soft Place to Fall / Tanya Christenson.
Description: Markham, Ontario : Red Deer Press, 2021.| Summary: "Creighton
Fischer is one of twelve teens finding themselves in an alternate school in a
small BC town, with a teacher who cares for and listens to them. But when
Ms. Hay goes on maternity leave, the kids feel abandoned, and things fall apart.
Somehow Creighton and Carin, the one girl in the class, manage to find their
way and emerge triumphant-- Provided by publisher.
Identifiers: ISBN 978-0-88995-638-4 (paperback)
Subjects: LCSH Alternative schools—Juvenile fiction. | Teachers – Juvenile
fiction. | Teenagers with disabilities – Juvenile fiction. | BISAC: YOUNG
ADULT FICTION / General.
Classification: LCC PZ7.1C575So |DDC 813.6 – dc23

Red Deer Press
www.reddeerpress.com

To Brad,
For being my soft place to fall

"A deep sense of love and belonging is an irreducible need of all people. We are biologically, cognitively, physically, and spiritually wired to love, to be loved, and to belong. When those needs are not met, we don't function as we were meant to. We break. We fall apart. We numb. We ache. We hurt others. We get sick."

–Brené Brown, research professor, University of Houston

BEFORE

We rolled into some little town the day before my fifth birthday, and the guys set up rides late into the night. I was the first to rise and wake Mom up. She sat on the trailer steps, wearing fluffy winter boots and a pink robe. She held her cigarette in one hand, while clutching a blue mug filled with coffee. I was bundled in my red snowsuit. She hummed "Happy Birthday" while I played with my cars on the ground in front of her, scraping the piles of frozen dirt together to form roads. I watched as she inhaled her cigarette. Her eyes closed and she raised her head, pulling her cheeks in tightly, before releasing a fume of smoke into the cold air. Mom took her last sip of coffee, which meant we could start our walk around the empty fairground. I liked the quiet of these winter mornings, just me and Mom, while the carnival slept.

Mom and Dad met when she was nineteen. Every May long weekend, the fair passed through Breton for Lilac Festival. Dad was one of the guys who traveled with the carnival—a carnie. He'd made his way around Canada with the carnival since he left home at fifteen, doing pretty much everything, from restocking Porta Potties with toilet paper to selling corndogs at the concession. When he and Mom talked for the first time, he was running the Zipper, still working his way up the ranks at the age of twenty-one.

Mom grew up in Breton. I guess she was one of the girls who hung out with the carnies each year, and their fling that May long weekend led to me. When she found out she was pregnant, she quit her waitressing job at Barkley's Bar & Grill, and joined Dad in the parade of trucks and trailers that moved from town to town. My destiny was decided. My first home was a carnie trailer, and I spent twelve years on the road.

Mom was kind of a celebrity at the carnival. One night, when all the guys were sitting around the trailer, she was singing along to one of Dad's cds. After the first verse, the talking stopped.

"Gracie Rae, you ought to make some cash with that

voice of yours," one of the guys said. "You sound like an angel!"

Dad's buddies persuaded her to stand out front of the fairgrounds with a bowl, and Mom nervously did. It wasn't long before money overflowed, and people came back the next day for more. Eventually, the carnival sold tickets, and people showed up just to hear her sing.

My fifth birthday was on Friday, February 24, 1989. My party started when the carnie guys woke up. I opened the tiny trailer fridge to peek at the cake Mom and I had baked the night before. I slammed the fridge door and accidentally dropped my cars on the floor, hoping Dad would get up earlier than usual. Finally, Mom let me take him a mug of coffee. I tucked his cigarette above my ear, like I watched Dad do, and held his lighter tightly between my teeth as I carefully balanced the coffee, spilling with each small step. He sat up sleepily and rescued the mug from my shaky five-year-old hands. I put the cigarette in his mouth, and he held it forward for me to light.

"I'm five today, Daddy," I reminded him.

"You're right, son, it's your birthday," he said, laughing as he scuffed my hair up with his free hand. "What you wanna do for your birthday?" he asked, blowing a perfect circle of smoke toward the roof.

"We're going to have a party, Daddy. When all the guys wake up, they're invited. Me and Momma made a cake last night."

"A cake? Well, it will be a party then, won't it?" Dad gave me another head scuff.

I waited for the carnival to come alive. By noon, Mom was banging on the trailer doors and yelling at Dad's buddies to hurry up. They dragged their lawn chairs over, one by one, till most of them were gathered in a circle in front of our trailer. Just as Mom headed in to get the cake, Bruno said, "First things first, Gracie. The little man's gotta light us up."

It was my job to light their cigarettes. I was their entertainment, the only kid living with the crew. They held their smokes between their teeth, and I made my way around the circle with a lighter.

Mom stepped out of the trailer with the cake, placing it on the small folding table in front of me, and everyone sang "Happy Birthday." Then I opened my Spiderman pajamas.

I didn't know this would be my very last birthday cake until I turned fifteen. I never imagined it was the last time

I'd ever bake with Mom.

That July, the carnival offered Dad the Manager of Operations position, which meant we wouldn't have to travel with the fair anymore. He'd divide his time between the four different units in Canada, and make sure things were running smoothly. We'd live three months in one place, before moving on to the next central office. The constant life on the road would slow down.

"It'll be good for Creighton," I heard Dad tell Mom. "He can start Kindergarten in the fall. He can go to school a few months in each city, get to see the whole country. And you can line up gigs wherever we are. You'll be a celebrity across Canada before you know it, Gracie."

Dad slapped Mom on the bum. He was laughing. Mom smiled. Her face was red.

"Our very own Gracie Rae. And the best part of this job means we can get out of this trailer. They'll line up a rental for us wherever we go."

Dad took the promotion and, a week later, we were living in a tiny apartment in a town across the country.

The new job changed everything. Mom worked late most nights, singing, just as Dad knew she would. I usually woke up to find him at the kitchen table, having his smoke and coffee, freshly showered, in his white T-shirt and blue jeans, hair tightly slicked back, reading the paper and listening to the news in the background. I'd climb onto his lap, still rubbing my eyes, and sit until he was done. I loved the smell of his aftershave, when he'd gently rub his face up against mine. When he pressed his cigarette butt firmly into the ashtray, it was time for our breakfast. He'd lift me down, so I could grab the box of cereal from the bottom cupboard, and he'd reach for our bowls. I was in charge of filling them, while Dad got the milk from the fridge to pour on top. He read the paper while we ate and, at seven, I was allowed to change the channel on the TV to *Alvin and the Chipmunks*. I'd know when Mom was home 'cause Dad would grumble, as he moved her leather purse and jean jacket off the kitchen table, to hang them on the hook by the door, so we could eat our breakfast.

This life lasted just less than a month. It's what I remember of Mom, until the August morning when Dad found the letter on the table.

I walked into the small kitchen of our apartment, wearing my Spiderman pajamas. Dad wasn't sitting at the table in his usual spot. He was standing, staring at a letter that leaned against Mom's mug. I watched from the doorway. He breathed deeply, scrunched up the paper, and tossed it on the ground. He kicked the table, and rummaged angrily through the pile of loose cds, before forcing one into the small stereo. Willie Nelson's "Always on My Mind" started playing.

I backed up into the tiny bedroom, crouched in the corner, and watched Dad. He ran his fingers through his dark hair, while pacing back and forth. He pounded his fist on the counter. He kicked the crumpled letter on the floor, and then picked it up to read again. There was no leather purse or jean jacket on the table, just Mom's coffee cup.

We didn't have cereal that morning. I didn't watch *Alvin and the Chipmunks*. Dad eventually noticed me huddled in the corner of the apartment bedroom. Lifting me onto his lap, he sat down on the edge of the double bed. He pulled me in close to his body and kissed the back of my head. "It's just gonna be you and me now, son. Looks like your momma had to go."

"Why did Momma leave, Daddy?"

He shrugged. "Don't know, boy, I just don't know. Your momma didn't really say."

I sat there on Dad's lap, afraid to move. I could hear his quiet crying as he listened to the song play, over and over and over again. It must have been on REPEAT, 'cause "Always on My Mind" is what I remember about that day.

He finally put me down and stood on the tiny deck to have a smoke. I climbed into their bed. I held onto Mom's pillow and breathed in her perfume. I could still hear her singing me to sleep, sliding her fingers behind my ears, ensuring each strand of hair was tightly tucked. I could see the long strands of her blond hair that were left behind on her pillow. The framed picture of me and Mom that sat on her bedside table was gone. My little mind told me she would be back. Her jean jacket and leather purse would be on the table the next day, like it always was after she worked late.

But I was wrong.

She just disappeared that August morning. Gracie Rae Waters was gone.

CHAPTER 1

Before Mom left, I had been excited about kindergarten. She talked about it all the time, telling me I would be going to three different schools a year, and how cool it would be, having friends across the country. But I didn't start school that September. Dad never registered me. He wasn't coping too well after Mom left. I tagged along with him, driving here and there, sitting in his office, or fixing rides at the shop.

At five, I didn't know my alphabet, but I could fix a Zipper ride's brake system when a seal gave way, and rebuild a caliper set. I could remove a Bellville spring, Wedge ring, and O-ring from a compensator assembly piston by myself. I took out the bleeder screws when Dad told me to, and passed him a 7/16″ socket and ratchet or box-end wrench when he put out his hand.

I could also cook up a box of mac and cheese, or boil up noodle soup for supper, because every Thursday, it was my night to cook. Then we'd eat in front of the TV.

Dad had never done the laundry, but I had learned from helping Mom. I threw our greasy clothes in the washing machine every single Wednesday and Sunday, dumped one scoop of powdery soap on top, before turning the dial to the little arrow. When the machine rocked itself to a stop, I put everything in the dryer. Dad sorted our clothes into two piles, and I stuffed mine into my dresser.

Every night, I gave my teeth a quick brush, like Mom taught me, then put on my Spiderman pajamas, until they became too small to squeeze into. Dad stood at the bedroom door and said the same thing: "Night, my boy, dream well," before heading back to his old recliner. I closed my eyes and sang Mom's songs to myself—what I could remember of them, anyway. "Night, Momma," I said, wondering if she was thinking about me.

Every few months, we packed up and moved to a different apartment or house in another city, to line up the next carnival unit. When I turned six, Dad's secretary said he better get me in school, or he'd get himself in trouble. Starting school a year late didn't help me much over the years. I was tall and skinny for my age, and also the new kid who was older than everyone else. Whenever Dad had a travel day, I missed school, making it tough to settle anywhere.

Without Mom around, Dad figured things out as best he could, never saying much of anything. Over the years, he signed permission slips for fieldtrips when I asked him, and gave me money when activities needed to be paid for. He took me shopping for school clothes, and stood in the aisle as I picked out the basics that I thought I'd need. He shook his head or gave a nod when I stepped out of the change room; then he paid for the items at the counter. We stopped at the gas station for a slushy every Friday. He threw a peanut butter sandwich, cookie, and apple into a brown bag each morning for me to take to school, and every so often, he told me to take a shower.

With Mom gone, this is how we lived, just me and Dad.

In Grade 6, I arrived home from school one day to find a present on the doorstep of our rental house. The butterflies in my stomach told me it was from Mom. I hoped there was a letter explaining why she left, maybe a message saying she was coming back. But there was nothing other than a tiny card that read, "To Creighton—Love, your Momma" stuck to the top of the small gift. I could barely untie the string, shaking, as I frantically ripped off the blue paper to find a red velvet box. Inside was a silver chain with a charm attached, a little circle with a cross at the bottom. I had no idea why, after so many years, she'd decided to torment me with a present and not stay to see me. I searched all over the neighborhood that day, rode for hours in a panic, desperately hoping to find her, but she was nowhere.

Dad arrived home that evening, and I was crying on the couch. He could see the necklace in my hand, the blue paper I had ripped off the velvet box, and the little card on the coffee table in front of me. He picked it up to read.

Dad was still for a moment, staring at the words. "Where did you get this?" he said.

I didn't reply.

"CREIGHTON!" he said again, sounding angry. "I said, where did you get this? Did you see your mother?" He ran his fingers through his hair, slicking it back, moving closer to me with serious eyes.

"No!" I said, wiping my nose with my sleeve. "It was

just on the front step when I got home." I threw my head onto one of the cushions and turned away from him.

Dad sat down on the arm of the couch and pulled me up to face him. "That's all there was? Just this card and necklace? Nothing else?"

I shook my head.

I could see Dad's eyes tear up as he re-read the small white card, before placing it back down. He took the necklace from my hand and stared at the charm. His chin quivered, as he struggled to open the clasp with his large, shaky fingers. As soon as he'd placed it around my neck, he turned away and bit at his fist.

"What, Dad? What is it?" I asked.

He ignored me.

Dad grabbed the card off the coffee table. He scrunched it in his hand and chucked it against the wall. He kicked the doorframe, shoved the screen door open, and stomped onto the small deck. Pacing around, he pulled his pack of cigarettes from his shirt pocket, reached for the lighter, and lit a smoke.

"Dad? You okay? What? What's the matter?" I called out.

I could see him sitting on the front step, his elbows resting on his knees, as he inhaled deeply.

I picked up my crumpled card and tried to smooth the wrinkles, before opening the screen door.

"Dad, why are you so upset?"

He would not talk. He just sat there, finishing his smoke. And then he snapped, "Leave it, Creighton. It's done! Just leave it now. It doesn't matter anymore."

I stood in front of the bathroom mirror, rubbing the shiny charm between my fingers, confused. It was a reminder that I was abandoned, even though I knew I would never take it off. Had Mom made a special trip? Did she live around here now? She'd told me once, if we were ever apart, to look up at the sky and find Venus. We'd both be staring at the stars and feel closer. Was she preparing me? Did she know she'd leave?

I walked to my bedroom, slammed the door, and cranked up the music. I wanted my mom, not a necklace.

I learned from Dad's rage on this day in Grade 6, seven years after she left, that Mom was something I should never talk about.

CHAPTER 2

Mrs. Fitzgerald scanned the class list to find my name. "This is ... um ... Creighton, everyone. Creighton? Is that right? What an unusual name."

I stood in front of my Grade 7 class, shaking, as my new teacher attempted to introduce me. It was my third school that year, since Dad was the Manager of Operations and we moved every few months, so he could set up the next carnival unit. Fairburn Elementary was by far the worst school I had attended. Luckily, it was the end of March, so I'd only have to deal with Mrs. Fitzgerald for three months.

Looking toward the perfect rows of desks, she continued, "Grade 7 students, please welcome your new classmate to our school." She turned toward me. "I will have to see what I can gather for you, since it's already the final term and there's not much left." I could see she was annoyed. She put the class list back on her pile of papers and managed to find a small desk. I was used to slumping in the leftover school furniture they dragged out of storage.

Aside from Mrs. Fitzgerald being the worst teacher, it was the year that Carlos Gromson entered my world.

Carlos had dark greasy hair that stuck out the sides of his black hoodie. His skin was white and pasty, with unhealed sores all around his mouth. Acne scars signaled a battle he had lost all too often, and his Guns N' Roses hoodie pressed tightly against the rolls of skin that hung over his ripped jeans. A heavy chain dangled from his pocket, pulling his pants down way below his waist. I could see the small black skull, a charm dangling from the chain. The soles of his black runners had separated from the tops. White socks, stained brown, hung out the front of his shoes. A bad smell seeped from his overweight body.

On my first day in Mrs. Fitzgerald's class, she led us down the hall for PE. Carlos jumped up and hit the top of each doorframe as we walked. He kicked the open lockers and laughed when they slammed shut. Some students were working on posters on the hallway floor. The rest of us walked around them, but Carlos stepped right in the middle of the papers and kicked the felt pens. He cut across the stairs and slid down the banister, then lunged over the bottom four steps.

Mrs. Fitzgerald looked back toward him. She pushed her glasses in place. She had a large brown mole on the edge of her lip that she rubbed nervously. But as soon as she turned her back, Carlos left the line and headed in a different direction.

Mrs. Fitzgerald didn't seem to notice that Carlos hadn't arrived in the gym with the rest of the class, until she lined us up to make dodgeball teams. Her eyes darted around frantically. She rubbed her fingers together, in between pushing her glasses higher on her nose and rubbing her mole. Her panicked look was interrupted when the gym door crashed opened and swung against the wall. Carlos stood there, eyeing the cart filled with Nerf balls. Mrs. Fitzgerald clutched her whistle, which hung on the gold chain around her neck. Ignoring her instructions, he grabbed a ball from the cart and threw it toward us, laughing. We ducked to dodge it, as he grabbed another one to fire off.

"Carlos!" she shouted. "Carlos Gromson, we aren't touching the equipment yet. Carlos, look at your classmates. See how nicely they're standing in a line?"

He didn't respond.

One of his stray balls hit me right in the chest. I grabbed it. I felt my knuckles tighten. I stared at Carlos, shaking my head.

Mrs. Fitzgerald cleared her throat. Carlos glared at me. She cleared her throat a second time, and tried again to number us off for the game, saying nothing about the ball that hit me.

I lowered it to the ground and held it securely between my feet. Everyone stared.

When the game finally began, Carlos threw every ball straight toward me, and I dodged them as best I could. And then he came from behind and grabbed my T-shirt collar.

"Get Mr. Harvey!" I heard Mrs. Fitzgerald say to someone. "Quickly, run and get him."

"Why d'you keep lookin' at me, freak?" Carlos said, staring into my face. "You've been lookin' at me since the moment you walked into this school."

The chain around my neck tightened, because it was caught in my twisted shirt as he shoved me along. I swung my fist back and punched him. He stumbled into the cart of Nerf balls. No way would I let him break Mom's necklace.

Carlos breathed in deeply. He looked red. He staggered toward me. The gym was silent, except for the sound of Mrs. Fitzgerald's whistle. Everyone stared. She blew it several times, hoping it would help regain control.

Just as Carlos's fist struck me across the jaw, Mr. Harvey, the principal, arrived.

As we sat in the office, telling our stories, I realized there was no justice when it came to Carlos Gromson.

"He's always staring at me, giving me the eye," Carlos said. "Then he just up and shoved me into the storage cart, punched me right in the face. Guy doesn't even know me."

"Creighton," the principal said, turning toward me, "at Fairburn Elementary, we have a Code of Conduct. There is zero tolerance for any form of physical contact. Is Carlos right? Did you punch him?"

"Y ... yeah, I did. But he ... he kept on throwing balls right at me," I replied.

"That's the game," Carlos interrupted. "That's what you do in Dodgeball—you throw balls at people. I'm not gonna just stand there and let some dude punch me in the face. Obviously, I'm gonna swing back. Self-defense!"

"I understand this is your first day, Creighton. You need to think of the reputation you are choosing for yourself." He shook his head. "I'm going to give your parents a call, let them know what happened today, and I'll leave it at that. Tonight, I want you to think about the kind of reputation you would like to have here at Fairburn, and see if we can have a fresh start. Now, can you boys shake hands? Can we choose to get along?"

"Yeah," Carlos said, looking back and forth at us. "If he stops picking fights, I guess, stops staring me down all the time."

We shook hands and the principal walked us back to class.

Neither of us said a thing.

Mrs. Fitzgerald was standing at the chalkboard, talking about how to convert improper fractions to mixed numbers, something I knew I'd never understand. I tuned her out right away. I was used to tuning teachers out, since I knew I wasn't staying long.

I grabbed a piece of paper from my desk and started sketching. That's what I did to pass the time in school. Carlos Gromson. I figured I'd draw him.

The lesson dragged on. I noticed the edge of my desk,

where scissors had gouged out a hole. I stared at it closely. It was the deepest one I had seen. I'd sat in many leftover desks, and they all had the same things in common. I knew the force some kid had used to claim this space. The carved letters on the top of the desk caught my eye. I traced them with my finger, and followed the chiseled groove formed by a compass, used for nothing other than destruction. DALLAS. The kid who'd sat in this same small desk, before my time, had tuned the world out to get through another day, just like me.

I reached into my hoodie pocket and pulled out my penknife. I dragged it deeply through the laminate surface, carving my name below his: CREIGTON FISCHER 1998. I made my mark in another Canadian city. Mrs. Fitzgerald didn't notice. I didn't exist to her.

She came around to collect our Math. I hadn't started. I quickly turned my sketch of Carlos over, and slipped the paper into the pile for marking, so she wouldn't notice my unfinished work.

That evening, Dad and I were watching TV, eating mashed potatoes with a can of chili poured on top. He mumbled something about the call he'd received from the school principal.

I shrugged. I almost told him that I'd saved my necklace from Carlos Gromson, but stopped. Dad wasn't listening.

I hated my three months at that school with Mrs. Fitzgerald, and was relieved when the end of June arrived. I figured I wouldn't have to deal with Carlos Gromson again.

But I was wrong.

CHAPTER 3

On my last day of Grade 7, I walked down the cracked sidewalk, and was surprised to see Dad sitting on the cement steps in front of our rental house in Fairburn. The lawn mower was out, so I knew he had at least contemplated cutting the grass, which had now taken over the abandoned flowerbeds. His white T-shirt was tossed to the side, and his skin was sweaty from the sweltering June heat. His dark hair, which he carefully slicked back each morning, had fallen to the side. I dropped my BMX on the lawn and rummaged through my backpack, searching for the large brown envelope.

"IIere! Got something for you," I said, tossing it onto his lap before continuing into the house. The broken screen swung back and forth as the door closed behind me. I dumped my backpack on the dryer, and walked into the kitchen to grab a cold pop from the fridge. Dad was still reading my report card when I plunked down beside him, pulling my T-shirt off and throwing it onto his.

He didn't say a word. Then again, Dad never said much.

Finally, he took a sip of beer, and inhaled the remainder of his cigarette longer than usual, before pressing the butt firmly into the rusted coffee can on the step. He fumbled the report card back into the envelope, leaving his greasy prints on it. Then he turned toward me.

"Think it's time we settle, Creighton, buy a house, stay put, stop this moving all over the country. You're headin' to high school in September. Don't think all this travel's been good for you." He slapped the envelope on my lap and crunched the beer can in his hand.

Dad was trim and muscular, even though he wasn't a really big man. He'd put in a hard day's work, then come home, shower the grease off his body, and take it easy for the rest of the night. He thrived on his down time, which pretty much meant drinking beer in front of the TV. Taking care of the house was not a priority.

He turned to open the screen door. It stuck, so he punched it hard as he pulled on the handle. Surprised at what I'd heard, I got up to follow. "You'd give up the carnival, Dad?"

He muttered something, still holding onto the door handle. I moved closer.

"Was thinking about going to Breton. It's only twenty-five minutes away from here. Cheaper real estate than Fairburn—might be something I can afford."

"Breton? Mom's town? Where you guys met?" I was surprised Dad would want to go there.

He ignored the question. "They were talking about me takin' over Distribution, anyway, instead of managing the whole operation. I'm gettin' tired of moving around. I'd still have the odd trip to drive a ride up, or deliver parts sometimes, but I'd be workin' a lot more here in the Fairburn office, making sure all the carnival units get the parts they need, you know?"

Before the door swung shut behind him, I stopped it with my foot and stood in the entrance.

"You're fourteen now, old enough to be on your own for short bits," Dad continued, as he kicked the fridge closed with his foot, while balancing two more beer cans, one on top of the other. "Just figured it would be good in a smaller town, staying in one place, not missing so much school, no more changing schools every few months." He cracked the top beer open. "Why don't you mow that lawn, since you got the whole summer now!"

He assumed his position in the old recliner in the corner of the living room, and started switching through the channels on the TV. I knew that was the end of any sort of conversation.

I didn't know what having a home would look like. I couldn't imagine the feeling of staying in one school, in one town, around the same people. It didn't matter, though. Dad's mind was made up. Maybe we were moving to Breton because my final report card stated that attendance was an issue, and I would not be able to move on to Junior High for my Grade 8 year. There were so many "gaps in my learning" that I needed "extra support to help meet the diverse challenges" I faced.

When Dad was called into the school to talk about my report card, they told him an alternate school would be a better fit for me. I had no idea what this meant. It seemed unfair that someone like Mrs. Fitzgerald, the Grade 7 teacher I despised, could send me to a school for "challenged students." She didn't even know me. But Dad told me there was nothing I could do. Lane Oslo School of

Educational Reform, located in the small town of Breton, is where I'd be going in September. And really, I was used to change. Why would this place be any different?

Once Dad made his decision to leave Fairburn and buy a house in Breton, everything came together quickly. He accepted the job as Manager of Distribution for the carnival, which meant we no longer had to move every three months. And exactly one month later, we arrived in Breton.

Dad pulled up to the curb in front of our new house. "This is it, son! Needs a little work here and there, but it's ours. Never thought I'd see the day." The small front yard was trimmed with what used to be a white picket fence. There wasn't much paint left on the posts, and many were missing. Dad climbed out of the truck and opened the wooden gate, which aligned with the cracked cement path leading to the front door. He struggled with the latch, shaking the gate, when it suddenly broke off in his hands. I grabbed the other side to help, but the loose posts dropped, one by one, onto the cement.

"Well, damn. Guess we really don't need a gate, anyway." Dad kicked the pieces to the side.

While he unlocked the front door, I stood on the steps behind him, scanning the yard. The house had been vacant for a while, and the early July heat had browned the grass. The rose bushes at the front of the house were dead.

I imagined what it once looked like. I could smell the freshly mowed lawn that bordered the garden. Lush yellow roses reached the window trims, which were now chipped, awaiting a fresh coat of paint. Inside the house, I breathed in the musty odor of a wet basement. Several tiles on the entrance floor were missing, and tiny black spots of moldy residue sat along the window trim.

"Isn't this great, Creigh?" Dad said, as he patted my shoulder with a beaming smile.

I kept walking until I found the smaller of the two bedrooms. The walls were a pale pink, and the My Little Pony curtains dangled crookedly along the curtain rod, which had loosened on one side. I stood at the window that looked out into the backyard. The small garage must have been the selling feature for Dad, a place to tinker on his truck and avoid all household duties. There was an overflowing compost bin in the corner, made with worn pallets of wood, heaped high with grass-cuttings, accumulated from years of mowing.

"Ya gotta see this, Creigh! Come check out this porch," Dad hollered eagerly.

Outside the back door was a screened-in porch. It was surprisingly intact, unlike the rest of the house. Maybe someone had done a small upgrade. Built-in benches lined the edges, and the green indoor-outdoor carpet was in good shape. Dad pulled out a cigarette, lit it, and sprawled out on a bench. He sighed happily, something I'd never seen him do before. He inhaled deeply and closed his eyes.

"Well, Creigh, we got ourselves a house! This is it, our very own place. No more moving, son. It's a block from your school, a quick bike ride to town, maybe a thirty-minute drive to Fairburn when I have an office day, but that's nothin'. Never thought this time would come," Dad said, shaking his head.

"It's good, Dad, real good," I replied, trying to convince myself.

Even though I felt nervous about never moving again, and I knew Dad would do little to fix the house up, he looked so relaxed. I sat on the bench across from him, and imagined Dad standing on the landing at the bottom of the steps, barbecuing pork chops. I could see the beer in his hand, a cigarette hanging out the side of his mouth, while he mumbled and danced away to one of his George Straight CDS. Maybe it would be okay.

CHAPTER 4

I never appreciated Dad's company before, but that August, I missed him, since he was working a lot in the Fairburn office. He thought it was a good thing, me being on my own. I'd "learn some independence," he figured. But it was a really lonely month.

I filled my summer days by exploring. Breton had one main street, and mountains surrounded the small town. I could jump on my bike and find a new trail in whichever direction I turned. I imagined Mom as a kid, riding the same streets with her brothers.

After a week, I discovered the best swimming hole. As I rode along the highway, I noticed the lines of parked cars on either side of the road. I stopped at the bridge, where a bunch of kids balanced on the railing in swimsuits. One by one, they jumped into the river below, then followed the well-worn grassy trail back up to the bridge. In the distance, I could see patches of fine sand in between the rocks and cottonwood trees, every small area of beach claimed by blankets, towels, and umbrellas.

I stood with one foot on the ground, balancing my bike between my legs. One kid kept staring at me. He was wearing cut-off jeans shorts and a pair of old running shoes. When he climbed up the path for the third time, and noticed me watching, he struck up our first conversation.

"Ya gonna jump?" he asked.

"How deep is it down there?"

"I dunno, ten feet, maybe. Deep enough. Jump!"

The boy, who looked about my age, landed in the water below. He flicked his wet hair as he surfaced, and looked up to see if I was following. I rested my bike against the side of the bridge and peeled off my shirt. I was about to take off my running shoes, but he stopped me. "Leave your shoes on. The rocks. There's a lot of rocks in here!" he hollered up to me.

I looked around at the others, realizing everyone had some sort of shoes or sandals on. Guess that's how it worked at the river. I climbed over the railing, just like the others were doing, and jumped, landing a few feet away from him. By the time I came up for a breath, he was laughing, kind of hysterically, excited that I'd followed.

"Ha-ha!" he shrieked. "You did it!" he said as we swam to the shore, side by side.

This was the beginning of my summer with Schooner.

Schooner was a blond kid, almost ginger-haired, with a ton of freckles. His shoulders were red and scabbed up from permanent sunburn. I could see each bone in his ribcage, and his concave stomach barely supported the light blue underwear that rested far above his waterlogged shorts.

After we jumped a second time, Schooner began to talk. He looked directly at my face, barely blinking. He leaned in hard, and his blue eyes had a piercing stare. I backed up, feeling like there needed to be a bit more space between us, but Schooner stepped forward again.

"You must be new here, hey?" Schooner asked.

"Yeah, only been here a week. Just moved from Fairburn."

"Schooner. They call me Schooner," he said, reaching out to shake my hand. "Everyone hangs out here. A bunch of us come down every day. You should start coming. The river's the best!"

"Nice to meet you. I'm Creigh. Creighton Fischer."

Most people move their eyes around, or look away or up or down when they talk. Not Schooner. He'd ask a question, and I'd answer and look away. When I turned back, he'd still be staring, with a small smile on his face.

"What about you? You been in Breton long? You live around here?" I said, a bit uncomfortably, hoping he'd turn his eyes in another direction.

And Schooner did. As soon as I asked him a question, he turned away.

"Come on, Creigh, let's go for another jump," he said, moving toward the bridge.

We'd jump off the bridge, body surf down a way, then swim to the side and sit on the rocky beach for a bit. Schooner talked steadily while we tossed rocks in, always trying to hit the small island halfway across the river.

"Yeah, me and my buddies do this all the time. We come here and hang out and do stuff, ya know. Last week there was a grizzly, though, right there on that island, so we were trying to hit it with rocks."

"You guys saw a grizzly and stuck around?"

"Yeah, there're grizzlies all over—you'll get used to it," he said.

It was late in the afternoon and the river was clearing. A few cars were left along the highway, and parents were picking kids up, one by one. I knew Dad wouldn't be home till late. The sun had moved, leaving us in the shade. We sat down for a break and, for a moment, Schooner was silent. No more talk of bears or the pet seagull he told me he had. I turned to look, assuming he'd be staring at me, but he was still, quiet, looking ahead with a serious expression.

"When you gotta be home?" I asked Schooner.

"Come on, one more jump!" he replied, getting up to head toward the bridge, ignoring my question.

I felt done with jumping and being wet, but figured I better join him. We stood on the roadside, leaning over the bridge railing, staring down at the water below. The highway was quiet. The beach had emptied, and I could see the belongings left behind after a sunny day at the river. A hat, some towels here and there, pop cans, a flipper that must have dropped from someone's bag, a baby's soother. Schooner didn't talk. He rested his arms on the railing, like he was in deep thought. He wasn't staring at me, and didn't have that eager little smile he seemed to wear all day long. Crows had found their place on the beach, fighting for the remnants of food left behind, and that was the only sound, aside from the rushing water.

Schooner didn't have any friends. I realized this as we stood there in silence. Not one person had said a word to him all day long, and it was a place where everybody knew everyone. I didn't believe he and his buddies saw a grizzly. In fact, I didn't think there were any "buddies." I knew I didn't have much in common with this kid, except for one thing. We were alone when everyone else went home to their families.

Every day, Schooner and I biked to the river. But first, we'd stop at the rail yard to wait for the ten o'clock train. Schooner had a secret obsession with trains. I figured this out when the temperature reached thirty-two degrees Celsius by ten o'clock one Monday morning, and the train still hadn't arrived. Both of us sat on the bank, sweat dripping from our bodies, but he refused to leave.

More than the train itself, Schooner was fixated on boxcar graffiti.

"Look at it, Creigh. Check it out. Can you believe that tag? That's the best one I think I seen. Holy man, Creigh, they did that in, like, five minutes." He'd comment on every boxcar that passed by.

The graffiti on the boxcars was pretty cool. But after looking at cars over and over again, every single day, it never excited me much.

"Remember that one? I swear that car was here last week. Check this out. This one's new."

After the train passed through Breton, we'd finally ride to the river.

Schooner and I collected bottles from the weekend river parties, and about halfway through the day, we'd ride our bikes into town for a pop and sandwich from the gas station. This was our routine, because everything with Schooner was that way. When we had extra cash, we'd splurge on a double pack of bubble gum, Schooner's favorite.

Even though his constant talking made me a little crazy, I liked the company. I just agreed, and listened, and knew not to ask him questions, 'cause I learned really quickly that Schooner would never tell me a thing about his own life. We were two totally different people, yet we had one huge thing in common. We were both alone, trying to find our way in the world. We could stay at the river till dark and nobody cared. Although we never said it, I knew we both wished we had someone who was worried we'd be late.

CHAPTER 5

The late August mornings made me feel anxious. They were a reminder that school was just around the corner. But this year felt different. I wanted to get on with things. I wanted routine, a place to go each day. And I liked living in Breton. It was small, but close enough to Fairburn if we needed anything in the city. I could get around on my bike when Dad was gone. I liked the mountains surrounding the small town, and I liked the fact Mom grew up here. And it was so near the river, where I spent my days. The idea of home was starting to seem more real.

Dad gave me a ride to school on the first day, even though it was only a block from our house.

The alternate school was a small building next door to Breton's high school. We pulled up and I sat in the truck for a bit. The smoke pit was right between the two buildings, so there were a lot of kids gathered around.

We sat in front of the small two-room building, and I read the sign: "Lane Oslo School of Educational Reform." Underneath, in smaller print, it said: "Building bridges for ALL students." I laughed to myself. I was officially becoming a L.O.S.E.R.

I got out and shut the door. Then opened the door again. "Thanks for the ride, Dad."

He nodded and drove off.

To avoid making an uncomfortable entrance into the classroom, I saw the *Boys* sign on a door and walked in. I washed my hands, because I didn't know what else to do. The smell of stale urine wafted over me. I stared at the graffiti on the walls. There was a hole in the drywall, as if a fist had made contact, and one of the mirrors was missing. I finally walked into the open classroom. The teacher moved toward me, smiling.

"Why, you must be Creighton? It's nice to finally put a face to a name. I'm Ms. Hayworth, your teacher this year."

Ms. Hayworth reached out her hand and gently took mine. Her clasp was firm and sincere, as she placed her other hand on my shoulder and patted it. She smiled.

She knew my name. I took a breath, relaxed a little. Ms. Hayworth seemed genuine, real, unlike Mrs. Fitzgerald, who had made no attempt to get to know me.

"I'm so excited to have you here, Creighton." Ms. Hayworth interrupted my thought. "You've traveled so much. What an adventurous life you've had. So much to share with all of us."

She seemed to know things about me.

"Creighton, I have to tell you, I found a drawing in your file. I have an old frame and was hoping for permission to hang it by the sink. I've been dying for you to explain it to me. It's a fascinating sketch. You're quite an artist."

I wanted to see the picture. What sketch did I do? Ms. Hayworth led me to her desk where she had set the drawing.

There it was. The sketch I'd done of Carlos Gromson. I remembered handing it in to Mrs. Fitzgerald, hoping she'd think it was my math. It was a picture of a ferocious bear standing on its hind legs. Its teeth were bared and claws outstretched. In the stomach of the bear, was a small jail cell with a lock on the door. Inside the cell was a boy clinging onto the bars, staring outward. In the distance was a key, dangling from a large, circular chain, unreachable to the caged boy, who stared at it longingly.

I had drawn the picture the same day I punched Carlos. He seemed like such a jerk, making me out to be the bad guy. I had stared at him a lot on my first day, unintentionally, of course, shocked by everything he did. I just figured he couldn't be as evil as he seemed. There had to be more to him.

Why had my drawing ended up in my student file at the Lane Oslo School of Educational Reform? Especially since Mrs. Fitzgerald never noticed anything I did. Maybe it was her evidence that I was a dysfunctional student.

Ms. Hayworth had long blond hair, tied back in a loose bun. Her eyes were kind and she smiled a lot. "My goodness, Creighton, I don't believe there's a desk in this room that will be comfortable for you. I know where I can find one, though, if you'll just give me a minute." I could tell Ms. Hayworth was nothing like Mrs. Fitzgerald, even though we had just met.

When Ms. Hayworth left the room, something crashed outside. Some of the kids ran to see what was happening.

They peered out the back window. One boy climbed onto the bookshelf to get a better view. As he did this, someone grabbed a meter stick and belted him across the back of his knees. He fell to the floor. While everyone laughed, the boy on the floor got up angrily, inhaled deeply, and soon the two guys had each other in headlocks.

The outside door slammed open at the back of the classroom, and in came someone on a bike, eating a breakfast sandwich. He dropped his bike, jumped over the desk that was blocking his view, burped loudly, and stood on a chair to watch the fight that was taking place.

A girl stood in the corner, with her arms crossed, shaking her head. "Chill out, you guys—give Ms. Hayworth a break," she called. The two guys fighting actually listened and settled down.

The girl had piercings through her eyebrow and nose, thick black mascara, and brown hair braided into dread knots. She noticed me watching.

"This is pretty much normal here. I'm Carin—who are you?" she said.

"Creighton. You've been here a long time, I guess?"

"Yeah, a couple of years. Grade 10 now."

Just then, Carin turned sharply and moved toward the door. A boy who was small for a high school student stood in the entrance with a woman. He was wearing a pair of shorts that were far too small for him, and I noticed that the waist and chest straps of his backpack were tightly fastened. His long white socks were pulled up to his knees, which bulged above his tiny calves. He stared at all the action and his mouth hung open. Carin ran to his side.

"It's okay, Hamilton. Let's go find your locker. Tell me about your summer," Carin said. "Hi, Mrs. Scarlet," Carin added, turning toward the lady with Hamilton. "You get to work with us again this year?" she asked.

"Yes, I'm so happy, Carin. I love being in this classroom," Mrs. Scarlet replied. And then she looked around at the disaster.

Mrs. Scarlet started to pick up items that were strewn across the room from the fight. She tried to get the class seated, but no one seemed to listen. She must have been the boy's support worker or something. He seemed to need extra care.

"I got new socks," Hamilton said, pointing to his legs. "I got new socks. White ones. See my new socks?"

"Yes, Hamilton, they are very nice socks—and you got a new blue backpack?" Carin replied.

"I got new socks. See my white socks. They're new ones. My socks are shiny and new."

"And where did you get your new backpack, Hamilton?"

Hamilton pulled the socks up as high as they could possibly stretch. He smoothed them out by rubbing his hands up and down his legs, and pulled one more time when his hands reached his knees.

"Hamilton, this is Creighton," Carin said, pointing at me.

Hamilton's focus moved from his socks to my feet, and then slowly made their way up my body to my eyes. He looked at me for a few seconds, and then smiled. He reached for my hand.

"My name is Hamilton O'Leary. It is a pleasure to meet you, Creighton. Do you want to touch my new socks?" he said in a monotone voice.

I looked at Carin, and right away, she reached down to touch Hamilton's socks.

"They are very nice, Hamilton. You picked yourself out a real nice pair," she said.

I leaned down hesitantly and touched his right sock with my finger. "Yeah, real soft, Hamilton."

Just then, Ms. Hayworth came back, awkwardly carrying a large desk. She put it down quickly, relieved.

"Well, my goodness, here you all are. It seems like a long time since I've been with you crew. I guess you aren't going to give me time to readjust, are you? You're throwing me right back in. Why don't you help me and Mrs. Scarlet put the classroom back together?"

Ms. Hayworth began picking up the books that had fallen off the shelf, while she cheerfully talked to everyone and asked about our summer. Slowly, each kid began to help, as they answered her questions and shared their stories. Then she looked around the room.

"I think we've got it all. It looks like our classroom again," Ms. Hayworth said to us. "Now, Frasier, are you okay? Are you and Will both okay? You don't think you could have found a better way to greet each other after being apart for two months?"

Both boys looked at each other, shrugged, and started to laugh. Then she turned her attention to the bike that was lying on the classroom floor, amongst the desks and chairs. She smiled, breathed in deeply, and said, "Ratchet, you got yourself a new bike this summer? Why don't you stand it up, so I can have a better look."

Ratchet stood up, lifted his leg to the side, and farted. Everyone laughed. Ms. Hayworth just kept on talking about the bike. She moved in closely and got down to examine Ratchet's workmanship, because the bike was clearly something he had built himself. As she knelt, he stopped laughing at his own rudeness, and the echoes in the room faded. I thought about Mrs. Fitzgerald and her whistle.

"Well, Ratchet, you never cease to amaze me. This is quite incredible. I'm glad to see you spent your summer doing something productive, aside from working on the farm, of course. Good for you. You're so skilled, you really are. Now, I have a lock you can use, so why don't you take it out the back door here—where you'll be able to keep an eye on it, just outside the window—and chain it up," she said.

Ratchet listened, and he moved toward the door with his bike. Ms. Hayworth casually took off his hat and put it on his desk.

She turned to Carin and Hamilton. Hamilton was playing with a box of pipe cleaners, several of which he'd linked together. Carin was doodling on her arm with a black permanent marker. Ms. Hayworth slipped a white piece of paper on her desk, and carried on asking questions. Carin smiled at Ms. Hayworth, and then started drawing on the paper instead.

"Carin, I've been thinking about you a lot. How's your mom doing?"

"I don't know," she shrugged. "Kinda up and down, I guess. She never says much."

"And I see you got your eyebrow pierced. Now that's one place I think would really hurt. Was it painful?" Ms. Hayworth asked.

"It wasn't as bad as my bellybutton. This one hurt the most out of them all." Carin lifted her shirt so Ms. Hayworth could see her navel piercing. Everyone got up to look.

"Carin will come to you. Sit down and wait for her," Ms. Hayworth said firmly, and everyone sat.

For at least five minutes, Carin walked around the room showing us her piercings. It was like "show and tell" in elementary school. Ms. Hayworth was watching Hamilton, as he smoothed his socks and pulled to get them right to the bottom of his kneecaps. "I think Hamilton also has something he wants to show us."

"Go, Ham Dog!" shouted Ratchet. "Show us what ya got!"

Hamilton smiled as he walked to the front of the room. "I got new socks. See my socks. I got new socks. White ones."

Everyone clapped. Ratchet pounded on his desk. Hamilton started jumping up and down, and everyone laughed. Ms. Hayworth put her hands on Hamilton's shoulders and guided him back to his seat, gently removed his backpack, and thanked him for sharing his new socks.

After she made her rounds and everyone shared

something about their summer, she turned to the two empty desks.

"Hmm, have any of you seen Schooner?"

Schooner? There couldn't be more than one Schooner. I couldn't believe it; he was in this class, too? How could we spend a whole month together, Schooner talking nonstop, and we didn't know we'd be in the same school?

"I think his grandma's sick, so he isn't coming back," Frasier said.

"Oh, that's worrisome. I'll have to find out what's happening," Ms. Hayworth said.

His grandma? I knew nothing about Schooner. I didn't have a clue where he lived, other than it was a long way out of town. I didn't even know who he lived with. I had learned never to ask him anything.

"And we're supposed to have another new student—besides Creighton, of course," she said, smiling at me. "All together, there will be twelve, but we know how it goes—more will come, eventually!"

Ms. Hayworth moved so she was sitting on top of one of the empty desks.

"I missed you all. I hope you're a little bit excited about school," she said. "I know I am!"

It was almost 9:30. We had spent half an hour hearing everyone's stories. But the room felt peaceful.

I'd never been in a class with so few students. Ms. Hayworth liked her job, I could tell, and she liked us. Her voice was full of energy.

In that first week, we painted murals on the bathroom walls. She figured that we spent so much time in them, we needed to make the bathrooms more "visually appealing." She brought us apples each day, and we ate them while she was teaching. Sometimes, when our desks became uncomfortable, we could spread out with pillows on the floor, and use clipboards for our work. If we hadn't eaten breakfast, Ms. Hayworth pulled out a toaster, a loaf of bread, and a jar of peanut butter, and told us to help ourselves. When we came in each morning, classical music played on the CD player. Even though none of us would admit it, I think we liked how calm it made us feel. She had magazines for us to read about hunting, motorbikes, skateboarding, animals, and other things we were interested in. If we were focused on our work, she made us tea in the afternoon. It was my first week, and everything about the place made me look forward to school.

But more than anything else, I was surprised how happy I was when Schooner walked in on my third day. When he saw me, his mouth dropped open. He jumped up and down and hugged me.

"Everything good? Where've you been?" I asked him.

Schooner ignored the question. Of course, he ignored it.

I'd grown to like hearing his dumb stories. Yet, at school, he annoyed everyone. They egged him on, trying to make him exaggerate more, poking fun at him. Schooner was definitely not a cool kid.

One day, he opened a plastic margarine container, and gently lifted out a woolly bear caterpillar that he'd named Isabella. His creature came to school with him daily, and sat on his pencil as he wrote.

Schooner was convinced that his caterpillar could tell us about the weather conditions of the upcoming winter. Its head was becoming darker, so he believed winter would be severe, right from the start. Had it been her tail end that was dark, the end of winter would be harsh. The black bands that encased her body were longer than average, so the winter would be colder, longer, and snowier than normal. Schooner had absolutely no doubt that Isabella's thirteen body segments were there for a reason. Each segment corresponded to one of the thirteen weeks of winter. He didn't need to check the weather channel. He'd look at a segment of Isabella and give us a weather report. When I asked him where he'd learned about the caterpillar, he shrugged and said, "I dunno."

But Schooner could barely read. He'd got all the way to Grade 9, and couldn't make out many words at all. Most of the time, when we wrote stories, Ms. Hayworth or Mrs. Scarlet sat by Schooner's desk and wrote for him. I'd hear her say, "Schooner, you have the best stories ever and, soon enough, you'll be writing them yourself." A big smile would grow across his face. Even though no one respected him, the class knew Ms. Hayworth demanded they show acceptance and encouragement.

During our silent reading time, she gave him a National Geographic, and Schooner looked at it for ages, even when Ms. Hayworth started teaching.

Schooner had a rash all over his body, and we tried telling him it was from the caterpillar that he let crawl all over himself. He scratched constantly but ignored our comments, and brought Isabella to school every single day. When Ms. Hayworth took attendance, she'd call

Isabella's name out, just to help Schooner start his day off on a happy note. For the first time in school, I felt like I fit in, thanks to Ms. Hayworth, even though I was in a segregated school for LOSERS.

I wondered what could take this peaceful feeling away, since it seemed too good to be true.

CHAPTER 6

During the third week at Lane Oslo School of Educational Reform, my world shattered in a matter of seconds. Carlos Gromson walked into the room as if he owned the place. He was the other new student.

He plunked himself in the one empty desk. I closed my eyes and shook my head. He would take all of Ms. Hayworth's time. Carlos would torment Schooner. Hamilton would be picked on, and Ratchet would end up fighting with Carlos. It would be a gong show.

Ms. Hayworth introduced us to Carlos, and he looked surprised that I was sitting in *his* new classroom. When she realized we knew each other, she said, "That's great. I know Creighton will be happy to show you around the school grounds at lunch."

I nodded, but silently cursed at the thought of spending ANY amount of time with Carlos.

The morning wasn't too bad. He didn't blurt out or freak out or kick a single thing. Ms. Hayworth kept checking in with him. She'd give us our work, then go to Carlos right away.

"So, what brings you to Breton, Carlos?" she asked.

Carlos shrugged. "Mom wanted to ... I dunno."

"Well, Fairburn is a big city, so Breton will definitely feel like a change. It's a great little town, though. Make sure you tell me what you need, or if there's anything I can do to help you settle in."

"Yeah, it sucks. There's no skatepark. Nothin' to do here," he replied, looking the other way.

"You're a skateboarder? Ratchet and Will skateboard, too. Did you bring your board?"

"Yeah, it's in my locker."

"Can you show me?"

Carlos looked confused. "You wanna see my skateboard?"

Ms. Hayworth followed him to the locker area outside the classroom door, and I could hear her chatting away to Carlos. She brought the board in to show Will and Ratchet.

"Look at this, boys—Carlos also builds skateboards. Maybe we'll have to do a project sometime, and the three of you can plan things out."

Ms. Hayworth was doing her best to make Carlos feel good on his first day of school, just like she had done for me. He would take advantage of her, though.

After a week, Carlos began to gather a following. He built alliances quietly, one by one. He used a story about his great uncle Rigsby, who was serving a life sentence for murder. Everyone at Fairburn Elementary knew the story, too. I had heard parts of it in Grade 7, even though Carlos had been banned from telling it at that school. A few of us were working on math, while Ms. Hayworth and Mrs. Scarlet were helping others. Carlos kept interrupting, giving us bits of information to get us curious, desperately wanting people to ask more about his uncle's crime.

He told us to meet by the willow tree at lunch. Its weeping leaves touched the ground, making it more secluded and private than the other trees that bordered the edge of the school grounds. It was also the furthest tree from the building, a place that supervisors rarely checked. I figured I should hear the famous story from start to finish, even though I didn't think it was true at all.

We huddled around as Carlos spoke, almost in a whisper. He knew how to build suspense. He had practiced the story many times, on a lot of different people.

"My uncle was the creepiest man alive. He was so weird, people were freaked right out. Like, seriously, everyone stayed away. He lived in this kind of old mansion. It was made of stone. So the house was real cold and there was no heat, except for a woodstove. It was filled with cobwebs, and sorta dark and real dingy, and there was dust on everything. Thick, thick layers of dust."

Carlos emphasized each word and talked slowly, making sure no one missed a thing. The more he talked, the more everyone leaned in.

"My great uncle Rigsby only wore black, but he had this white cat. It was real skinny, and you could see its ribs and everything. Its fur was kinda patchy, too. Like chunks were sorta missing in spots, and it had one red eye and the other one was ripped out. Like, seriously, there was a hole right through the empty eye socket and into his head. Think it got torn out in a catfight or something. Anyway, Uncle Rigsby's black clothes always had white cat hair all over. My uncle would pet the cat. Like, REALLY pet it hard, till it screeched."

Carlos shivered and hunched his shoulders up to his neck, as if disgusted by the thought of his uncle's sickly cat.

"His yard was big, 'cause it was pretty much a mansion. So he had this gardener dude who took care of it all. Rigsby made the guy wear white, like a uniform. He'd yell at the gardener, and make him trim all the shrubs and keep everything perfect. My uncle would freak out if he didn't do it just right, the way he wanted. He'd stand there and watch over the guy. Poor dude would be shaking, trying to do a decent job, but slipping up lots 'cause he'd be so nervous. My uncle kinda got crazier, and he wouldn't even leave the house. The gardener did all his shopping, and ran around and did whatever he needed. I think he was trapped, scared to leave my uncle."

Schooner interrupted, "This ain't real. You're just messing with us, right?"

"No, seriously, man, like, my uncle is still in jail. He's there for life 'cause of what I'm gonna tell you next. So Rigsby had all these routines. He was kinda mental."

I could see Schooner tense his shoulders.

"For breakfast, he warmed up a tin pot filled with apple juice. Then he laid two pieces of white bread on top of the woodstove to toast. After it was almost burnt, he'd spread it with a thick coat of Marmite, that black, bitter stuff." He scrunched up his face. "And then my uncle went outside."

Carlos stood up to demonstrate the scene.

"You guys ready for this?"

No one said a thing.

"Well, my uncle started singing. Like, in a kind of delirious way. Sorta in a loud cackle, just random stuff."

Carlos paused, adding to the suspense.

"So, he sang all the way to the shed, with that shrieky voice of his, and then he grabbed his chainsaw, like this," he said, suddenly lurching toward Schooner.

"... the saw the gardener used to cut my uncle's firewood. He started revving it up, trying to get it going. He was dancing and singing with the saw, too. Then he cut up the garden. Next, he moved to the wooden stairs. Well, he chopped those up, too. Even the flowerpots and birdbath. Nothin' was spared! *Not ... even ... the ... gardener!*" Carlos said slowly in a deep voice.

The more Carlos leaned in toward us, the more Schooner backed up, staring.

"Rigsby took each body part and tied it up on the clothesline. Legs, arms, everything!"

Schooner covered his ears.

"The neighbors lined up along the street to watch the arrest. Rigsby was covered with blood, and that white cat was sittin' below the clothesline, lickin' up the drips. My uncle just raised his arms and surrendered."

"He sounds like one messed-up dude, man!" Ratchet said, staring at Carlos. I could tell Ratchet was playing along, seeing where Carlos would go with things. He was doubtful, like me.

"So, is that cat still alive?" Schooner asked.

"Yeah, and now that he's got a taste of human blood, that's all the cat's after. He'll attack anyone. And that stone house is still in Fairburn, and no one will go there."

The bell rang and we made our way back to class. Schooner shivered the whole way, scared to death.

On Carlos's third day at school, Ms. Hayworth walked into the classroom to find Hamilton crying in the corner. Carin stood by Hamilton with her arms crossed. Will and Frasier were laughing. Ratchet stood on a chair, swearing at Carlos, because he'd flung all of Hamilton's pipe cleaners across the room.

Ms. Hayworth walked toward Carlos with her arms crossed, her eyes filled with disappointment.

"Carlos, I do NOT tolerate unkindness toward other people. Look at Hamilton. Look at the fear you have caused him. You need to return his pipe cleaners and apologize."

Carlos kept snickering.

"Carlos, I have asked you to help Hamilton by returning his things."

Carlos laughed some more, plunked himself in his seat, and turned toward Frasier and Will to see if they were still laughing. They looked away.

"You'll need to leave, then. To be part of this class, you need to care and respect others. You are welcome back when you're sure you can do that."

Carlos did not move. He grabbed onto the side of his desk tightly. I had seen his temper back in Fairburn. I tensed up.

I thought about Mrs. Fitzgerald, and wondered how she would have handled this situation—knowing it would have been totally ineffective. With Ms. Hayworth, though, I felt badly. I hoped she could find her way out of the mess, like she always seemed to do.

"Well, it looks like we'll have to run our class elsewhere. Can all of you bring your writing folders and pencils? Carlos, I'm certain you will be joining us shortly.

You seem to like telling stories, so I'm sure you'll be a good writer." She must have heard him talking about his freaky uncle in class or something. "Once you've gathered Hamilton's things and placed them on his desk, you can join us next door."

Ms. Hayworth signaled us to follow. We walked silently into the other classroom.

The room had no desks, but there were some individual cubbies. There was a kitchen, where we had baked cookies in our first week. There were two large tables with chairs, and a carpeted area surrounded by several old couches.

Ms. Hayworth pulled out the box of clipboards, and gathered us around her on the floor. As she passed them out, we could hear Carlos in the other room, throwing things against the wall. Ms. Hayworth got up and closed the door to dull the banging, and returned to her spot on the carpet.

"We'll just give him some space, time to cool down. He'll come around."

She carried on teaching.

Once we started writing, the noise from the other room stopped.

After a few minutes, Carlos entered with his writing

folder, and plunked himself heavily onto a couch. Ms. Hayworth never said a thing. She helped Schooner, who always got frustrated during writing. Then she moved to Hamilton, who usually linked waves of lines together for his stories. Ms. Hayworth asked Hamilton what his story was about, and wrote the words above his swirls.

After several minutes, she moved to Carlos. She asked if he had an idea of what he wanted to write about. Carlos muttered something in a rude voice, and Ms. Hayworth asked him to tell her again. He said it louder, but still quite rudely. She wrote a sentence or two on his paper and asked him to continue.

When the lunch bell rang, everyone started to leave. I helped Carin gather the clipboards and put the pillows back in order.

We could hear Ms. Hayworth. "Thank you for joining us, Carlos. What can you do about Hamilton's feelings now? You hurt him this morning, by taking things that were important to him."

"They were stupid pipe cleaners," Carlos snapped.

"They were not yours to take or to toss about the room. You need to apologize. You can talk to him, or maybe write a note."

She took an apple out of the fridge drawer, and placed it on the arm of the couch beside him.

"I'll leave you for a while, Carlos, and let you decide how you want to deal with the issue."

"He's a retard. He can't even read, so why would I write a note? This is so stupid!" Carlos called out.

Ms. Hayworth left the room, ignoring his comment. I entered the other classroom to grab my lunch. Surprisingly, Carlos had piled the pipe cleaners on Hamilton's desk.

At lunch, we could do our own thing. The high school was across the courtyard, so Carin went to meet her friends. Schooner and I walked with Ratchet. He usually bought a burger somewhere.

When the bell rang and we piled back in the class, Carlos was sitting at his desk. Ms. Hayworth glanced at him, and then scanned Hamilton's spot. There, on his desk, was a stickman on a skateboard, all made from pipe cleaners. When Hamilton saw the gift, he giggled, jumped up and down, and clapped his hands.

Maybe Carlos wasn't actually evil. Like Ms. Hayworth, I wanted to believe there was good in everybody. I had a bad feeling, though. Carlos could never let Ms. Hayworth win.

CHAPTER 7

"Hey, you!"

I turned around and Carin punched me on the shoulder, smiling. It was the last week of September, the first time we'd ever run into each other outside of school.

"Oh, hey," I replied, surprised. "You must live around here."

"Yeah, just on the next block ... Ninth Avenue. What about you?"

"Wow! We're almost neighbors. We're on Eleventh, couple more blocks over. Can't believe I never saw you walking before."

"Well, I have to admit, I'm a little lazy. Sometimes I get a ride with Mom, if she has an early house to clean. But if I knew you were walking this way, I'd wait for you—if you want me to, that is."

"That'd be good. Maybe that would get me going on time."

"Hah, you're always on time, Creighton. You've never been late for school," Carin said.

"Yeah, true. Guess 'cause we have a decent teacher. I'm surprised you noticed."

"You're surprised I noticed? You're, like, the only normal guy in the class. Of course, I'd notice."

"You and Ms. Hayworth seem pretty tight," I said, changing the subject as we walked together.

"Well, it's my third year. And yeah, she's great. She's kinda been big in my life, that's for sure. So, what brought you to Breton, anyway?"

"Dad ... he got tired of his old job. We moved around a lot, so he figured it was time to settle somewhere for good. Mom grew up here," I added, 'cause I liked how normal that sounded.

"Just you, your mom and dad, or you got brothers and sisters?" she asked.

"Just me and Dad. You?" I asked, changing the subject.

Carin was wearing a black hoodie and pair of faded blue jeans, with rips all the way up her thighs. She always wore some kind of baggy sweatshirt over a pair of old jeans. Her eye makeup was black, making her brown eyes stand out against her pale skin. With all her piercings and dark dread knots, she looked tough. But it was confusing, because underneath it all, she seemed soft, almost delicate.

"No brothers or sisters, either, just me and Mom. Only met my dad a couple of times." Carin laughed. "Mom was pretty young when she had me," she continued, shaking her head with a smile.

I nodded. I wasn't so great at conversation at the best of times. But talking to a girl, I felt useless.

We stood at our lockers. She reached into her backpack and took out a plastic cup. Slowly, she unwrapped the wet paper towel she had used to protect a small bouquet of flowers. I pretended not to notice. I tossed my backpack into my locker.

"Nice walking with you this morning, Creigh. Wanna meet tomorrow?"

I liked how she called me "Creigh."

"That'd be good," I replied. "I'll stop at the corner of Ninth, if you like—8:20-ish?"

"That'd be awesome." Carin said.

Her eyes crinkled up when she smiled. She didn't do it

often, I realized. Usually, her face seemed tight. She'd bite the inside of her cheek and twist her lips with her fingers. She looked serious most of the time, quiet, like she was thinking or something.

I turned the other way. I didn't know what else to do when she smiled like that, staring at me for what seemed like forever.

Carin walked to the sink and filled the plastic cup with water. She placed it on Ms. Hayworth's desk, and fiddled with the small handful of flowers, making it look perfect.

"You brought her flowers?" I said. It was a dumb comment because, of course, she'd brought her flowers.

"Yeah, Ms. Hay loves flowers. She told me that once, and we have a ton growing wild in our yard. Not much left now, but I try to bring some when I see decent ones."

"You always call her Ms. Hay?"

"Ha!" Carin laughed. "Yeah, Ms. Hay, Ms. Hayworth, just whatever, I guess."

She walked to the carpet and pulled her Walkman CD player out of her front pocket. Sitting, curled up in the corner amongst the pillows, she adjusted her headphones and buried her head into her knees. She closed her eyes as she listened to music. She did this most mornings.

Schooner came in the door, looking grumpy. He walked to his desk, slumped into his seat, then put his head down, pulling his hood overtop. I grabbed the hood and yanked it back, teasing him a bit.

"What's up, bud?"

Looking up at me, he said, "Not much, Creigh. Frickin' tired is all. Too early, man."

"Want a game of crib?" I asked, thinking maybe I could lighten him up a little. Crib was something Ms. Hayworth had taught us the first week, and she was pretty happy to let us have a couple games before the day got going.

"Yeah, guess so," Schooner said, dragging himself to the back table.

Ms. Hayworth walked in, carrying a bunch of papers she'd photocopied, and smiled when she saw me and Schooner sitting there with the crib board all set up. "Aw, that's great, boys. I love coming into the room when it's so peaceful and calm—thank you for that." Then she walked to the carpet where Carin was tucked away in the corner. Ms. Hayworth crouched down and lifted Carin's hood off gently, moving the headphones off to the side so she could hear. Carin smiled, and Ms. Hayworth put her hand on her shoulder. They were talking quietly. I could hear Ms.

Hayworth ask something about Carin's mom. And then Ms. Hayworth walked to her desk.

"Carin, you brought me fresh flowers again. So thoughtful! Always makes my day. It's the end of September and you still have poppies?" she called across the room.

"Well, that's the last of them, I think," Carin called back.

"Want to help put up this artwork?" Ms. Hayworth asked, carrying a stapler and the pile of construction paper.

Together they stood at the bulletin board, chatting, while Carin stapled each collage onto the wall.

"You let me know what you need, Carin," I heard Ms. Hayworth say to her. "There are supports in the community for things like this. You can't take on everything alone."

I wondered what Ms. Hayworth was talking about.

Maybe she and Ms. Hayworth were tight because she was the only girl in the class. Since I'd started at Lane Oslo, I'd noticed that everyone depended on Carin, because she cared a lot. Like Ms. Hayworth, she paid attention to the small stuff. She could tell when Hamilton was scared, or when Schooner was nervous. She'd bring Ratchet little snacks, 'cause she worried about his never-ending hunger. She knew Ronnie liked order, and helped him get things in place when he started to stress. She even went out of her way to talk with Carlos, and try and get to know the guy. Ms. Hayworth had a soft spot for Carin, too. In a class full of guys, Carin was her saving grace.

Just after the bell rang, a tall lady came to the door, holding a clipboard.

"Can I help you?" Ms. Hayworth asked.

"Yes, I'm the new counselor at Breton Secondary. I think I'm in the right place," she said, looking around, puzzled. "I'm here to pick up Karen Reiner. I will be taking her each week for about an hour. I took over for Mrs. Donnis, who used to see her."

"Do you mean Carin? It's *Car-in Rainer*," Ms. Hayworth said, correcting her pronunciation.

I knew Carin was super picky about her name because she'd corrected both Schooner and Carlos when they said it wrong the first time they met. She told them, "It's like a car you drive and then you just add IN."

"I'm good," Carin replied, looking at the woman. "I think I'll just stay here today."

Ms. Hayworth walked to Carin's desk. She knelt down and spoke quietly to her.

"Fine!" Carin said, groaning. "I'll go. Whatever, I guess."

She stomped out of the room, following the lady. I

wondered why she needed to see her, anyway.

After school that day, Ratchet and I both happened to be grabbing our bikes from the rack outside the back of the classroom.

"Hey, you wanna go for a ride?" he asked. It was the first time he'd said much to me. I felt kind of nervous, since I'd never hung out with people after school before. No one had invited me anywhere, throughout elementary school.

"Maybe go to the river, hang out for a bit," he continued.

"Sure, man," I said, knowing I had nothing better to do.

I followed behind. We rode to the bridge, the same place Schooner and I had hung out during the summer, about a ten-minute ride from school. Ratchet rested his bike against the bridge, then stood, looking out over the river, resting his arms on the railing. I did the same. He pulled a box of smokes from the sleeve of his T-shirt, grabbed a lighter from the front pocket of his jeans, and lit a cigarette. He held the box toward me, offering one. I shook my head.

"I'm good, thanks."

We stood there for a bit while Ratchet finished his smoke. The air was cool, and the trees that lined the rocky beach were now yellow and orange.

I pictured Schooner taking a jump. I could feel the summer heat and see his blistery skin, from endless hours spent at the river.

Ratchet tossed the butt onto the road, and stepped on it with his brown work boots, pressing it firmly before heading to the path. We made our way down to the empty beach, where the fall leaves scattered themselves along the shore. We started skipping rocks, when suddenly Ratchet stopped. He kicked the ground below, rubbing the sand with his boot, and tossed the last pebble he had in his hand.

"This is where it happened."

"What happened?" I asked.

"You know, with Carin."

I didn't know what Ratchet meant. He sat down on the log, balancing his arms on his knees in thought, before taking out another cigarette. He inhaled deeply as he lit the smoke, cupping the cigarette with his hand, so it wouldn't blow out in the wind, then looked ahead toward the water. He was quiet. I waited, because I knew Ratchet was the sort of guy you couldn't rush.

"What an ass! She was just a kid." Ratchet mumbled to himself.

"I never heard. What happened to her?"

"He took her, dragged her into those bushes." Ratchet stood up and turned to the shrubs behind us, pointing. "Can only imagine what he did to her."

I didn't move. I could see it in Carin's eyes now. The pain.

"He beat her pretty bad. Pervert just left her there when he got what he was after. Think she was in those bushes alone for hours, before she staggered to the highway. Some lady saw her and drove her to the hospital."

I thought about Ms. Hayworth, standing at the bathroom door each time Carin needed to use the washroom. She had also jolted back when Ratchet pushed Devon against the wall and accidently fell into her. All the flowers she brought Ms. Hayworth, and the quiet conversations they seemed to have. She'd always drift off, sort of into a trance, whenever Ms. Hayworth was teaching.

"When did this happen? What do you mean?" I felt nauseous.

"It was a couple years back. July, the summer before she was in Grade 8, that's when he did it. She was different back then. She started up in the high school and didn't last a week. He messed her up real good. I was in Grade 9 when she came to Lane Oslo."

"Who did it, Ratchet? Did they get the guy?" I was angry and couldn't sit any longer. I started chucking rocks with more force.

"I don't know the man. He got caught and they locked him up. An old dude in his sixties or something. The bastard couldn't even prey on someone legal age. Still chokes me up. I can't even look at her sometimes."

As vulgar as Ratchet seemed, he was pretty soft, too. We carried on skipping rocks and didn't say a thing.

"Well, you dip-wad, should we get out of here?" he asked.

I wondered if that's why Ratchet had brought me to the river, to tell me Carin's story, a fact I needed to know in order to attend Lane Oslo. Ratchet's way of protecting Carin. He seemed like that kind of guy.

I couldn't sleep that night. Carin was all I saw. I replayed the awkward conversation I'd had with her as we walked to school. I could see her deep brown eyes.

I got up to get a glass of water. Dad was still sitting in his recliner.

"What's up, son?" he said, when I walked past the living room.

"Not much, just having trouble sleeping tonight," I

replied, standing in the doorway with my glass of water.

"Ah!" Dad said. "Something on your mind?"

"Yeah. Just this girl in my class—I guess she was raped a couple years back. Hard to stop thinking something like that happened to her."

Dad leaned forward as he pulled in the footrest of his chair. In the upright position, he kept his hands on the armrests staring at the floor.

"How old's this girl, Creighton?" Dad asked, still not looking at me.

"I don't know ... fifteen. She's in Grade 10 now. She was only thirteen at the time, though. Who'd rape a thirteen-year-old, Dad? Seems crazy. And I guess he was an older guy."

Dad didn't say anything. He was still leaning forward in his chair, staring at the carpet.

"Dad?" I said. "Dad, what's the deal?"

"What's her name?" he said, standing up.

"Carin. Carin Reiner."

He turned toward me, leaning his hand on the door frame. "Hmm, so she's in your class? You're friends with this girl?"

Dad never showed much interest in what I had to say. He rarely asked me questions or made conversation.

"Yeah, she's a really nice girl. Do you know her or something, Dad? I asked.

"No, no, I don't know her," Dad replied. He didn't look at me, as he brushed past through the doorway. "Well, you best get to bed. Try and get some rest, shut your mind off."

"Yeah," I said, confused. "Night, Dad."

He stood at the kitchen sink, both hands holding onto the counter, his head down. Then he gave the cupboard below a firm kick, rattling the dishes that were waiting to be loaded into the dishwasher.

I backed up and turned toward my room.

Lying in bed, I realized I hadn't thought of Mom all day. My mind usually drifted to her, but not lately. I felt guilty. Was I forgetting her? Sometimes I struggled to imagine her face. How could I forget what Mom looked like?

The night was clear. Venus was out. I wished I could call Mom and talk to her. I'd ask about Dad, his reaction to my news. "Night, Momma, I love you," I whispered. Then I thought about Carin, hurt, alone in the bushes. Afraid.

The next morning, I could see Carin walking in the distance. She was at the corner of Ninth, waiting, just where we had planned to meet. Her dark hair, the black hoodie covering her fragile body, her gentle smile. When she saw me turn the corner, she sped up. She looked happy.

"You remembered," she said, surprised.

"Of course, I remembered." I wanted to say more. I wanted to tell her how sorry I was. Nothing came out. I could see her crawling up the steep river path to the highway, bleeding, crying, and waving helplessly at the cars passing by. I swallowed. "You got some flowers in that bag of yours?" I said, not knowing what else to say.

I could not focus that day. I didn't even hear when Ms. Hayworth asked me to help Hamilton put his backpack away.

"You okay, Creigh?" Carin asked softly, as she put her hand on my shoulder. "You've hardly said a word today."

CHAPTER 8

It was a couple of weeks after the pipe cleaner incident, the beginning of October, when Carlos arrived at school earlier than normal. He was not in his typical grumpy mood, and he had been extra quiet since he'd done what Ms. Hayworth expected of him, and made amends with Hamilton. Ms. Hayworth was teaching us a lesson about the Earth's crust. She got sidetracked, and talked about a mountain that had erupted back in the eighties, when Carlos jumped in like he was an open book of knowledge.

"It was Mount St. Helens," he interrupted. "It happened on May 18, 1980—at 8:32, I think. A 5.1 earthquake triggered the volcano to slide. It was one of the largest landslides in recorded history. It traveled, like, 175 to 250 kilometers an hour."

We were all stunned, especially Ms. Hayworth.

"How do you know about this, Carlos?"

"I don't know. Discovery Channel, maybe?" He shrugged.

"I didn't know you had an interest in this sort of thing," she said.

"I don't."

"I'm so impressed." She patted Carlos's shoulder as she walked by his desk. He pulled back.

For the rest of the lesson, Ms. Hayworth tried her best to maintain our focus, but engaging everyone was impossible.

Hamilton linked his pipe cleaners into various shapes, and on occasion, he blurted something out. "I'm getting a red bike and I'm gonna go FAST!" He used hand actions as he spoke, and his interruptions were welcome entertainment.

Devon carved away at the underside of his desk with scissors. Ms. Hayworth acted like she didn't notice.

Ronnie lined up his supplies in two parallel lines, creating a pattern. Eraser, pen, paper clip, eraser, pen, paper clip, eraser, pen, paper clip …

Schooner drew and sketched his name, attempting each letter with background shadows and symbols, just like the tags he saw on the boxcars.

Carin used a paper clip to scratch her initials on her arm, and traced over the letters with a black marker. Ms. Hayworth walked by and took the paper clip off her desk.

Ratchet fiddled with the parts of an old VCR player that Ms. Hayworth had given him. He was building some sort of contraption.

Will's grandfather had taught him how to carve, so he worked away on a block of cherry wood. Ms. Hayworth had asked him to make a post for our classroom. It would stand like a small totem pole at the door and represent each one of us. She was happy for him to carve while she taught, as long as he contributed and listened.

Carlos usually made rude remarks, but today he was quiet, other than his Mount St. Helens comment.

We took off at lunch as usual, and Schooner and I walked with Ratchet to the smoke pit in front of the high school, next to Lane Oslo. Hamilton went with Mrs. Scarlet, and I saw Carin meet her friends.

When we returned, there was a police car in front of our building near Ms. Hayworth's vehicle. An officer was talking to her. The high school principal, Mr. Roland, stopped us before we got close to the scene.

"I need you all to gather here," he said, directing us.

"We're just going to take a little walk to the high school this afternoon, instead."

"Why can't we go in our school?" Ratchet interrupted, pushing his way toward Mr. Roland. "You said you didn't want me in the high school."

"No questions right now, Matt. There's been a little situation that's getting sorted out," Mr. Roland said to Ratchet. "Come on, all of you, follow me."

I had never been inside Breton Secondary, but Mr. Roland seemed to know each kid from Lane Oslo. They must have attended before transferring to the alternate program. He took us to the back of the library. We'd each be interviewed about "the situation" and, until it was our turn, we could play on the computers.

Ratchet started to freak out, and demanded Mr. Roland tell us what was happening. Schooner got defensive and his face grew redder with panic.

"I did nothin'. I swear to God, I didn't do a thing this time. I shouldn't have to stay here. This is so stupid." Schooner kicked the computer chair. "Stop lookin' at me, you freak!" he said to Devon, who started to snicker as Schooner's temper grew.

"Come on," I said to Schooner, "it's okay. You're not in

trouble. They're talking to all of us."

"I'm not staying here. No one can make me stay here. I hate this frickin' school," Will muttered as he exited the Library.

"Come back here, Will. You need to stay with me for a while," Mr. Roland pleaded.

It was obvious that Will didn't care. He kept walking right out the door, and Mr. Roland didn't stop him.

Hamilton was crying, so Mr. Roland told Mrs. Scarlet he didn't need to be questioned, and she could take him for a walk somewhere.

Carin looked at Carlos with dagger eyes and said, "What did you do, Carlos? What did you do to Ms. Hayworth? You did something to her car, didn't you?"

Carlos looked away. She was right, though. We both knew it. Carlos could never let Ms. Hayworth win a battle. That's why he'd been so quiet for a couple weeks. He was brewing up this plan, waiting to get revenge.

"You're an asshole, Carlos. If you did something to her, I'll kill you myself. Tell me. What did you do to her?" Carin continued.

"Now, Carin. Watch the profanity. Remember where you are," Mr. Roland said.

As Carin walked closer to Carlos, never taking her eyes off him, she muttered back, "Oh, I know where I am, all right. He's an ass, though," she said, pointing at Carlos, who actually seemed to cower. "There's only one person you need to talk to, Roland, and that's this asshole right here."

"You need to leave this instant. You cannot use such foul language here. Come with me!" Mr. Roland grabbed her arm.

She shook it roughly away from his grasp and said, "You gonna leave the rest of these guys alone, Roland? You gonna take me and leave everyone here in your library? Don't you remember? We're DANGEROUS!" she taunted.

Mr. Roland started to sweat. He clearly didn't know what to do. He jingled the change in his pocket. With his other hand, he smoothed the remaining strands of his brown hair over his balding head.

Just then, Carin was called out of the room by a police officer. As she walked away, she looked at Carlos and said, "You are *so* going down!"

"Now, everyone, get back to the computers," Mr. Roland said.

Devon was on Napster, downloading music. As others noticed, they logged on, too.

"You cannot be on music sites at school. That's not what the computers are for. You all know that. Now, come on. All of you, let's get it together."

No one logged off.

He removed Frasier's toque, but after Mr. Roland walked away, Frasier put it back on his head and adjusted it. "Don't touch me!" he muttered under his breath.

And then it was my turn to go to the office for questioning, like the others had. They led me to a small room. The tall lady, the school counselor who saw Carin each week, stayed in the room while a police officer asked me questions.

He wondered who I was with at lunch, and where we were. He wanted to know how long I'd been at Lane Oslo, and why I got sent there. He wrote my answers in a small notebook.

After about ten minutes, the officer asked the counselor to walk me back and grab Schooner next. I was worried about him, knowing he'd never handle any type of questioning too well, especially from a police officer.

Schooner cried as he left the library. Carin never rejoined us. I wondered what they'd done with her. Carlos was the fastest of all. He looked totally composed when he returned from the office. Mr. Roland escorted us back to our building and handed us over to Ms. Hayworth.

"You certainly have your hands full, Ms. Hayworth. Will you be okay with them for the rest of the afternoon?" he asked.

"Of course. Thank you."

"I am sorry about that, everyone, but I'm afraid something happened to me today that wasn't very kind," Ms. Hayworth said apologetically.

Just then, Carin walked in, and slumped into her desk.

"Hi, Carin. I was just saying, something was done today that really hurt me. It was distasteful, inhumane, and completely disrespectful. It made me feel unappreciated. Something like this erases everything I've done, and makes me not want to be here. But I am here. Because it wasn't all of you. I know whoever it was will feel badly about it. I know they will re-think what they did. I know they will have remorse. So, we're going to get on with our day. And whoever you are, I hope you realize ..."

Ms. Hayworth swung her head back, tucked the loose strands of hair behind her ears, and took a deep breath, crossing her arms as she spoke, close to tears.

"... I hope you realize that I choose to be here with all of you. I love my job, and I care a lot about you. We're kind of like a family, and it only takes one to destroy what we've created. That's all I want to say. I just hope you're hearing me."

"What happened, Ms. Hayworth?" Ratchet interrupted the silence.

"You know, Ratchet. I don't feel right about discussing it, because I have always dealt with each of you privately. It wouldn't be fair to the person responsible, if I shared what was done."

"Who cares if they're embarrassed? They screwed you around, so just say it." Ratchet demanded.

Ms. Hayworth wouldn't discuss the situation further. She carried on as she always did.

When the bell rang, we left quickly, hoping to learn what had happened. We knew the police car had been parked by Ms. Hayworth's vehicle after lunch, so we headed in that direction. In a perfect circle, around her car, were small pools of blood and bits of flesh that had obviously been left after a cleanup.

Carlos was not with us.

Just then, kids from the high school started running over. Word had spread that something big had happened at Lane Oslo.

Billy Jacobs was the first to arrive. He was a buddy of Ratchet's from the high school, always at the smoke pit when we hung out.

"Holy crap, did you hear what happened?" he said as he ran toward us. "I heard the police talkin' to Roland when I was in the office. Some creep killed a bunch of mice and plastered the crap out of the parking lot. Guess he slit open the stomachs, pulled out the guts, and spread them all over a teacher's car, even dumped hunks of flesh in a circle around it—so weird. Frickin' sick!" Billy scanned the ground. We all started looking around her car. We even found bits of bone, and chunks of soft gray fur scattered beside it.

Schooner wanted to check the dumpster right away. "Come on. They must've chucked the crap in there."

"You're gross!" Ratchet said, following anyway. We all followed.

Schooner boosted himself up and climbed over the edge. He opened the black garbage bag that sat on the top. As he opened it, he turned his head back, gagging. We all boosted ourselves up on the edge so we could look in.

"Ah, raunchy, man. Close that thing." Ratchet pulled back and jumped off the edge of the dumpster.

The bag was half-full of hollowed-out mice and their innards. Carin had stood back underneath the tree with her arms crossed. She twisted her lip every so often with one hand and scraped the ground with her foot.

As we walked away, we talked about Carlos. We all figured it was him. He was the only one who treated Ms. Hay badly, always challenging her, trying to get her upset.

"What would Carlos be doing with so many mice, anyway? Where would he even get them?" Will asked.

"Pet store, bro. They got craploads of mice to feed snakes," Ratchet replied. "You know, he has a python."

Before leaving the school grounds, I walked back in to grab my hat, which I'd forgotten on top of the lockers. Mr. Roland was talking to Ms. Hayworth in the classroom and didn't notice me in the hall.

"I need more time with him, Jim. I can't just let him go; it's not been long enough," she said calmly. "And really, we have no confession or proof it was him. It's a feeling. I'm certain Carlos was responsible, but it's not a confession that I need."

"That was an evil crime. That was a threat in my mind. You could press charges. Aren't you concerned about your safety?" Mr. Roland asked.

"No. It wasn't a threat. It was a statement. He's obviously used to pushing people away, and he's been successful. He will not be successful with me, Jim. He needs someone even more than I realized. I know it's disturbing. But if I abandon him, who will he have, and what will I have taught him? What will I be teaching the others?"

"By keeping him here, what message are we sending the students? It's okay to kill animals and shred them into pieces, and you get to stay in school?" he asked.

"I am showing my students that I will be here for ALL of them, whether they fail or they succeed. If I send him away, then I'm doing what everyone before me has done. Instead, I want to keep him here, because he doesn't expect me to do that. Plus, the kids have to know they can't just give up on people. How will they learn resilience if I don't show it myself? He knows I know. He knows the other students know. That, in itself, is big and he will suffer the guilt."

The next morning, when we walked into the building, no one said a thing about the incident. Ratchet started calling Carlos "Carcass," and we all followed. This was our statement, I guess. It was our way of telling him we knew.

CHAPTER 9

The more I got to know Ratchet, the more I realized, he'd do whatever was needed to look out for us. He seemed to know a good person when he saw one. There was another side to Ratchet, though. I'd heard kids talk about his freak-outs, but never watched one happen. After Christmas break, I saw the anger for the first time.

Ms. Hayworth gave us blank world maps to label and color. She coached us through each step, telling us what to put in the legend, and demonstrated how to color the map, ensuring the pencil-crayon lines were going in one direction.

Ronnie excelled in activities like this, and was completely focused on his map. He formed each letter perfectly and used his ruler to underline every word. He organized his pencil-crayons on top of his desk in the order of rainbow colors: red, orange, yellow, green, blue, indigo, violet—Roy G. Biv. The rest of our papers looked like a dog's breakfast.

Schooner crumpled his map. He sat with his head down. Hamilton turned each continent into happy faces and added legs and arms, labeling each one as members of his family. Will gave up and worked on his carving, instead. Ms. Hayworth turned to Will and said, "That's fine, Will, but you do have to complete this map. If you want to carve now, you can do the map for me at lunch."

He tossed his carving tool onto the floor and roughly grabbed the map, placing it abruptly on his desk.

Ratchet shouted, "I don't get it. Can you say that again? What color did you say Greenland should be? If it's called Greenland, shouldn't I color it green?"

Ms. Hayworth kept moving around the room, trying to give us some sort of knowledge to help us survive in the real world.

Ronnie was the first to finish, and his map looked like a masterpiece. Ms. Hayworth held it up and praised his detail. He remained as expressionless as always. Carcass got up, walked over to Ronnie's desk, and with the point of his compass, dug right into the center of the map, dragging the needle through the paper, leaving an imprinted scratch along the top of the desk. Ronnie's arms flapped as he attempted to fix his page, taping it with sticky tape, oblivious of Carcass.

Ratchet got up. His nostrils flared. "What did you do that for? You ripped his page right in half?"

"Not your business," Carcass said and stomped toward the door.

Ratchet cut across the open seats to get to the door faster. "I'm making it my business," he said, as he grabbed Carcass's T-shirt at the neck. Carcass attempted to get out of his hold, but Ratchet had him firmly pinned.

"Don't touch me, you faggot!" Carcass demanded, as he punched the side of Ratchet's head.

"What you just call me? Did you say faggot?" Ratchet held the front of Carcass's shirt and shoved him against the wall. "Say it again, Carcass. Say it. What did you call me?" Ratchet banged Carcass's head against the wall. Carcass looked scared. His stocky, overweight body couldn't withstand Ratchet's strength.

"Ratchet, let him go!" Ms. Hayworth maneuvered herself between them.

"Carcass just destroyed Ronnie's map—then he called

me a faggot." Ratchet's eyes did not move. They remained fixed on Carcass, who was starting to gasp for air, as his T-shirt tightened around his neck.

"I never said nothin'," Carcass wheezed.

"Yeah, I think I heard you pretty clearly. Hey, boys?" Ratchet said turning toward the class. "Did you hear what he called me?"

No one said a thing.

Ms. Hayworth tried to direct Ratchet out of the classroom, but he dragged Carcass with him. They moved through the doorway and into the hall. Hamilton had his hands over his ears, hovering at the back of the classroom, and Carin went to sit with him. The rest of us followed the fight into the hallway, even though Mrs. Scarlet tried to stop us.

Ms. Hayworth shouted, "Call the office!" which Mrs. Scarlet did, using the phone that was attached to the wall at the back of the classroom, where Hamilton was huddled beside Carin.

Ratchet shoved Carcass to the floor and straddled him. He held Carcass's arms down with his knees, swinging punches at his face, one after another.

"You think you can treat us like this? Is that what you

think? You can just walk into this school and act like you run the place?"

Mr. Roland entered through the main doors. He could see us gathered in the small hallway outside of the classroom, watching Ratchet and Carcass.

"Stand up, Matt. Get off him now!" Mr. Roland shouted as he approached. Ratchet started to get up. Beads of sweat poured off his forehead and he wiped them with his bleeding hand. He stumbled, catching himself so he wouldn't fall, and gave Carcass two more kicks in his ribs. He headed toward the school entrance.

"I'm not done with you yet!" Ratchet hollered, as he pushed the steel door open, exiting the school.

"I'll be back for you, Carlos," Mr. Roland called out, as he raced to catch up with Ratchet. Carlos was curled up on the floor.

Ms. Hayworth knelt beside him. "You okay, Carlos? Let's get you up," she said, lifting his arm. He rose slowly, holding his side as she walked him to the sink in the other room. "We'll clean you up and see how you are."

Ratchet was suspended for one week and Carcass was back, sitting in school the next day. I knew Ms. Hayworth had spoken to him privately, because he placed an envelope on Ronnie's desk the next morning. Inside was a new map he'd colored himself. Ronnie didn't understand that sort of apology. He wasn't a kid who needed one. He really had no understanding of what had taken place. His focus was on his own map and the tear, which appeared through its center. That was it.

After I watched Ratchet defend Ronnie, I knew he would protect each one of us. But I also realized what he was capable of. Even though we couldn't stand Carcass, Ratchet took his anger to a new level.

And then I thought of the story Dad had told me months earlier.

Ratchet had been at my house one afternoon. We were supposed to be working on a school project, but ended up watching a movie instead. When Ratchet left, Dad asked me about him. "Was that the Radcliff boy?"

"Yeah, Matt Radcliff. But no one calls him that," I said. "Why?"

"He's that kid who made the papers years back. You know, he got taken away from his parents. They beat the kid, I think. Almost killed him. Kept him in a cupboard or some darn thing. Guess a social worker got wind of it and took the boy away. Nice kid now, though? Guess it worked out in the end."

Dad finished the last slug of beer, then piled the can in amongst the empties on the porch, grabbed his keys as he called back to me, "Just headin' out to get the mail," and he left.

After Dad told me the story, I thought about it a lot.

Ratchet arrived late most days. Ms. Hayworth would finally get the class settled and start her lesson, then he'd crash in with his bike and destroy the silence. Although he lived in a group home for teens, he also spent a lot of time at a dairy farm, where he worked. It was a ways out of town. When he had shifts after school, he stayed in the hired man's tiny house, since it wasn't being used. Ratchet called it his "shack." Once Ratch got his "N" and was allowed to drive on his own, he sometimes used the old farm truck. The owners seemed to take good care of him. It didn't seem to matter if he rode his bike or drove the truck, he was always late for school.

"Glad you made it, Ratchet," Ms. Hayworth would say patiently, as she waited for him to take a seat. "Did you sleep okay last night?"

"No, I couldn't fall asleep. It's these stupid pills. I tried to tell the doctor they mess me up, but he makes me keep taking them."

The staff at his group home had put him on some sort of pills to help control his violent outbursts. In the morning, they would kick in at about ten o'clock, so he'd sort of be on a rampage till then, and always starving.

Ratchet talked openly to the whole class about the pills he took. He told us his social worker was sending him to a bunch of different doctors.

"They figure I'm some mental case or something. Gotta see some psychiatrist to figure out if I got a messed-up brain."

When he happened to bring food to school, Ms. Hayworth let him eat in class. She even brought little plastic bags filled with trail mix that she'd give to him throughout the day, trying to help him fill his hunger. Ratchet finally took a stand.

"That's it! I'm not taking these stupid things anymore. I'm throwing the pills in the dumpster. They make me crazy—I swear they do. I got a pounding headache. My guts are rumblin' and I wanna puke. All they do is mess me up."

"Ratchet, you're interrupting. Everyone is quiet and focused. This isn't the time to share what's going on in your mind."

He stopped talking but dug noisily through his desk, rummaging around until he found the container of pills.

"Found them!" he blurted out again. He marched out the back door, slamming it as he left, and we all turned our heads to watch.

"Let him be," Ms. Hayworth said. "Let him do his thing—he'll be back."

We heard the lid of the dumpster slam shut and we started to laugh. Ratchet was done with meds, just like that.

I knew I could depend on Ratchet for anything. But his anger worried me. How far would he take it? I didn't want it to cause him any trouble.

CHAPTER 10

On Monday, February 22, two days before my fifteenth birthday, death struck Lane Oslo.

There's no doubt Schooner was a different sort of guy. He'd been carrying a caterpillar to school for five and a half months. Even when he stayed at my place, Isabella came along. It was during the first month of school when he invited himself over for the first time. It wasn't long before he was staying the night at least a couple times per week, afraid to bike home in the dark.

I think Dad liked when Schooner was around. He talked more, even smiled sometimes. He seemed to go out of his way to make Schooner feel comfortable, offering him things like chips or pop. He even started putting the sleeping bag out on my bedroom floor, assuming Schoon was staying the night. He didn't like that Schooner ate so little, so he made more of an effort to cook dinners. Schooner never finished his plate, though. He'd mix the food around a bit with his fork, have a few bites here and there in between his talking, and then scrape the remainder into the garbage under the sink.

"The kid doesn't eat, Creighton," Dad said. "He's skin and bones. Wonder why? What's the deal with his family, anyway?"

"None of us know much, Dad. Think he just lives with his grandma. He never eats at school, either. Just the odd snack Ms. Hay gives him."

"Well, you'd think if he didn't eat much at home, the boy'd be starving. Must get what he needs, I guess," Dad said, turning back to his newspaper.

Schooner was a mystery. But one thing everyone knew about was his short fuse, which made him a target in school. Carcass especially liked to see him blow, and constantly provoked him with things like bad "Mom" jokes.

"Shut up, man! Don't even look at me," Schooner said, as Carcass intentionally tried to trigger him in the bathroom one afternoon.

But Carcass kept going. "Yo momma is so fat ..." he

continued, looking at Schooner, trying to push him further over the edge.

"Carcass, stop, man. Leave him!" I said.

Carlos walked out the door, looking back, laughing.

"Don't ever talk about my family!" Schooner screamed, as the door slammed closed behind Carlos.

Schooner sat down against the bathroom wall next to the urinals. One hand on his knee, he ran the other through his sweaty hair. "I hate that kid. He doesn't even know."

"It's all good, Schoon! Carcass thinks those stupid jokes are funny. He tells them all the time," I said, kneeling beside him on the chipped cement floor.

It was these sorts of moments that told me Schooner didn't talk about his life for a reason. Sometimes I wondered if that's why he was so attached to his caterpillar, because he didn't have much else.

He'd been bringing Isabella to school since September. Ms. Hayworth brought in peat moss and a spray bottle of water to help him make a better habitat for the little thing that lived inside a margarine container. He talked obsessively about the Isabella Tiger Moth she would become, and waited anxiously for the day she would form her cocoon. He said he'd learned all about her on Discovery

Channel, which made sense because, for a guy who could hardly read, he knew a lot about caterpillars.

When the days grew colder, Ms. Hayworth helped Schooner research the caterpillar on the Internet, so he understood that his pet actually needed to hibernate in order to pupate naturally. During the day, she encouraged Schooner to leave it outside the school under the overhanging roof, away from the snow, but still in a much cooler location. He added leaves, so she had a place to hide and curl up into her natural ball.

He checked the poor thing all the time, and carted the container to and from school every single day. It was probably his love for Isabella that eventually caused her death. Her life ended one Monday morning, two days before my birthday, and I worried Schooner would never be the same again.

We all knew her death was inevitable, because there was no way a caterpillar could survive being touched so much by a human being. In the morning before she died, he sprayed the peat moss with water and tickled Isabella to watch her curl into a ball. But she didn't move. By ten o'clock, after checking her constantly, Schooner put his head down and started to whimper.

I walked over and put my hand on his shoulder. "It's okay, buddy," I said.

Ms. Hayworth crouched down beside him. "You gave her a good life. I don't think there's another caterpillar in the world who was given so much love."

"Really?" he asked. "You think she was happy?"

"Schooner, buddy," I said. "You carted the thing with you everywhere you went. How could she not have been happy?"

"She was so alone when I found her crossing the road ... not another caterpillar in sight. She was going to be killed if I didn't take her. I wish she didn't die alone. I shoulda kept her with me when she was sick."

"Caterpillars are very solitary, Schooner. In times like that, they prefer aloneness," Ms. Hayworth said sympathetically. "Come, we'll find a place to bury her and have a little ceremony."

Will and Frasier were whispering to one another, and Carlos was imitating Schooner crying.

"Shut up, man!" Ratchet said. "Have some respect."

Carin was sitting on top of her desk, arms and legs crossed, rubbing her elbows. She was biting her cheek and sniffled quietly. When Ms. Hayworth gave the cue to have a ceremony, Carin took the lead.

"We can bury her by the rock garden," she said to Ms. Hayworth. "Out back. I have a tiny box from my belly-button ring. Let me grab it."

Carin ran to her locker and back. She also grabbed some carnations from a vase on Ms. Hayworth's desk. Turning to Will, she said quickly, "Get those tiny wood scraps you threw out and glue them together to make a cross."

Will's face grew serious. He did as he was asked.

We followed Ms. Hayworth outside. None of us put our jackets on and we traipsed through the deep snow in running shoes, until we arrived at the small rock garden at the back of the alternate school.

We all stood around a woolly bear caterpillar, lying dead in a belly-button-ring box, prepared to watch it lowered gently into the ground.

As Schooner tried to control his sobs, I think we were changed by his emotion. We just stood as he said goodbye to little Isabella. No more teasing. Somehow Schooner gained everyone's respect, because it was impossible to ignore his pain.

Carin held Hamilton's hand tightly and whispered softly to him. Mrs. Scarlet also tried to distract Hamilton. Ratchet's eyes welled up with tears as he scraped his boot around, forming a small pile of snow with his foot. Frasier and Will were quiet. Even Carcass made no snide comments. The twins, Gabe and Cass, patted each other's shoulders, trying to look sympathetic. Ronnie turned his back because, I figured, he couldn't really feel emotion. He always looked stone-faced, no matter what was going on in the class. When a kid was freaking out, or even when Ms. Hayworth was upset, Ronnie never changed his expression. Devon looked at everyone curiously, smiling a little, because he wasn't too comfortable with serious things. I stood next to Schooner. I gave him the occasional shoulder squeeze when I heard him sniffle. All twelve of us, the most messed-up kids in the district, who were unable to function in a regular classroom for one reason or another, stood together in a circle.

Ms. Hayworth broke the silence.

"You taught us all a good lesson, Schooner. You noticed a caterpillar alone and felt something for that little creature, while others might have walked on by. You took her in and made her feel safe."

I glanced at Schooner. He had that piercing stare, like he often did, holding onto every single one of Ms. Hay's words. Once in a while, he'd gasp in air as his crying slowed down.

"But loss," she continued, "it's a very painful thing."

I looked around the circle and my eyes met Carin's. She was staring at me. She blinked. A small drop of water slid from her deep brown eyes onto her cheek, leaving a trail of smudged black makeup down the side of her face. She caught it with her hand. I swallowed. Her cheek crinkled, forming a small smile. She twisted her lip with her fingers. I smiled back, and this time I didn't look away.

I didn't understand why Schooner's sadness affected all of us. No one mocked him at all. Whatever the case, our class pulled together when we placed a little caterpillar into the frozen ground, marking Isabella's spot with a tiny crooked cross and some old carnations.

CHAPTER 11

Two days after Isabella's death was my fifteenth birthday. Even though Schooner talked nonstop about the secret present he'd planned, I didn't think he'd pull through, not after the loss of his caterpillar.

Since Mom had left, my birthday was just another day. Every couple of years, Dad handed me something he figured I needed, like a Swiss Army knife, tossing the gift to me when it was convenient for him. He left them in the shopping bags, sometimes even making an effort to sticky tape the top of the bag closed. But this year, I was excited.

Dad didn't say a thing that morning. I got up like I always did. He was on the porch, having his smoke. I grabbed a bowl of cereal and plunked myself at the table.

"Mornin', son," he said, as he walked toward the front

door to grab the *Breton Bi-Weekly* newspaper.

"Morning, Dad," I replied.

"I'm going into the office today, so you go ahead with supper tonight. I'll be late," he continued.

"'K Dad."

I thought about the cake Mom and I had made, and the small trailer fridge we'd stuffed it into for the night. I remember waiting for the carnival guys to wake up and then lighting their cigarettes. I could see Mom sitting on the trailer steps in her pink robe and fluffy boots. I could hear her voice humming "Happy Birthday." I wondered if she remembered, too. Did she wake up and think about her little boy in his new Spiderman pajamas?

I walked into the school, like I had done every other day for six months. I tossed my backpack in my locker. No one else was in the hall. I walked into the class and saw no one there, either. Ms. Hayworth wasn't running around getting stuff ready. Schooner wasn't following her, chatting, like he did every single morning. There was no Mrs. Scarlet helping Hamilton. Carin wasn't buried in pillows on the corner of the carpet, listening to music with her hood covering her face. I looked outside the window and saw Ratchet's bike. He was never early, but the bike was already there in the rack. I noticed Hamilton's pipe cleaners all linked together on his desk. I realized he must be here, too, because he would *never* leave his pipe cleaners at school overnight.

I started to leave, thinking I'd check out the other room, when suddenly everyone jumped out from behind the large bookcase and started singing "Happy Birthday." Carin was holding a cake with fifteen candles on top. She walked toward me. I smiled awkwardly, while she placed the cake on my desk. My name was written in blue icing, *"Happy 15th Creigh."* I stood there uncomfortably as the song finished.

"Well, blow them out!" she yelled, laughing. "And don't forget to make a wish," she added.

"A wish?" I asked, confused.

"Yeah, Creigh, you make a wish when you blow out candles." Carin explained.

"Wait, wait!" Ms. Hay interrupted. "All of you stand behind Creighton. Let me get my camera. We definitely need a picture of this special moment."

I waited for everyone to squeeze in behind me. I puffed up my cheeks nervously, unsure how to actually blow out fifteen burning candles.

"Cake for breakfast, everyone!" Ms. Hayworth said excitedly. "Smile!" She took the picture and then Ms. Hay handed me a card. I opened it and read the front:

"If you gently touch a nettle, it'll sting you for your pains; grasp it like a lad of mettle, an' as soft as silk remains."
Sanskrit Proverb

"I love the meaning behind these words, Creighton. It's something I definitely believe in myself."

"Thanks, Ms. Hay. I'll have to try and figure them out."

Carin brought over a knife and a pile of plates, and I basically butchered her perfect work as I cut the cake. She passed everyone a piece, and we all sat on top of the desks, eating. Everyone talked and the room felt calm. Ms. Hayworth was smiling. Carlos was even talking back and forth. He seemed happy, like the rest of us.

"Thanks, Carin. You did all this, didn't you?" I asked as she walked by, collecting the finished plates.

"You deserve it, Creigh," she replied. "You needed a little party." Ms. Hay and Carin were good about making birthdays special in the classroom. Ms. Hay always had cards for her students. But there'd never been a cake or a party.

Even though Schooner was more quiet than usual, he'd reminded me to be at the tracks by five o'clock if I wanted my birthday surprise. While I walked there, I couldn't wipe the smile off my face. I'd had a party. Carin had made me a cake.

I felt a little guilty, though, thinking about Schooner's sadness. Why did he get so attached to a little caterpillar? I couldn't erase Ratchet's teary eyes from my mind, and wondered how a guy like him could feel emotion at a caterpillar's funeral. What stopped Carcass from making fun of the situation, and turning the funeral into something of his own? He let the moment belong to Schooner. What was Carin thinking, as she stared at me with that little half-smile?

And I'd had a party of my own. I loved how she wrote "Creigh" with the blue icing—my name on a cake! I was never given a card before. Ms. Hay had picked one out just for me. I stopped and pulled it out of my backpack. I read the words again as I walked. I still didn't understand them, but I liked that it said: *"Happy 15th Birthday, Creighton. So happy you joined our family. Ms. Hay."* Not Ms. Hayworth, she had written, *"Ms. Hay."* I liked its familiar sound. She called us a family. I hadn't had that, either.

The train arrived later than its normal five o'clock time, but Schooner still hadn't shown up. Then I heard him screeching from somewhere. I stood up and ran to the bottom of the bank, trying to see along the edge of the tracks, where the train would pass as it slowed down.

There, in the distance, on top of a boxcar, was Schooner, just a small figure getting larger as he approached. His hands were flailing in the air, and he was jumping up and down, yelling at the top of his lungs.

"HAPPY BIRTHDAY TO THE BEST FRIEND I EVER HAD!" he shouted.

Had he really done it? I strained my eyes, trying to see what he was yelling about.

"Look at it! I did it! I made it for you; I got it done," he shouted, pointing below him at the freshly sprayed tag that read: VENUS.

"Venus?" I thought. I didn't get it. Why did he write VENUS? He didn't know why Venus was important to me. I'd never talked about it at all.

The train was coming to a stop and Schooner's boxcar passed. I could see him looking back at me, still yelling. I tried to catch up to him. As I approached, a police car pulled up to the intersection and flashed its lights.

Schooner did not look scared. His focus remained on me, his body intense, anticipating my reaction.

I pointed to the police car, and then cupped my mouth, as I screamed for him to jump off. Schooner didn't seem to care. He swung himself down the side of the car, tightly holding the handle of the steel ladder, while his body dangled, legs flailing, as they tried to make contact with the top of the step. He jumped off the slowly moving train, falling into the pile of gravel alongside the track. He stood up, dusted himself off, and raised his arms proudly.

The police officer walked toward Schooner.

"Young man, you'll be coming for a ride with me," he said. "Not sure what you thought you were doing, but you can't be riding on top of trains. That's a long ride from the Fairburn station. Someone reported you climbing up there."

Schooner looked at me as he walked toward the police car, arms above his head in surrender, just like you'd see in a movie, and he continued to holler.

"It's all yours, Creigh, your own boxcar, man!" he repeated.

Schooner climbed into the car, still smiling and waving at me as the vehicle pulled away. He had done it. He'd created a tag and never looked prouder. I couldn't believe he rode all the way from Fairburn. He must have caught the bus there after school.

Because of his so-called vandalism, he was given community hours under the supervision of a probation officer. Ironically, he thrived on the work he was assigned. Each day after school, for two hours, he cleaned up the tracks that passed directly through Breton. The best thing about his new job was a fluorescent orange vest, making him feel important, like a uniform. Even though he could slip it over his clothes once he got to work, he'd proudly put the vest on at his locker after school.

"Why you putting that thing on now?" Ratchet asked.

"No time! I gotta be at work right away," Schooner replied, racing out the door.

We all knew Schooner could put that vest on in a matter of seconds, but he loved his uniform, and proudly wore it through town to get to the "job site," as he liked to call it. Schooner's punishment was actually a blessing.

Once the RCMP released him on the day of his arrest, he rode over to my house.

I wasn't sure what to say. Schooner, the guy who was so afraid of getting in trouble, had vandalized a train in my honor. And the crazy part of it was, I didn't even understand what he wrote. It didn't say Creighton or Creigh or Happy Birthday, Buddy. It said VENUS, and I had no clue why he thought of that.

"Just out of curiosity, Schooner, why'd you choose to write VENUS instead of my name or something?" I asked.

Schooner reached toward my neck and grabbed the charm in his hands.

"Your necklace, man—the symbol of Venus," he said. "I know how much you love that thing from your mom."

I clutched the charm that had dangled from my neck for two whole years. For at least seven hundred and thirty days, I must have stared at that thing in the mirror, once in the morning, then again at night, whenever I remembered to brush my teeth. In all that time, I'd never thought about what it stood for.

I'd known Schooner for eight months, but he kept on surprising me. He couldn't read much, he had a pet caterpillar in Grade 9, and he told a lot of lies. Then suddenly, out of nowhere, he'd come up with things that would blow my mind. It took a guy who was supposedly dumber than a stick to make me see the obvious.

After he left, I unhooked the necklace and held the charm in my hand, turning it over and over. "Venus," I thought.

I remembered standing in front of the trailer with Mom, searching for the bright light. She'd remind me, if we were ever apart, to find Venus. She'd be staring at it, too. It worked when I was young; knowing we were under the same sky made me feel closer. But not anymore. I tried to picture her face, and realized the image was fading. I tried to recall the songs she sang, as she tucked my hair behind my ears, and struggled to think of the words.

I made sure I arrived early for school the next day. I couldn't wait to get on the computer. I typed in "symbol of Venus" to see if Schooner was right. There it was, the charm that I wore faithfully each day, unaware of what it stood for.

As a horoscope symbol Venus represents the drive for togetherness and is associated with love.

It was perfect. How did I not realize this?

I continued to read. Ms. Hayworth entered. She'd been photocopying materials in the small office next door.

"My goodness, Creighton, you scared me half to death. I didn't realize you were here. Is everything okay? You're so early."

She rested her hand on my shoulder. Staring at the screen, she noticed the symbol and the description I was reading, and she saw the necklace I held in my other hand. Taking a deep breath, as if she'd wanted to talk about my mom before, she pulled a desk closer to my chair and sat down.

"Creighton? The necklace, it was from your mother, wasn't it?"

I nodded.

"I knew it must be something special, since you've worn it every single day since we met."

I looked up at her.

"I know your mom left when you were a young boy. I'm sure it's been painful sometimes."

I nodded again, looking down at my lap.

"But, Creighton, we're all searching for the same thing, you know."

I clutched the charm, rubbing it between my fingers. A lump formed in my throat. I couldn't cry, not in front of Ms. Hayworth. I continued to look down and turned my head away.

"I guarantee, a day has not gone by without your mom remembering what she left behind, Creighton. But it's hard to give to others what you haven't received yourself."

Ms. Hayworth had one arm on the desk where she sat, and one hand on me. She seemed to know so many things about all of us.

"You're an intelligent boy with a deep understanding of people. You'll figure it out, Creighton. You'll be able to put these feelings to rest eventually."

I couldn't say a thing. I just nodded, keeping my head down, wiping my nose with the sleeve of my hoodie.

"What are we all searching for?" I wondered. Ms. Hayworth was right—loss is a really painful thing.

CHAPTER 12

"Guess what, guys?" Ratchet said to Schooner and me, as he rushed in the back door of the classroom. "I got the truck tonight." And when he got the farm truck, it meant freedom for all of us.

Mr. Sullivan, the owner of the dairy farm where Ratchet spent most of his time working, seemed to look out for Ratchet. He'd give him rides to school when Ratchet spent the night out at the farm and, eventually, gave him an old truck. Probably felt bad for Ratch, since he had no parents taking care of him, and he spent so much time biking to and from town.

It was Friday, March 19, the last day of school before spring break. The plan was to meet at the sawdust pits. We usually did something if Ratchet got the truck on a weekend.

"I'll stop by your house. Grab you guys there," Ratchet said, kicking his locker shut.

"You're staying at my house, hey, Schooner? You good with that?" Of course, Schooner was good with that. He always stayed at my house on weekends.

"Yeah, I can probably stick around if you want me to, Creigh," Schooner said, like he was sacrificing some other important event for my sake.

As she listened to the three of us making plans, Carin jumped into the conversation. "I'll see how my mom's feeling, and maybe we can drive everyone out to the farm." Carin had got her Learner's License in January, so she was always looking for opportunities to drive, as long as her Mom could be in the car.

"Sounds good. I gotta work first, though, so don't come till after seven," Ratchet replied.

Carin drove me and Schooner to the farm just before eight. Her mom was in the passenger seat, since Carin still needed an adult in the car in order to drive anywhere.

"Thanks, Mom," Carin said as she got out of the car, "I'll get Ratchet to bring me home, so please don't worry."

"Well, I don't want you walking anywhere alone," Mrs.

Reiner replied. "You make sure he drops you off right at the house. And you wake me up when you come in."

Mrs. Reiner had a thick layer of makeup on, and a brightly colored scarf wrapped around her head. The makeup was so thick, she probably had to peel it off before she went to bed. Maybe she figured the makeup would hide her poor health.

"Mom, I'd never walk alone. Trust me."

"Appreciate the ride, Mrs. Reiner. Don't worry, we'll make sure Carin gets home okay," I said.

It seemed like a big effort for Mrs. Reiner to walk around the car to the driver's side. She was such a frail looking woman, so tiny, you could almost see through her. I quickly moved in and opened the driver's door for her, feeling bad that we'd dragged her out to the farm at all.

Carin had been to Ratchet's place before, but this was the first time for Schooner and me. As we walked toward the shack, a loose cow wandered toward us. Schooner grabbed onto me.

"It's after us! I think it's a bull. He's gonna charge us, I know it," he said, squeezing his way between me and Carin.

"Jesus, Schooner, get a grip!" Carin said impatiently. "You're at a dairy farm. There's gonna be the occasional cow out here. They're not going to kill you."

The cow picked up her pace and mooed. Schooner started screaming, and ran ahead to get inside Ratchet's shack. We shook our heads, laughing.

Ratchet opened the door to let us in, holding a pot in his hand, as he ate his remaining mac and cheese. Beside the door, heaped in a pile on the floor, were his coveralls and gumboots. I could smell the manure.

"Just gotta jump in the shower. Be a sec," Ratchet said, as he tossed the empty pot in the sink.

Carin was helping herself to the bag of sunflower seeds Ratchet had left on the counter. "Are we still hitting the pits tonight, or what do you feel like?" she asked, as she spit the shells into the half-full dish.

"Doesn't matter to me," I replied, looking around, impressed that Ratchet kind of had a place of his own.

The shack was basically one big room with a small, separate bathroom. Schooner made himself comfortable on the single bed in the corner. He grabbed Ratchet's Walkman off the bedside table and fiddled with the CD. There was no sheet on the bed. I could see the pillow scrunched in the corner of the thin mattress, and the worn-out comforter draped over the end of the bed, falling onto the floor. Next to the bathroom was a washing machine. On top was an open box of laundry soap, with a heap of clothes piled next to the box. A towel was jammed underneath the washing machine, to stop the leaks, maybe, and a mousetrap sat beside the empty laundry basket on the floor.

The shower stopped.

The small window beside the bed had a sheet nailed up like a curtain. I imagined Ratchet grabbing the only sheet on his bed, in frustration, and hammering it up there, probably after a late Friday night, when he couldn't deal with the sunlight pouring in the next morning. The clock beside his bed was flashing *12:00*. Carin walked over and set it to *8:42*, the correct time. On the cement floor, beside the bed, was an open bag of potato chips. Schooner kept reaching in, grabbing a chip, and then wiping his cheesy hands on the mattress as he fast-forwarded the CD.

"That's disgusting, Schooner!" Carin said. "You're getting crap all over the mattress. Wipe your hands on your pants or something."

But Schooner had put the headphones on and was singing along to Guns N' Roses' "Knockin' on Heaven's Door." His eyes were closed, and he was belting out the words, drumming with his one free hand on the side of the bed, while swinging a chip in the air with the other. Carin and I laughed.

A toolbox sat on the small kitchen table beside a pack of cigarettes. There was a bike chain and a drive train on an old towel. Beside it, there was a small ratchet set and a tube of oil. I was impressed that Ratchet rode his bike to school when he stayed out here. No wonder he needed a breakfast sandwich when he got to town. Next to his toolbox was a cheque from Sullivan Dairy for $114.29, with his name on the top: *"Pay to the Order of Matt Radcliff."* It seemed strange, seeing his name.

"Mind grabbing me those pants?" Ratchet said, pointing to the jeans that lay in a heap on the floor beside his bed. He was standing by the bathroom door with a towel wrapped around his waist. "What's with him?" he said, pointing to Schooner, who was dancing pretty hard, as he sat on the bed with his eyes closed.

Ratchet came back out of the bathroom, wearing his jeans. "Give me that!" he said, ripping the headphones off Schooner. He popped the CD out of the Walkman and put it in the CD player that sat on the kitchen counter. Ratchet skipped the song to Guns N' Roses' "November Rain." He sang along as he opened the fridge, took out a Corona and cracked it open, using the edge of the counter. He sliced a piece of lime and pushed it into the bottle with his thumb, still singing. I was surprised he had a fresh lime in his shack. I thought he was going to take a slug, but he didn't. Instead, he handed it to Carin, familiarly.

"Thanks, Ratch!" Carin said, and smiled as she swung her head back to take a sip.

He washed his pot and the other dishes piled in the sink.

Ratchet shook his head to the beat, singing along. Schooner stood on the bed and joined in. He grabbed the pillow and pretended he was dancing with a girl, smiling as he belted out each word. Carin and I had never seen this side of Schooner. Out of the blue, Carin reached for my hand and pulled me up from the chair, singing.

Next I knew, we were dancing, and I had no clue what I was doing. Schooner jumped on the bed, clapping when he saw us. We all sang together.

When the song came to an end, Carin's hand was still in mine, and she was laughing hard. I had never seen her look this happy. I pulled her in, gave her a little squeeze with my free arm, surprising myself. I noticed Ratchet watching us.

"Hey, let's get out of here, then," he said, and turned off the music.

I dropped Carin's hand and walked toward the chair, where my jacket was draped over the back. I felt bad. The way Ratchet had glanced over made me feel uncomfortable. Even though he was in Grade 11, older than all of us, he seemed grown up. You could tell he'd been shaving for a few years, because he had a full shadow on his face after a day. He grabbed the truck keys off the counter and gave them a little toss in the air, catching them and shoving them in his pocket, as if he'd been tossing keys and catching them for years. He rummaged through the laundry pile on top of the washing machine, gave a T-shirt a quick sniff, then put it on. Ratchet kicked the cupboard below the sink, closing it with his foot, then he walked toward the door and grabbed his plaid jacket off the hook. The way he moved around in his own little shack made it seem like he'd been an adult his whole life.

We piled into the front of the farm truck, heading to the Sawdust Pits for a party.

"Need to stop anywhere?" Ratchet asked, reversing along the narrow driveway that led away from his shack.

I was thinking about Ratchet as we drove to the party.

How could the same guy who danced around happily in his little farm shack get so violent sometimes? He seemed like a different kid when he stayed at the shack. Or maybe he was a different kid since he'd tossed his pills. At the farm, no one was controlling him or telling him what to do; he was free, on his own, living life. Maybe it was the group home that had wound him up and pushed him over the edge. Or was it school, sitting there all day in such a tightly confined space? If Ratchet was the kid Dad had read about in the papers, the kid who'd lived his first few years in a closet, having no one to depend on, that life would have messed him up. Why would doctors think a pill could fix that?

By the time we made our way up a gravel road to the sawdust pits, a crowd had already gathered around the bonfire. A pile of old pallets burned, and people were standing around, drinking. When Carin got out of the truck, a bunch of girls ran over. Carin had lived in Breton her whole life, and went to school with the girls until Grade 8, when she was transferred to the alternate school.

Ratchet also seemed comfortable. He had no problem talking, and seemed to know everyone at the party. Schooner made his rounds, too, trying to bum drinks off guys he didn't even know. Most people just ignored him.

I found it hard to mingle. Carin was good at pulling me into conversation, but I felt bad she took on this responsibility, like I was a burden or something, when she probably wanted to hang out with her friends.

"Creigh," she said, tugging at the side of my jacket, "I need you for a sec." She pulled me away from the fire. "I gotta pee bad. Can you come with me?" she whispered.

Of course, I could go with her. I would go anywhere with Carin.

"Wait here, 'K?" she said as her eyes darted around, looking for a private spot where she couldn't be seen.

Standing there, waiting beside the bushes, I wondered why she'd asked me. I kept my back to her. She continued to talk, but I couldn't hear a thing she said.

"Oh, my God," she said, rushing out of the bushes, zipping up her jeans. "I thought you left. You didn't answer me." Carin grabbed my arm. "Seriously, I thought you left me in those bushes," she repeated.

"I wouldn't leave you, Carin. You okay?" I asked, worrying. Carin's eyes were wide with fear. She held onto my arm and her grip didn't loosen. Of course, she would feel scared, alone in the bushes. Why hadn't I made her feel safer?

"Sorry, Creigh, I just ... it's just that I ... it doesn't matter. Thanks for waiting for me."

As we walked back to the fire, cars were starting to leave, and news spread quickly that the party was moving to the river.

"I can't go to the river!" Carin said, pulling at my arm. "I need to get home. Where's Ratchet?"

"It's okay, we'll get you home," I answered, as my eyes searched around for his truck.

Ratchet was talking by the fire, and looked like he was in no hurry to move.

"I'm sorry," Carin said. "I don't want to ruin your fun."

This was my opportunity to say something, to tell her I knew, that I'd heard the story. Instead, I led her to a log by the fire. Ratchet was standing there, too.

"Ratch, you mind dropping us off at Carin's on your way to the river?" I asked.

"You guys aren't coming?"

Then Ratch looked at me, like he remembered. Of course, Carin would never go to the river.

"Yeah, sure, man. I'll get you home, Carin."

Carin didn't say a thing. She sat there on the log, holding her clenched hands between her knees, shivering.

"Here, put this around you," I said, taking off my jacket and resting it on her shoulders. I sat next to her, waiting to see if Ratchet was ready to go. She leaned her head on me.

Ratchet glanced over.

"Why are you so sweet?" Carin said softly. "You're the quietest guy I've ever met, but you're so good to me."

She stood up and turned to face me, her knees touching mine, still wearing my jacket. Reaching for my hands, she pulled me up from the log. We walked toward the truck to wait for Ratchet. She leaned her back against the door, grabbed onto my hands, and pulled my body in toward hers. We were still for a bit, just staring at each other, and then I leaned in to kiss her. I'd never kissed a girl. Carin moved her head in toward mine. Just as our lips made contact, she jolted back, turning her head abruptly away.

I didn't say a thing. Maybe I should have. I just stayed still.

Carin turned her head back to look at me, still holding my hands, waiting for a response. It wasn't the toughness I was used to seeing. She took a breath. I tucked the loose strands of her brown dread knots behind her ear. I couldn't take my eyes off her. I gently wiped her face with my thumb, catching the small tear. Her cheek crinkled, forming a tiny smile. The same smile I had seen at Isabella's funeral.

"Jeez, thought you forgot me," Schooner said, jumping in the driver's side of the truck and scooting himself into the middle. I climbed in through the passenger door and Carin followed, moving onto my lap. Schooner pounded on the horn, laughing, holding it down to get Ratchet's attention.

"Knock it off, Schooner!" Carin snapped. "He's coming; give him a sec."

Ratchet was good at navigating the bush roads in the dark, as we bumped our way down the gravel road. I held onto Carin with one hand, and pressed my other against the window to protect her head from hitting the glass, with each pothole we tried to dodge. Ratchet looked over, just as Carin interlocked her fingers with mine.

"I better drop you off here," Ratchet said, as he pulled over to the side of the road, just as we entered town. "I don't want to drive down Main Street. Too many cops, and I only got one headlight workin'."

"It's all good," I said, turning toward Carin. "Schooner and I will walk you," I added.

We stepped out of the truck. Carin and Schooner were talking on the sidewalk, and I leaned back in the window to Ratchet. "You good, Ratch?" I asked.

"Yeah, man, why wouldn't I be good?" Ratchet replied, looking at me, then turning away to hold onto the steering wheel.

"You like her, don't you? I asked.

"It's all good. You two are good, man," he said, clearing his throat. Ratchet kept looking forward. He gave the engine a few revs and pulled away.

CHAPTER 13

The last week of school before summer holidays, Schooner really started to worry me. He always had the occasional outburst of anger, but Ms. Hay was usually good at calming him before the blow-ups got too big. He seemed to be losing respect for her, sometimes even ignoring her completely when she spoke to him. We didn't know what his issue was, until the huge incident, the worst blow I'd seen him have.

Ms. Hay always made an effort to keep Schooner interested in school. She'd find topics he liked, so he'd be motivated to read. When things mattered to him, he'd catch on. When he had Isabella, Ms. Hay made all of his work about Woolly Mammoth Caterpillars. Between Discovery Channel, National Geographics, and the nonfiction kids' books she signed out from the Public Library, Schooner learned what he needed to. He memorized words if they had some importance in his life. Like my Venus tag on the train.

A week before the end of school, Schooner was slumped over his desk with his head down. He often kept a jacket or hoodie on, even on sweltering June days, when the classroom was unbearably hot, ensuring his face could barely be seen.

We were getting settled after the bell rang, when Ms. Hay walked over to his desk with a book in her hand. "Schooner?" she said, kneeling down beside him. "I found a book in the library yesterday—it's about graffiti. It's a form of art, you know. You're always drawing tags on your work, so I thought you might like to learn more about it."

Schooner did not move. His head remained face down, with his hood pulled tightly over top.

"Some graffiti artists make a living with their work," she continued, even though Schooner seemed to be ignoring everything she said. "It's not the kind of graffiti used in vandalism. People actually hire graffiti artists to paint."

Schooner looked up drearily. His eyes seemed red.

"So, what you're saying is, you think I'm going to vandalize things?"

"Not at all, Schooner. I know how good you are. I see your art on your schoolwork every day. I just thought ..."

"You thought what?" Schooner replied. "You thought I'd start vandalizing things, didn't ya? Ha? Ya figure I'm gonna start wrecking stuff?"

Schooner's voice was aggressive. His face was red. Ms. Hay put her hand on his shoulder gently as she stood up.

"Schooner," she said slowly, "take a breath. I want you to take a slow breath. You're fine."

He stood up, holding his fists tightly at his sides, breathing deeply between his bared teeth, while staring at her intensely. Ms. Hay took a step back as she moved her arm off his shoulder. His eyes were bloodshot with fury. We all knew to stay back when Schooner had an episode. He was like a raging bull awaiting release from his stall.

"You WILL be okay!" She kept talking to him in a calm and soothing voice, never taking her eyes off him. "Mrs. Scarlet," she said, pointing toward the door, still looking at Schooner, "take them to the other room." We knew the routine. It wasn't the first time we'd had to evacuate the classroom when someone freaked out.

Just as we were all getting up, everyone whispering and watching closely, Schooner stood up, too.

"I can't wait to get out of this hellhole!" he yelled, as he kicked the leg of the desk in front of him. He paused only briefly, like he was revving up. He marched toward the open door, pushing all the books off the top shelf as he passed by, sliding the pottery cup filled with pens off Ms. Hay's desk, kicking the legs of the table, even throwing the chairs that were in his path. Beside the door was a bulletin board, neatly covered in blue paper and borders. He reached up and tore it down the middle, leaving the ripped paper dangling. And then he put his fist right through the glass window at the top of the door.

"I hate this place," he yelled. "I never wanted to come to this dumb school, anyway."

He swung the door closed behind him, and the remaining shards of glass fell onto the classroom carpet and hallway floor. He continued into the boys' bathroom, the door swinging shut behind him. No one moved. Ms. Hayworth stood motionless. We waited for her guidance, but she said nothing. I could see her swallowing. She was biting her lip. It wasn't Carcass who made her eyes water. In the whole year, with the many outbursts and fights, she'd never got emotional. It was Schooner. Schooner was the one who made her crack.

Everyone was scattered around the classroom, since we had all been making our way to the door to evacuate. Schooner just got there first. He made sure of it!

"It's okay," she said as she took a breath. "You can all sit down. He's just having a hard time right now. He didn't mean what he said."

The room was silent, which was a rare thing at Lane Oslo. Even Ratchet didn't say a word. He just got the dustpan and broom and walked toward the door, to clean up the shards of glass that were spread throughout the hallway and classroom.

"Thank you, Ratchet," she said. By then, Carin had made her way to Ms. Hay's desk, picking up the pens and the broken pieces of pottery from the cup Schooner had pushed off her desk. A few of us started picking up the books and chairs, straightening the classroom, unsure what else we should do.

"Ah," Ms. Hay sighed with a smile, brushing strands of her long hair out of her eyes. "When Schooner comes back to class, I need all of you to do something for me. We aren't going to bring any of this up with him. I don't want you to tease him, or say a word about what just happened. I need Schooner to be here for the last week, to get through the rest of this year. He and I will quietly have a chat. But I trust you can all let this go, and not make it into something bigger for him."

She turned to me. "Creighton, do you mind going to check on Schooner?"

Schooner was crouched on the floor of the bathroom. His head was between his knees, and I could hear him crying.

"Come on. We'll hang out at the river and stuff. It'll be good."

"She's not comin' back, you know." Schooner looked up at me, throwing out his hands before running them through his greasy hair.

"What do you mean? Who's not coming back?" I asked.

"Ms. Hay. She's going to leave us. She's gonna have a baby ... can't you tell?" Schooner said.

I never noticed, but Schooner was right; Ms. Hayworth did look bigger. But she would have told us, given us some sort of warning.

Carin knocked on the door of the bathroom. "Can I come in?" she said, and pushed the door open enough to see me talking to Schooner, who was still sitting on the floor, with no intention of leaving the bathroom.

"Oh, gross," she said looking around. "It's disgusting in here. Schooner, how can you sit on this floor?" Carin said, pretending to gag. "Come on, Schoon, we only have a week left. Let's make it a good one for Ms. Hay. Come back to the classroom. She says she isn't starting until she has you there."

"Tell him! Tell Creigh. You know everything about Ms. Hay," Schooner said, looking up at Carin.

Carin looked at me, then back at Schooner. "Tell him what, Schooner? What do you want me to tell Creigh?"

"Ms. Hayworth's pregnant, isn't she? Tell us the truth, Carin," Schooner said, raising his voice.

Ms. Hayworth slowly opened the door. "Why don't you all come back to the class?" she said quietly. "I'll talk to everyone at the same time."

Schooner got up off the bathroom floor, and we followed Ms. Hayworth into the classroom. There was silence as we entered. The three of us walked to our seats. Ms. Hayworth stood at the front, her bun falling apart earlier than usual. Her baggy shirt hung over her black leggings. There was a bulge, as Schooner had said, but she often wore loose-fitting clothing. And the rest of her body remained as thin as ever. I'd never have noticed.

"I have some news for you all," Ms. Hayworth began.

I looked over at Schooner. He had resumed the same position, hunched forward, with his hood pulled tightly over his head.

Ms. Hayworth cleared her throat. Her voice was shaky.

"I was going to wait until the end of the week to talk to you, but I think it's best I share some news now. Next year will be exciting for all of us. I'm having a baby in September. I'll have to take some time to be a mom, which means you'll have someone new as your teacher for a while." She stopped again. No one moved or said a thing.

"I'm sure some of you will like the idea of a little break from me," she said, laughing, "... because ... well, some of us have been together for years."

Ratchet interrupted, as he usually did.

"You can just bring the baby. We'll help you, Ms. Hay."

She laughed.

"Mr. Roland hasn't said who my replacement will be, but I'm sure he'll find someone good, someone you'll like."

Hamilton was oblivious to the news. He had a new purple comb that he ran through his hair, occasionally stopping to rub his fingers along its teeth.

Ronnie was crouched on the floor beside his desk,

gathering the paper bits that had fallen out of the hole-punch. He took each circular piece and formed patterns on his desk. Will had his carving knife in his hand, and he held it above the miniature totem he was balancing between his legs, making the finishing touches. He was silent, as if thinking. And then he pressed the blade firmly into the post that was almost complete. He dragged the knife down the faces of the thirteen animals he had so carefully carved, destroying months of work.

Ms. Hayworth noticed at the same time.

"Stop, Will! It's almost finished. We're going to put it in the showcase at the end of the week," she said, quickly walking over to him.

Ms. Hayworth had asked Will to carve the post, so that it could be displayed in the cabinet in the entrance to the school. She wanted something to represent our Lane Oslo family.

She grabbed the knife. "We'll fix this," she said to Will. "We'll put this post up at the front of the school, just as we planned."

Carin twisted her lip, running her tongue along her teeth. I'm sure she had known, too. She wasn't saying a thing, though. She wasn't looking at anyone.

Carcass smirked as Ms. Hay took the carving away from Will.

Ratchet was talking to Gabe and Cass, still convinced that his idea of having the new baby in the classroom would solve the problem.

Schooner was right. This safe room, the place Ms. Hay had made for us, was coming to an end.

CHAPTER 14

"Get up, Schoon! Come on, man. We gotta get going," I said, rocking Schooner with my foot as he rolled over in his sleeping bag. "Last day, bud, it's summer. Get in the shower."

Our last day of school before summer vacation, my final day of Grade 8, and Schooner would not get off my bedroom floor.

"Leave me alone. I'm not going to school today," he replied, his words muffled by the scrunched-up pillow pressed against his face.

"You gotta go, Schooner. Everyone will want to see you. Ms. Hay will want to say goodbye."

"Yeah? Well, you tell her I said 'Bye.' Now let me get some sleep," Schooner replied.

I walked into the kitchen. Dad sat at the table. He was sipping his coffee, reading *The Globe and Mail*, when I interrupted.

"Can't get Schooner out of that sleeping bag today," I said, grabbing a bowl from the cupboard.

Dad looked up from his newspaper and took another sip. "Isn't it almost your last day?" he asked.

"It is our last day. We get dismissed at lunch. He knows that. I told him everyone will want to say goodbye, but he says he's not going. Ms. Hay won't be back in September. She's having a baby. Think it's really bothering him."

"Hmm ... probably hard for the old boy," Dad said, continuing to read. "Goodbyes would be tough on a kid like him. Seems like a lonely fella to me," Dad added, as he stood up to put his mug on the counter.

I ate my bowl of cereal. Dad folded the newspaper in half and gave me a tap on the head with it. He pushed his chair in with the other hand and moved toward the coffee maker, where he started to fill his old thermos with the remaining coffee.

"You going out of town today, Dad?" I asked, knowing that when he filled his thermos, it meant he was traveling.

"Won't be too late tonight. Delivering a ride to

Strasville, then home. Maybe five or six," Dad said as he screwed the lid on.

He walked down the hallway. I assumed he was going to brush his teeth, but instead he entered my bedroom. I could hear him talking to Schooner.

"Hey, my boy, I need you to get up and give me a hand this morning."

Schooner mumbled something back.

"Get dressed and I'll meet you on the porch," Dad added, before continuing on to the bathroom.

I poured the remaining milk from my bowl into the sink, holding the last few bits of soggy cereal with my spoon to avoid another plugged drain. I filled my glass with water from the tap and gulped it down. I rearranged the supper dishes in the dishwasher, so I could squeeze in my bowl and glass, and also made room for Dad's coffee cup, which he *always* left on the counter. As I was filling the dispenser with soap, I noticed the porch door swing shut. Schooner was up.

"I need you to help me carry these empties out to the truck," Dad told Schooner, who had actually listened and met Dad on the porch. We had been living in the house since July, almost a year, and not once had Dad made a trip to the bottle depot with his empty beer cans. Yet today, out of the blue, he decided Schooner needed to load them up. They were stacked neatly in their cardboard trays, twenty-four packs, filling two of the four benches right to the roof. They were also piled below the benches. I knew the last thing Dad was thinking about, before a trip to Strasville to deliver a ride, was to clean up his empties.

"Schoon, you got up!" I said to him, as I joined them on the porch.

Schooner didn't say a thing.

"You're going to get a lot cash for these, Dad," I said, trying to break the silence, as we all hauled piles of cardboard trays to Dad's pick-up.

"Ha! Yeah, probably should have got on this a while back," Dad muttered as he closed the tailgate. "Good thing we have Schooner here to help."

After the porch was cleaned off, I wondered how long Dad would drive around with the empties in the back of his truck. I knew he had no intention of stopping at the bottle depot on his way to pick up the ride he had to deliver.

"Thanks, boys, appreciate the help," Dad said as he opened the driver door. Just before he climbed in, he turned to Schooner. "You'll go to school today, won't you, my man?" Dad said, not giving Schooner an option to refuse. "You'll be here tonight?" he asked.

Schooner didn't talk. He looked down at his feet and nodded.

"Good, crib tournament, then. You go to school, and when I get home, the challenge is on with you boys." Dad didn't wait for a reply. He tossed his thermos on the passenger seat, climbed into his truck, and drove away.

Crib was something Schooner understood right away. He couldn't figure out math, but when Ms. Hayworth had taught us how to play the game earlier in the year, Schooner caught on before any of us. He noticed the dusty crib board on our living room shelf one evening, and challenged Dad to a game. I was surprised Dad agreed, since he was comfortable in his fully reclined chair, a beer in hand, watching TV. Since that night, Schooner often got us going in a game when he stayed over.

"Let's go—we're going to be late," I said, as I turned toward the porch door that led to the kitchen.

Schooner followed me in. I tossed an apple toward him as we headed out the front of the house, but noticed him set it on the dryer as we walked out.

Schooner was sullen the whole way to school, unlike

the usual mornings, when I wished he'd stop talking, just to take a breath.

When we arrived, things felt different. Carin wasn't in the corner of the carpet buried in the pillows, listening to music. She had gone to school early and was taking paper off the hallway bulletin boards. Ms. Hayworth had put plastic bags on our desks, and Will, Cass, and Gabe were piling their belongings into them. Ms. Hayworth had put a garbage can in the hallway, and was helping Carcass empty his locker.

"That's disgusting!" Ratchet said as Carcass pulled out a plastic bag, oozing with some unidentifiable liquid.

Ratchet had just arrived. He opened his locker to show Ms. Hay that he had nothing in it. I don't think he ever brought a thing to school, other than the breakfast sandwich he bought on the way.

"What's up with you today?" he said, turning to Schooner, who stood at his locker, staring blankly.

Just then, Carcass started laughing. He pulled out a moldy orange and held it up to Schooner's face. Carcass's eyes were wide, and he was using his high-pitched annoying laugh.

"Want some b-r-e-a-k-f-a-s-t?" he said to Schooner.

Schooner slammed his locker closed and walked into the classroom.

"Goodness, Carlos, we should have dealt with this locker sooner. Did you eat any of your lunches this year, or are they all piled at the bottom?" Ms. Hayworth said, as she continued to pull out plastic grocery bags, one after another. She was wearing rubber gloves and scrunched up her face, holding her breath, each time she disturbed another bag that had been resting in the pile for several months. Next, she held up his Agenda, which had been missing for ages.

"Well, surprise, surprise, look at this discovery," Ms. Hay said, shaking her head with a smile. The sticky Agenda was also moldy. She held it up above the garbage can, shaking it to see if the pages would open, but they were dried together, sealed shut, probably from one of his spilled slushies, which Ms. Hay refused to let Carlos bring into the classroom after lunch.

I didn't have much in my locker. I tossed my binder, a few pens, and a pair of brand-new running shoes that I had never worn, into the empty grocery bag. A change of shoes for PE was on the school supply list, but none of us had ever used them. Actually, I don't think anyone else brought school supplies, except for Ronnie and Hamilton. When I walked back into the classroom to gather the rest of my things, I could see Schooner sitting at his desk with his head down. His hood was pulled tightly over his head, and his grocery bag was still empty.

Hamilton was oblivious to all that was happening. Mrs. Scarlet was trying to get him to help her with his desk. However, he had recently discovered gel and was completely focused on his hair. He had taken to combing it firmly to one side. His new purple comb, which he continually used to smooth his hair throughout the day, was his latest obsession.

"I got a new purple comb. Look at my purple comb. My purple comb is so pretty and shiny. See my purple comb?" he said, leaning in too closely to Schooner.

No one was listening to Hamilton's comments. Usually, we kept him talking, but today everyone was annoyed. Hamilton continued.

"Look Schooner! You can touch my hair, Schooner. You can use my shiny purple comb." He reached his comb above Schooner's strawberry blond head, ready to slide it through his un-brushed hair, when Carin grabbed it, just before it made contact.

"Give me that comb, Hamilton!" she said, yanking it out of his hand.

Hamilton stood with his mouth open.

"You comb your own hair today ... okay, Hamilton?" Carin said sharply, as she placed the comb back in Hamilton's hand.

He slowly lifted the comb and placed it in his own hair, sliding it firmly down one side, using his other hand to smooth the slicked strands tightly against his head, as he continued to mumble quietly.

"See me comb my hair? My hair has a purple ..."

The sound of Schooner's deep breathing interrupted Hamilton, who started to back up toward the wall, because even Hamilton knew the early signs of Schooner's rage. Schooner grabbed the edge of his desk, clenching both fists until his knuckles turned white. His eyes grew smaller as he inhaled and exhaled, dragging the air through his tightened jaw. He lifted his desk. He looked directly at Hamilton and yelled, "Shut up, you retard. Nobody wants to hear about your stupid comb and look at your ugly hair." He smashed his desk down and returned to his slumped position.

The room was silent. Hamilton finished the stroke in

his hair, still leaning against the wall he had backed himself into, and slowly sat down on the floor. No one said a word.

Dad was right. The last day of school was tough on a guy like Schooner. But it wasn't just that school was coming to an end. Schooner must have been worrying for some time, because he'd already figured out Ms. Hay was pregnant. The news was a big deal for all of us.

I thought about my other schools, the many classrooms and teachers. But I had never had a teacher like Ms. Hay. No one before had made me feel so cared for. Dad's words, the moment he told me I had to attend a special high school, rushed through my head. I remembered how nervous I felt when I walked into the boys' washroom for the first time. I saw the graffiti and the hole in the drywall.

And then I saw Ms. Hayworth.

No one was as kind as her. No one had ever welcomed me like she did. No one loved their students the way she loved us.

As soon as the bell rang at twelve o'clock, marking the beginning of summer holidays, Schooner walked out the back door. He didn't say goodbye to anyone. We crowded around Ms. Hayworth, trying to convince her that Ratchet's idea was not such a bad thing, and she could bring the baby to school each day. Finally, we shut up and just stood, uncomfortably, waiting for the hug she was giving each of us.

Surprisingly, Carcass waited, too. Just as Ms. Hayworth reached out her arms for him, he looked at her and pulled back. He walked away, and then turned toward Ms. Hayworth before exiting the classroom. "See, you're just like the rest of them!" and he continued out the back door.

Ms. Hayworth swallowed.

"I hate that kid!" Ratchet said as he jumped over the desk, moving quickly in an effort to catch Carcass.

"Leave it, Ratchet!" Ms. Hay said. "It's okay, you guys. You don't need to worry about me."

"Why does he say crap like that?" Ratchet said, punching his own hand with his fist. "I don't know how you take it, Ms. Hay. If I were you, I'd have beat the kid to death by now."

And then Ms. Hay turned toward me.

"I'm glad you found your way to us, Creighton. You were just what we needed at Lane Oslo," she said, holding onto me. "You'll be busy this summer, it sounds like—with your new job."

I had started working at the local butcher shop. One of Dad's buddies gave me the job. He called me in whenever he needed an extra guy to package or clean up. The pay was decent, and it was nice having a bit of cash sometimes.

"Yeah," I said. "Trying to save for a truck. Maybe by the time I turn sixteen, I'll have one."

"Well, good for you. I'm so happy you ended up in Breton after all of your travels."

"I never stayed in one place as long as I've stayed here," I replied. "I've had a lot of teachers, but none like you."

I waited outside for Carin, who was, of course, the last student to leave Ms. Hayworth. She came out the front door, wiping the blotches of mascara from underneath her eyes.

"Come on, you," I said, putting my arm around her shoulders.

At first, neither of us said a thing, as we walked toward Carin's house, and then she broke the silence.

"It's not going to be the same, Creigh. I don't care who they hire, there's never going be another Ms. Hay! And who would ever take the job, anyway? They'll never find someone decent."

"I don't understand why she didn't say something earlier. You knew, didn't you?" I said, turning toward Carin.

"Yeah, I asked her a while back. She never answered me, though. She just kind of smiled, so I knew. I don't think she said anything because of Schooner. She probably knew he'd just 'check out' as soon as he got the news. Maybe she wanted to get him through the year."

We stood outside Carin's house, like we did each day when I walked her home.

"Wanna come in, Creigh?" she asked.

I'd sat on the steps of her house before, and Carin had come over to my place a few times, but this was the first time she'd invited me in.

"Yeah, I can come in for a bit," I said, even though I had absolutely nothing better to do. I had no curfew. No one was at home waiting for me. Even if Dad were home, he'd never question where I had been. And, of course, there was no one else I'd rather spend time with than Carin.

Carin lived in a duplex with her mom. She opened the gate of the fenced yard, and we walked up the front steps. The strand of Christmas lights, which were once secured around the doorframe, had loosened and dangled over the doorknob. Carin held them out of the way with her thumb, as she awkwardly fumbled with the key to unlock the door. I started to slip my shoes off.

"Don't worry about your shoes," she said, not taking hers off, either. "Sorry, it's a bit of a mess," she added, as she attempted to clear a small space on the counter with her arm. She signaled for me to sit down on one of the bar stools.

"Iced tea or something?" she asked.

"Sure, that would be good, thanks."

I wasn't sure where to look first. A wooden shelving unit divided the kitchen from the small dining area. It was filled with hundreds of knickknacks—little porcelain dolls, some sort of decorative fan, maybe from China, vases of all shapes and sizes, some filled with silk flowers, candle holders, a large ceramic elephant with one broken tusk, several wine glasses, all covered in dust. A collection of silver spoons was attached crookedly to the wall, and surrounding it were many small plates, decorated with a variety of painted animals. Above the cupboards were green plants—fake ones, I figured—and baskets, a lot of baskets! The table had pill bottles scattered about. Some were open and tipped over, leaving a mix of colored capsules amid the rest of the clutter.

Carin sat down on the stool beside me, as she placed two glasses of iced tea on the counter in front of us. She must have noticed me looking around.

"I know, she has a lot of stuff. My mom, I mean. It's her stuff."

"Ha! And my dad has nothing," I replied. I looked around some more. "She kind of made a home for us, hey? Ms. Hayworth. She was so organized. It was like a home there," I said, changing the subject, still looking around.

"What do you mean, Creigh?"

"I don't know," I said. "I don't know what Schooner's got for a home, but it can't be good, since he's at my place so much. Ratchet? Well, he doesn't really have anyone. We're all a bunch of mess-ups. You know what I mean. And Carcass. What's his story, anyway?"

None of us knew a thing about Carcass, but his final words to Ms. Hay were stuck in my head. She wasn't like all the others—Carcass was wrong. But I don't even think he believed that himself.

"Yeah," Carin said. "If it weren't for Ms. Hay, I wouldn't even be in school."

Leaving the classroom for summer holidays was one thing, but knowing Ms. Hayworth wouldn't be there when we returned was something else. I thought about what she'd said—that we're all searching for the same thing. Maybe that's why it was hard to say goodbye. We had all found a little piece of what we were looking for. And lost it.

CHAPTER 15

"Hey, young fella," said a man standing in front of us at the checkout. "Hope you don't mind me asking, but you look awful familiar. You aren't a relation of Gracie ... Gracie Rae, are ya?" He stared at me some more, leaned in closer, his head tilted to the side.

It was a hot summer afternoon in July, and Carin and I had stopped at the grocery store to grab some gum. We stared back at him. He shook his head, as he continued to eye me up and down. I felt uncomfortable.

"Sorry, kid, I haven't been around for a lot of years. Just trying to find my place again, see where's all my family's at." He continued, "I seen ya standing there and, by darn, you're like a spittin' image of my sister Gracie. Look exactly like she did when I got sent ..." He paused. "Ya just look like my baby sister, is all."

I looked at Carin, unsure whether I should answer. When I was eight, my grandfather had wanted to meet me, but Dad canceled his visit at the last minute. I remember him telling me, "It's for the best, son. You don't want to get involved with those people." Dad told me Mom didn't want her family in my life at all.

The guy kept talking. "Thought I'd come back to this little town. I grew up here, ya know. But can't seem to locate where's all my brothers and such."

I finally nodded. A part of me was curious. I liked that he recognized me as Gracie's son. I wondered why he was in town. Maybe he'd know where Mom was.

"Creighton Fischer," I answered, reaching out my hand toward his. "This is Carin," I said, relieved she was with me.

"Hah!" He laughed, rolling back his head, hand extended toward mine. "So, I'm right, ain't I, kid? Gracie's your momma, ain't she?" he said, as he shook my hand aggressively. "I knew you had to be hers. Guess that makes me your uncle. Cullen. Cullen's the name," he said, still shaking my hand.

I had never been told the names of Mom's four brothers. I knew nothing about her family, other than the small comments Dad made once in a while.

"Nice to meet you, sir," Carin interrupted, keeping her hands firmly in the front pockets of her jeans. She looked worried, biting the inside of her lip, as she scanned him up and down. It's what Carin did when she was unsure.

None of the Waters boys were living in Breton anymore, which made it easy for Dad to keep Mom's family out of my life. Dad figured they'd been forced out of town for one reason or another, 'cause they were bad, "real bad," he'd said. We didn't know where they'd disappeared to, although Dad figured they were likely in jail. I just knew never to mention my connection to the Waters family. Mom told Dad that the best gift she ever received was her baby's last name. Guess she was relieved I became a Fischer, breaking the Waters' family curse.

I could see Carin staring nervously at him. His black muscle shirt had a white skull on the front. A tattoo extended all the way up the side of his neck, some sort of snake wrapped around a young woman. Strands of the woman's wavy blond hair draped over the large reptile, and her tiny red bikini barely contained her curves. His dark hair was greasy, and he had a long deep scar that stretched across his left cheek. His front tooth was missing and, as he talked, he pushed his tongue through the open space. He smelled of oil, as if he had worked on a car or something, and his hands were filthy, stained with grease.

The cashier said, "A dollar seven please." It was my turn now. I fumbled through my pocket for a loonie and some change.

"Finally got my ass here to see that pretty sister of mine sing. I missed a lot of good years," he said, shaking his head. "I was told she has a voice of an angel, so figured I needed to hear it for myself."

Carin grabbed my hand. Her grip was firm.

"Guess you'll be at the Strasville show tomorrow? Maybe see you there?" Cullen kept talking, as he lifted his grocery bag off the counter. I tried to concentrate and pay the cashier for my pack of gum. It didn't look like Cullen was in any rush to leave the store.

I didn't know what to say. Carin squeezed my hand again. I wondered what that meant. She crossed her legs and scraped the floor with her foot. I had so many questions. I felt frozen. And then he placed his grocery bag back down on the counter, as if he had another thought.

"Don't tell her, though, boy. I wanna surprise the hell outta her."

I nodded, even though I had no idea my mom would be singing in a nearby town. I was unprepared. Was this real? Was he really Mom's brother?

"Yeah, we'll be there," Carin jumped in. "We can't remember which pub she said. Do you happen to know?" Carin continued.

Maybe she was suspicious, too. Or she was helping me out because I was failing miserably.

"Strasville Station! Can't wait. Man, you look like your momma, boy. Soon as I saw those eyes, I just knew you had to be my Gracie's."

I wasn't sure what to think about. Butterflies enveloped my stomach. I was recognized by a stranger as being Gracie's son. Strasville was only a three-hour drive. I began to shake.

Cullen gave a salute and headed toward the door. I stared at him, trying to decide what to make of the situation. He turned back, several times, to have another look at me.

"Creigh?" Carin pulled on my hand. "You okay? You're shaking to death. You're all sweaty. What's the deal?" She dragged me out the door and toward the concrete barricade in the parking lot. "That guy seriously gave me the creeps.

Something about him, he looked so familiar," she continued, as she pulled me down to sit next to her. "So, you never met him? You never met your uncle before? You think he really was your uncle?"

"Never met anyone in Mom's family. Just knew she had a dad and four older brothers. It's funny. Now that I think of it, I never heard a word about her mom. I honestly can't even tell you if she had one," I said, still shivering.

"Creigh," Carin whispered softly. "What ever happened to your mom, anyway?"

I swallowed. No one had asked this question before.

"There's not much to tell. She just up and left one morning when I was asleep. I woke up and she wasn't there, like she normally was. That's what happened," I said, turning toward Carin. "I honestly don't know why she left."

"How old were you?" she asked.

"Five. Five and a half, I guess. Dad didn't seem to know it was coming. At least, that's what he told me. Left a note for him, never even said goodbye."

"And you've never seen her since?" Carin wondered.

"No," I said as I lifted my necklace. "But she dropped this off when I was in Grade 6. I never saw her, though; she just left it on the step."

"Venus. That's the sign of Venus, right?" Carin asked, as she lifted the charm from my neck to examine it more closely. "So that's why Schooner sprayed that tag? Why Venus?"

"Well, when I was a kid, I liked to look at the stars. Mom would show me the Big Dipper and the Little Dipper—you know, all the constellations. I'd sit on her lap in my jammies on the front step of the trailer. Dad would still be at the carnival till late. I could never get to sleep, because it was so loud at the fairgrounds."

I stopped talking for a bit. Had Mom known all along she wasn't going to stick around?

"She'd be wearing her pink robe. It had this fur on the front." I paused again, thinking. "I liked to rub my fingers on it. I could hear kids screaming on the Zipper. I can still smell the corn dogs and popcorn. I could tell you the sound of every single ride at that fair. They were always running in the background, late into the night. I'd never want to go to bed until I found Venus. That was the challenge—like a little test for me each night. 'You always need to know where Venus is, my Creigh,' Mom would say. 'If you and Momma are ever apart, you just look up at the sky and find our planet. We'll both be watching it—okay, my boy?' she'd tell me once in a while."

Carin didn't ask me any more questions. It was quiet for a while. And then she grabbed my hand. I was embarrassed because it was wet with sweat. She squeezed it tightly and we sat some more, still not saying a thing.

"So that's where your mind drifts to," she whispered. "Well, we better call Ratchet. We have to get to Strasville tomorrow night," Carin said as she stood up, pulling me off the barrier.

"No. We can't go to Strasville. I can't see her, Carin, as much as I wish I could. She doesn't want to see me."

"Do it, Creigh. Here's your chance to talk to her."

Carin and I were walking toward her place. I could feel my heartbeat finally slow down, once we got moving and the uncontrollable shivering stopped.

I imagined the Strasville bar, my mom on stage, holding her guitar. She was wearing her tall brown boots and little white skirt, her long blond hair loosely falling onto her denim jacket. She'd play a few chords, then brush her hair behind her shoulder, so that it wasn't in the way of the strings. I could see the audience clapping along to the beat, like they did at the fairgrounds. She'd tap her boot on the floor, keeping the rhythm. And then she would notice me in the audience. Her voice would get raspy, and she'd choke up a little and try to finish the song. She'd come walking down off the stage toward me ...

No. I shook my head.

"We can at least see if Ratch can take us. There's no harm in trying. You have to go, Creigh."

"Why, Carin? Why do you want me to see my mom so badly?" I asked.

"'Cause it's driven you crazy for a lot of years. I know you, Creigh. I've always wondered where you disappear to, just out of the blue."

Carin's mom came out of her bedroom. She was in her robe, even though it was two o'clock on a hot summer afternoon. I had met her a few times now. She was usually reading a magazine or lying on the couch, watching a soap. I knew she wasn't well. There were many times Carin mentioned things about her mom's poor health. And Ms. Hayworth always asked Carin how her mom was doing.

"Mom, we're going to Strasville tomorrow night. We're getting Ratch to drive us up there," Carin blurted out. "Creigh's mom is singing in the pub. He hasn't seen her since he was five."

I could feel my face heat up. I didn't expect Carin to say anything. I didn't like her mom knowing about me.

Carin's mom never really said much to either of us. She was just kind of there. Sometimes, when Carin and I were talking, I'd see her look up as she filed her nails.

"Ratchet can't drive you over those mountains in that truck. It's too unreliable," she interrupted.

"Mom, we have to get there somehow," Carin argued.

"It will be dark. It's just dangerous. And none of you are nineteen, so how do you plan to get into a pub?" Carin's mom continued. She tightened the knot of her fleece belt, and took a sip from the mug that rested on the kitchen counter.

"Mom, you totally don't get this. Creighton NEEDS to see his mom. We have to get there. Maybe you can come—I could drive if you come, or Ratchet can drive our car?" Carin suggested doubtfully.

"It's okay, Carin," I interrupted. "We don't need to go. Don't worry, Mrs. Reiner. I don't know if I want to see her, anyway."

Carin's mom scratched her head and tapped her long, polished nails on the counter. She started to stack the opened envelopes and bills that were scattered about the kitchen. There were some large crumbs of soda crackers left on a plate by the sink, which she picked up, piece by piece, nibbling at each bit. She busied herself in the kitchen, moving dirty dishes around, without actually putting them in the dishwasher or sink.

"You know I'm nervous about the mountains, Carin," she said, looking around the kitchen. "And I don't have the money for gas."

"It's fine, Mrs. Reiner," I said. "Carin, don't worry about it. Just let it go."

"It might do you good to get out of the house for a bit. Some fresh air ..." Carin suggested.

"Well, I suppose," she said, as she chewed nervously on her knuckle, thinking. "It's just, my doctor's appointment that day and ..."

"Mom, seriously, your doctor appointments aren't that long anymore. You don't need to make this into a big deal," Carin continued.

"Fine, you sort it out," she said and left the room.

Carin and I stared at each other, shocked that she had sort of agreed.

I couldn't sleep that night. I knew Carin would be lying awake, too, thinking about me. I couldn't stop replaying how it might go.

I also worried about Dad's reaction. What would he

say if I told him the plan? He would not want me to go see Mom, even though he'd probably want to see her, too. She was something we didn't talk about. It was a topic I learned was out of bounds. There was no way I could tell him. I knew that.

In the morning, I called Carin.

"This is a bad idea," I said.

"Look, Creigh, it's all organized. Ratchet's coming into town at five. They're letting him off early. Schooner's going to meet here, too. Mom's even willing to go, and that's a big deal, 'cause you know she hardly leaves the house anymore. And seriously, if you don't go, you will regret it," she pleaded.

"Not a big deal? Schooner's coming, too? This is like a big group thing now? We're all going to see my mom sing? And I feel bad, dragging your mom over the mountains when she isn't well."

"Come on, Creigh. You know they'd never miss this. We all know how important this is for you. Just go with it. It'll be okay. I know it will."

I had to work at the butcher till four that day and, just as I expected, I could barely focus. Once in a while, I'd start shivering, like I did when I saw the guy in the grocery store. I'd feel the sweat on the back of my neck start to build. I was terrified that if Mom saw me, she would turn and walk away.

But everything was organized. We were going to see my mom that evening.

CHAPTER 16

I felt sick as I waited on the front step for Mrs. Reiner's car. Would I really be seeing my mom in three hours? Each time I heard a vehicle, I got more butterflies. At least Dad was out of town, so I didn't have to say a word to him about the trip to Strasville.

Ratchet was driving, and Carin's mom was sitting in the passenger seat, when they pulled up twenty-five minutes late. Schooner rolled down his back window. I could see his smile from ear to ear. I gave him a fist bump and noticed his collared, button-up shirt.

"You're all dressed up. Looking good," I said.

"Yeah, show him your bow tie," Ratchet called out, laughing. "Or did you take it off already?"

"Shut up!" Schooner yelled.

"Leave it, Ratchet," Carin said. It was obvious Ratchet had been working Schooner over, since he had never dressed up for any occasion.

I opened the back door and Carin slid into the middle, toward Schooner, leaving me a space beside her. The floor of the car was piled with junk: a snowbrush, magazines, some newspaper flyers, crumpled tissues, a tube of lip balm, and some empty pill containers. I tried to push the items aside to make room for my feet. Just as we were pulling away from the curb, Schooner stuck his head out of the window and yelled, "R-O-A-D-T-R-I-P!!!!!"

I knew they cared. I knew Schooner had dressed up because he figured this was the most important event in my life. But I was embarrassed by the attention. I enjoyed helping them out, but I didn't like them doing the same for me.

"Don't get too excited. We don't know what's going to happen," I said.

The three-hour journey felt like days. The car struggled over each mountain pass. I didn't talk at all. Guess that was the one bonus of bringing Schooner along. He didn't stop yapping the whole way. I managed to chew the skin around the outside of my fingernails down to the inner layer. Had Carin's mom not been with us, I would have told Ratchet to turn around. But I didn't have the courage to do that to her. It all felt wrong. Ratchet was playing CDs, singing along to the blaring music, and drumming on the steering wheel.

"Jesus, Creigh, you're so uptight! Loosen up, dude," Ratchet said, looking at me in the rearview mirror.

Carin squeezed my hand.

"Stop the car!" Schooner yelled at one point, looking out the window. "I just saw the hugest creature in those trees."

"It's an elk, dude! It's a frickin' elk," Ratchet said.

As Schooner talked, he also looked around. He sat forward, upright in the seat, his head bobbing. He was holding onto the hand rest, his knuckles white, like he was afraid.

"Schoon, did you ever drive through the mountains before?" Carin asked.

"Nope," Schooner answered, looking around with wide eyes. "Farthest place I've ever been is Fairburn. Always wanted to go on a road trip."

I saw the sign that said: *Strasville City Centre, next right*. My heart beat faster. I rolled down the window to let some air into the car.

"Hmm," Mrs. Reiner said, "I haven't been here in years. I'm sure the pub is just around the corner, though."

She was right. There was the sign: *Strasville Station Pub*, just as we went around the bend.

As we pulled into the parking lot, the neon sign was flashing:

Welcome Home Gracie Rae! 8 PM

I swallowed. Was this her home? It was already 9:10. I panicked, thinking we'd missed her.

"Darn, we're so late," Mrs. Reiner continued, looking around as Ratchet circled back and forth. I'd been worried, since they'd picked me up later than we had planned.

The parking lot was full, and cars were also parked along the side of the road on both sides.

"Creighton, your mom must be a popular singer—there's nowhere left to park," she said.

Ratchet decided to drive around to the back alley, and managed to find a spot along the edge of the dirt road.

"You wait here. I'll go in and see what the setup is. Some pubs allow minors in before ten," Carin's mom said, as she closed the car door.

Schooner kept leaning over Carin, reaching toward the dashboard, skipping the songs he didn't like, trying to get back to Britney Spears.

"Leave it!" Ratchet said, hitting Schooner over the head.

After what seemed like ages, Carin's mom returned, and said there would be no way to get us through the front door. IDs were being checked, and several staff manned the entrance.

Ratchet opened the car door. "Screw this, I'm going in!"

He walked directly across the alley where we were parked, to the steel door at the back of the pub. He went in. It was that easy. Ratchet just opened the back door and walked through. Carin followed, with Schooner close behind her. She signaled for me to come, but I could not seem to lift my body out of the car.

"I never knew your mom, Creighton," Carin's mom began.

She had never really acknowledged me before. In fact, I wasn't sure she liked me at all. Luckily, Ratchet stuck his head out of the pub just at that moment, frantically signaling me to come. I'm not sure if I got out of the car to avoid the awkward conversation, or if I actually wanted to see my mom. But I did get out.

Ratchet pulled me in, catching the steel door with his foot before it slammed shut. Nobody was around. It was the back of the pub, and directly inside the door where we entered was a steep staircase, leading up toward what seemed to be the ceiling. Ratchet dragged me onto the narrow stairs, which seemed slightly sturdier than a ladder, and then guided me onto a metal catwalk, just above the tables that faced the stage. The heat from the lights that protruded from the edges of the mesh bridge was intense. I could see Carin motioning us toward her, as she crouched in the dark corner of the ceiling next to Schooner, staring down toward the stage.

Below the catwalk of theatrical lights, I could see the blond of my mother's hair, and her slim silhouette reflecting through the aluminum rails. Echoing from wall to wall was the soft and raspy voice that had lulled me to sleep, night after night. I could feel her fingers running through my hair, as she ensured each wisp was tucked tightly behind my ears. I could smell the perfume on her neck as she guided each strand into its resting place.

"Creigh, don't stop! They'll see us here. Move it. Go to Carin," Ratchet whispered as he shoved me.

I could still smell the half-empty cup of coffee on the table that she'd left behind. I'd smelled it for days, until the coffee had turned into a thick sludge of green cream. I could see Dad, holding his head in his hands, listening to Willie Nelson's "Always on My Mind," over and over.

Ratchet managed to drag my frozen body across the catwalk to where Carin and Schooner huddled. I was sweating from the heat of the lights. Each step toward the corner was exhausting.

"She's gorgeous, Creigh. Your mom is truly stunning!" Carin whispered, as she grabbed my hand, pulling me in toward her. "Your uncle was right; you totally have her eyes."

She had the same wavy blond hair. She was holding her guitar like she always did, with long strands getting in the way of the strings. She flipped her hair behind her shoulders between strums. She was wearing tan cowboy boots with a heel, not the ones she used to have. She wore a ruffled white blouse and a denim skirt. I didn't know any of the songs. They weren't any I remembered.

"Quit stepping on me, Ratchet," Schooner said loudly.

"Shut up! That's the last time I'm gonna tell you to shut your mouth, dude!" Ratchet snapped, frustrated by Schooner's constant chatter. "They're gonna see us if you don't keep your mouth closed."

Mom reached for her glass of water when the song was done. It sat next to her on the tall wooden stool. She waved to the audience and walked off the stage. It was her last song. Everyone in the pub stood up, clapping, giving Mom a standing ovation, hoping she would come out again. People were chanting, "Gracie, Gracie ..."

And then she came back on stage, sipped her water, and lifted the microphone out of the stand. People were still cheering as she began to speak. I wanted them to stop so I could hear what she was saying. She waited, and finally the pub was silent.

"This next one is kinda special to me, so I saved it for the end. It's one of my own. It sorta reminds me of ... well ... my life. It's about searchin' for something. Trying to find some light, when darkness keeps following ya around. And regrets of sorts, and not really knowin' how to fix 'em. I guess we're all looking for something. A soft place of some kind, just a soft place to fall, I guess."

She paused for a long time, looking up at the ceiling, before she signaled her small band to begin.

Her voice broke unevenly. She wasn't strumming the guitar, which stood in the stand beside her. She held the microphone tightly, with both hands. They seemed to be shaking. *"Behind blue eyes there is dark,"* she started singing. *"A curse that follows like a cloudy day ..."*

She paused to regain composure, cleared her throat, and then continued.

Her eyes were closed. When the first verse was done, she placed the microphone in the stand and picked up her guitar for the chorus, still singing.

That's what Ms. Hay said, too. We're all searching for something.

I didn't hear all the words. People were loudly clapping along.

The audience cheered at the end.

"Thank you all! Thank you all for coming to see me sing again. It's always good to come back to Strasville," she said to the audience.

Mom waved. She walked toward the edge of the stage and blew kisses. She waved some more and made her final exit.

"Let's go!" Ratchet said. "We gotta get down there."

Carin pulled my hand. "Schooner, stay right behind Ratchet. Don't let him out of your sight," she said.

We followed Ratchet and Schooner off the catwalk, to the small staircase on the other side of the ceiling, and then I grabbed Carin, pulled her back. Ratchet and Schooner had already made their way down.

"I can't do it. Let's just go to the car," I told Carin. It was so hot from the lights, my T-shirt felt soaked. Was the song about Dad? Maybe me? Why did she say it was a song about regrets? She could have come back. We would have let her.

"Whatever you want, Creigh." Carin whispered. "But I can go with you if that helps. We can walk backstage together."

We huddled at the top of the narrow staircase, out of view. I buried my head into Carin's neck, and she held me tightly.

"Come on," Carin said slowly. She gave my back a little rub. "We can climb down and go straight out the back door. It's right at the bottom of these stairs."

Ratchet climbed back up the stairs.

"She's right there, Creigh. As soon as you get to the bottom, you'll see her behind the stage. Come on!" Ratchet said.

Schooner had followed Ratchet back up. "What's happening? Aren't we going to see your mom now, Creigh?"

"We'll meet you guys in the car. Just head out and we'll follow," Carin said, trying to help me.

"No way!" said Ratchet. "You came all this way, you gotta go talk to her. Don't chicken out now."

"Leave it, Ratchet! He said he wants to go," Carin replied.

Ratchet shook his head, disappointed. "Come on, Schoon, let's get out of here."

Carin and I made our way down. At the bottom, I peered toward the back of the stage, where Ratchet had said he could see Mom. He was right. There she was, talking to a man. He handed her a drink. I could see the small glass, the bottom filled with ice cubes and maybe brandy. This was it, my chance to walk straight through the door toward her. Carin stood beside me, watching, too, not saying a word. Just then, the guy put his hand on the back of Mom's skirt. She was laughing. He gave her a pinch and slid her skirt up her thigh. She put one hand around his neck, swinging her head back, as she poured the entire drink down her throat. She seemed unbothered by the groping. I turned my head. I didn't want to see her touched that way.

"Let's go!" I said to Carin, turning toward the steel door. "Let's get out of here."

Carin wasn't moving. I looked at her face. She was biting the inside of her lip like she did sometimes. She was staring at a poster on the wall that read: *Gracie Rae Waters, 8 PM, Strasville Station Pub—Saturday, July 10.*

"Coming?" I said.

She backed up toward me, still staring at the poster that was tacked to the wall at the bottom of the stairway. I held the steel door open, and pulled her through toward the alley. Carin was quiet.

"You okay?" I asked, giving her shirt a gentle tug. She pulled away.

"Your mom, her last name is *Waters*?"

"Yeah, Gracie Rae Waters," I said, puzzled.

"She had four brothers? There were five of them, altogether?" Carin continued, still staring at Mom's name on the poster. "She's Basil Waters's daughter, then? Basil is your grandpa?"

"Yeah, he is. But I never met him. I never met anyone in her family, except the guy we saw at the grocery store," I replied, confused.

She didn't say any more.

"Gosh, Carin," Mrs. Reiner said, as we joined the three of them in the car. "I was so worried. None of you were in the pub when I checked. Ratchet just told me you were up on the ceiling catwalks. You could have got caught. That sounds so dangerous. You should have at least come to let me know what was happening. I've been waiting in the car for ages." Mrs. Reiner seemed upset.

"Sorry, Mrs. Reiner," I replied, since Carin completely ignored her. "We didn't plan on any of that happening. Once we went through the back door, Ratchet found a way for us to watch the end of the show."

"Well, it wasn't up to any of you to let me know. But Carin knows my expectations. Right, Carin?" she said, looking back from the passenger seat.

Carin turned away. She did not sit in the middle on the way home. She made sure Schooner was tucked between the two of us. She did not talk. She looked out the window, biting the inside of her lip, twisting her dread knots. I'd let her down. She'd put all this effort into getting me to Strasville, and I hadn't talked to my mom at all. I wanted to believe that's why she'd turned cold so suddenly. But it was something bigger. Something about Mom's last name.

CHAPTER 17

I rang the bell like I usually did. Carin's mom opened the door slightly. Peeking through the small crack, she said, "Carin is not wanting to see you right now, Creighton. Maybe it's best you don't come by for a while," and she closed the door. I didn't have a chance to speak. I walked home and went straight to my bedroom, cranking up a CD Ratchet had burned for me. All I could think about was Carin.

It had been three days since our trip to Strasville, and she had ignored all of my calls. Just when I felt like I understood her, everything got confusing.

I had been cautious with Carin. It had been four months since I'd tried to kiss her at the party. She'd pulled away, so I'd let her take the lead since then. Sometimes she'd grab my hand or give my back a rub, but I tried really hard not to touch her first. Even after she got a waitressing job at the Depot Diner, and we were both working a lot, we managed to spend all of our spare time together. But I still wasn't sure what I was to her, even though I knew what I wanted to be.

Carin's arrival in my world had even helped my daily thoughts of Mom almost disappear. But now, since Strasville, I wondered if all women were complicated. How could they just leave, without explanation—my mom, Ms. Hay, and now Carin—people that mattered?

Dad knocked on my bedroom door. I figured he'd be wondering why I hadn't come out for so long. I ignored him and turned my music up. He let himself in. For some reason, I started to cry when I saw him. I pulled my knees into my chest, grabbed at my hair in frustration.

"What is it, son?" he asked.

Dad rarely asked me questions about my life. When I offered information, hoping for some kind of conversation, he seemed uninterested. He'd go back to reading his paper or watching TV. I was used to dealing with things on my own.

"Why did Mom hate her last name?" I yelled over my music, feeling angry. "You said that once, that she was glad I got your last name, that it was the best gift she ever received. Why was the name 'Waters' a curse?"

Dad turned the volume down. "What's all this about, Creighton? Why are you upset about your Mom's last name? Did something happen? Did someone ask you about her family?"

I knew I would never tell Dad about Strasville. He would be upset, probably hurt, that I hadn't let him know. I didn't want to deal with all that.

"No. It's Carin. She asked me if Mom's last name was Waters. When I said it was, she wanted to know if Basil Waters was my grandpa? He is my grandpa, right, Dad? He was the one coming to meet me, and then you told him not to come. Why? What's the deal with her family?"

Dad stared blankly ahead. I could see his hands shaking. And then he turned to look at the ceiling as he cleared his throat, not wanting to make eye contact with me.

"Don't ignore me this time. You never talk about Mom."

"It was your grandfather, Creighton," he said, still facing the ceiling. "Basil Waters. He's the man who hurt Carin."

His voice cracked as he spoke, and he started to breathe more heavily. He turned toward my dresser, which stood near the door, and he rested his hands on top. Gasps emerged deep from within his throat. He was crying. His knuckles were white from his tight grip, and he sniffed loudly in between quiet sobs.

"What?" I said, confused.

"You had just started Grade 6 when it came out in the papers. He assaulted Carin in July. But it all came out that September—guess that's when he got caught. That's when he was charged. Remember when Mom left the necklace?" Dad continued, still facing away. "It came out in the news just after that."

"So ... my grandpa ..." I stopped talking, trying to make sense of what Dad said. "It was my grandfather, Mom's dad, who sexually assaulted Carin?" I said slowly.

"Wait here," Dad said, leaving the room. He came back with a folded piece of paper, a newspaper clipping he'd obviously saved, probably stashed away in the small wooden box on his dresser. He sat on the bed beside me as he unfolded it. And then he read it aloud:

"Basil Waters was charged Thursday, September 17, with sexually assaulting a thirteen-year-old girl in Breton, 54 kilometers outside of Fairburn."

"'The father of five, who had faced drug charges in the past, was arrested early Thursday,' said Constable Jack Hilterman, of the Fairburn RCMP."

"Hilterman said Waters was cooperative when police woke him up around 4 AM. He was arraigned Thursday on charges of sexual assault. His attorney, Bill Carson, said, 'Waters is a loving family man who did not harm the young woman. My client was not involved with her,' Carson said. 'Basil is not the kind of man who would hurt another human being.'"

Leaning over the wastebasket beside my bed, I heaved. Nothing came out of my mouth, but I gagged again, feeling the need to vomit. I could see Carin standing in the Strasville pub, staring at the poster. While I watched my mother being groped, disappointed in her weakness, Carin had read her full name on the ad—Gracie Rae Waters. Of course, "... the father of five," it said in the newspaper article. And Cullen, my uncle. I had told Carin that Mom had four brothers, when the guy recognized me in the grocery story. She must have figured it all out in Strasville.

I stood up, pacing around the room. "Why didn't you tell me?" I demanded. "You knew all this time? When I told you about Carin being raped, you knew it was Mom's dad? You knew it was my grandpa?"

"I know, Creighton," he replied, shaking his head. "I just couldn't say it. I didn't know you knew the girl, till you mentioned her name that day. I didn't know who she was. Just heard the name through the carnie guys, after it happened. Some of them knew your mom way back. They knew it was her dad."

"Why is everything about Mom such a big secret all the time?" I stood up, yelling. "Everything! I can't even say her name, without you freaking out or going completely silent. Why did she hate her last name, Dad? She hated the name 'Waters' way before her Dad raped a thirteen-year-old girl!"

"He was not a good man. I figure he must have hurt your mother, too, when she was growing up." Dad got up and tossed the newspaper clipping on my bed. He walked back to the dresser and slammed his fist on its surface. My CD player vibrated, skipping to the next song on its own.

He turned toward me, holding his hands out in despair, and then ran his open fingers through his hair.

"Sit down, Creighton," he said, as he sat back down on the bed himself.

I slumped down on the end of the bed, away from him.

"There's a lot I don't know. Your momma never liked to talk about her past. Right from the start, as soon as I met her, I learned real quick not to ask her much, especially about her family."

Dad paused, picked the newspaper clipping back up, folding and unfolding it in his hands. Every now and then, he'd use the side of his thumb to wipe a tear as he breathed in.

"You know, she always wanted me to marry her." Dad stood up again. He moved toward the window, looking out into the backyard. "I didn't understand it at the time. I mean, I didn't have much money. I figured I'd marry her one day, when I could get her a good ring. The time just never came."

I had no idea Mom and Dad weren't married. I'd never thought about it at all.

Dad's hands gripped the windowsill. He kept shaking his head as he talked.

"Now, piecing things together, I'm guessing she didn't want to be a Waters anymore. Always kick myself for not getting my crap together. Probably would have helped her out a lot, made her feel more secure, maybe, after all she went through growing up. How hard would it have been to marry her?"

"But why, Dad, why did she hate her name?"

"I think all those boys hurt your momma in some way or another. I just don't think she got over it. They were known all over town. Pickin' fights, drugs, stealing, and I guess assault, too. None of those boys treated women well. Not sure how your mom turned out to be such a good woman, raised in that home without a mother to protect her from it all."

"Where was her mom?" I asked.

"She wouldn't say, Creighton. I asked her once. But I could see there was pain in that question. She just couldn't say anything about it, not to me, anyway. I'm sorry, son. I know I've never been too good at this."

He stopped talking for a moment.

"I guess your mom needed more—more than I was giving at the time."

I thought about what Mom said, before she sang her final song in Strasville.

"She probably didn't know what she was looking for, Dad. She didn't know what she needed."

"You go now. Go talk to Carin. Tell her what you know. Don't be holding things back like I have. You like this girl a lot, don't you, son?"

I nodded.

"Well, you be there for her, then. Even in the tough times, you gotta notice the small stuff, give her what she needs. She's gotta be your number one."

I looked at Dad and nodded. He wished he'd done that for Mom; I could hear it in his voice. It was a perfect opportunity to let him know about the concert, to tell him I saw Mom. But I couldn't. It would bring up a whole lot more pain for him. And it was Carin I needed to deal with, not Dad.

He left the room.

I picked up the newspaper clipping that he'd left on the bed. I read it a few more times, folded it carefully along its creases, and tucked it in my pocket. I hopped on my bike, knowing exactly where I needed to go.

CHAPTER 18

I knocked on the door of Carin's house. Like she did before, Mrs. Reiner opened the door, just enough to see me through the crack.

"Creighton, what did I tell you last time? She's not ready to see you."

"Please, Mrs. Reiner, I have to talk to her."

Carin came up from behind her mom, pulled the door open wide. "What is it, Creighton? There's really not much to say."

I stepped into the house and Carin took a step back, so I stopped. Her mom moved to the side, watching me.

"Carin, I didn't know it was my grandpa. I promise you, I didn't know. I never met the man. No one told me it was him."

All the times I'd held back, making sure I didn't touch her, this time I leaned forward to wrap my arms around Carin. But she pulled away, leaving my arms extended. I dropped them slowly to my side.

"You don't get it, Creighton. You don't get what that man did to me."

"I know, Carin, I understand. Ratch told me the story."

"No, Creighton!" she yelled. "Don't tell me you know the story. Don't ever say that you understand. No one knows anything, Creighton."

Carin started to cry. Her hands were flailing around as she shouted at me. I didn't move. I just stood there, unsure what to say.

"What happened to me that July is something you will never understand! The fact it was your grandfather makes me feel ill. How could you not have known? You'd have heard his name. It was in the news. That's all people talked about." She crossed her arms angrily, pausing to catch her breath. She bit the inside of her cheek, and occasionally reached up to give her lip a twist.

"I lived in Fairburn when it happened, Carin. It may have been all over the news in Breton, but I never heard about it there."

"Well, you've been in Breton for almost a year now, Creighton. I know you knew the story. Your dad would have known. He would have said something about your grandfather."

"No, Carin. Dad didn't say a thing. He doesn't talk about Mom's family. He showed me the newspaper clipping today, for the first time. Until I read the story myself, I never knew it was my grandfather."

"And that sick uncle of yours, who met us in the grocery store. I knew he looked familiar." She threw her hands out again. "I knew I was creeped out for a reason."

She seemed to be getting angrier. I'd never seen Carin show such rage.

"Your uncle is just like his sick father. Who puts a tattoo of a half-naked woman on his neck, Creighton? They are sick, sick people, all of those Waters men. They make me sick!"

I nodded. I wanted to say, "I know," but figured that would be the wrong response.

Carin's mom had backed herself against the counter, still watching us. She probably had no idea what to say, either.

"You don't know what it's like to come home every day, and feel so afraid of being alone, to have to check each room, just to make sure no one is waiting to pounce on you. You don't know what it's like to be afraid of the dark, afraid to go out with your friends at night. You'll never understand how much fear you can have, for a place you once loved ..." She was screaming now.

I nodded again.

"And why, Creighton? Why, if you knew what happened to me, even if you didn't know it was your sick grandfather, would you not have said a word? You just pretended it never happened. You didn't ask me one single question."

"Carin!" I finally interrupted. "I didn't want to upset you. I worried about it all the time. But I didn't know if you wanted to talk about it."

"Yeah, well, that's what everyone thinks, don't they? You all just brush it under the rug, like it never happened at all." She was looking at her mom, too, yelling at both of us now. "And I just have to go on, every single day, pretending like nothing is wrong."

Carin's mom interrupted. "Carin, that's not true. I've always been here. I'm always here to talk about it if you need to, you know that. I will always be here for you."

"Seriously, Mom? What did you expect me to say? *'Hey Mom, can I talk about how I got raped for a bit?*

I'm feeling kinda sad.' Did you really think I'd ask? And no, you don't know that you'll always be here. Stop saying you'll always be here for me. It's like you say it to reassure yourself or something."

Mrs. Reiner started to cry. I wanted to back up, open the door, and jump on my bike, get out of their house. But then I thought about what Dad said before I left. "Well, you be there for her, then. Even in the tough times, you gotta notice the small stuff, give her what she needs. She's gotta be your number one," Dad had said.

"Your cancer, Mom. Think how many times it's come back already. Just stop telling me, over and over again, that you will be here for me. Because you don't know that, Mom. Stop trying to convince yourself that everything will be okay, when it isn't," Carin shouted, thrashing her hands around as she paced the kitchen.

Mrs. Reiner put her head down on the counter, as she sat on one of the barstools. She was crying quite loudly now.

"I'm sorry, Mom, but you've gotta be realistic at some point. You've got to face the truth."

Carin sat down on the other barstool beside her mom. She sighed heavily, probably from exhaustion.

I slowly moved behind her, putting my hands on Carin's shoulders. I waited, thinking she would brush her shoulders off. But she didn't this time. I rubbed them gently as she reached for a tissue from the box on the counter. I pulled a second one out and handed it to Mrs. Reiner. She nodded, blowing her nose, as she walked away, down the hallway to her bedroom. I swiveled Carin's bar stool around so that she was facing me. I pulled her head into my chest, waiting again for some form of rejection. I slid one hand into the back of her hair, weaving my fingers through her dread knots. She let me hold her, her hands firmly by her side.

We didn't move. She didn't say a thing, but I could feel her tears soak through my T-shirt. I could feel her stiff body relax in my arms.

I loosened my grip and pulled her head away from my chest, so I could look at her, gently moving the loose strands of brown hair off her face. She had no makeup on. There were no black streams of mascara running down her cheeks. She had tiny freckles on her nose. I caught her tear with my thumb and her face creased, allowing a small smile to form.

"Carin," I said quietly. "I think he hurt my mom as well. I don't want to lose both of you because of that man."

Carin stared at me. "You think he abused your mom?"

I nodded. "Don't think Mom ever got over it. I remember Ms. Hay telling me, *'It's hard to give to others what you haven't received yourself.'* She couldn't be a mom. He's not going to take you down, too."

She stood up and buried her head in my neck. I held her for a really long time. We didn't say anything to each other.

I understood why Mom hated her last name now. People would assume the worst of her, just like Carin did of me, when she realized Basil Waters was my grandfather. How would she ever escape the damage her family had done?

I could hear Carin quietly sniffling and felt the wetness on my neck. Finally, I pulled her off to kiss her forehead.

Looking into her eyes, I said, "Later, we're going to the beach. Ratch is picking Schoon and me up at three. Why don't you come with us?" I asked, still holding her face in my hands. "It will be good to get out for a bit. You're probably really tired. It's been a long three days. Let's get some fresh air, sit in the sun for a while."

She nodded.

"I'm sorry he hurt you, Carin," I said softly.

She nodded again.

I slid my finger across her cheek, wiping the last tear.

The small lake was about a fifteen-minute drive from Breton. Ratchet had a way of finding the best beach spots. We'd drive around until we came across one without any people. We liked to make a fire when the sun went down. Even though the river was right in town, with a decent beach, we didn't go there if Carin came along. Usually, the lake drive was a little cramped, with the four of us piled in the cab of Ratchet's truck. Today I didn't mind it at all.

Carin was squished between Schooner and me, partially balancing on my lap. She was quiet. But she let me hold her hand when we turned off the highway onto the dirt road to park.

We dragged a large log along the sand, so we had a place to relax. Ratchet took off his T-shirt and lit a smoke. He balanced one foot on the log, inhaling as he peered out toward the lake. Even though it was a hot July afternoon, he kept his jeans and work boots on. He always did at the beach.

Schooner ran down the shoreline, gathering rocks to skip. He was in his cut-off jeans shorts, the same ones he wore last summer. His shoulders were red and peeling from the few times we'd made it to the river in between our jobs.

Carin stood at the edge of the water. I sat on the log, beside Ratchet, trying not to watch her. She bunched her dread knots together and tied them loosely at the back of her head. She was wearing a short white dress and flip-flops. She'd never worn a dress before. She stepped closer to the water and started to lift it over her head, revealing the brown bikini she was wearing underneath. I looked away, toward Ratchet, who was squishing his cigarette butt into the sand with his foot. I heard a splash and turned to see her disappear under the water.

I imagined myself jumping in after her. I'd hold her partially naked body against mine.

"Wanna cook some dogs?" Ratchet said, interrupting my thought.

We started gathering driftwood for the fire.

Carin waded out of the water, quickly grabbing her towel to cover her body, patting it dry. She walked toward me, smiling, the towel now wrapped around her.

"We're making a fire this early? You hungry already, Ratch?" she said as she approached me.

Ratch had his knife out, carving a roasting stick. He scraped the bark off the end to form a sharp point.

"Creigh?" Carin said as she turned toward me. "I thought you'd come for a dip."

"I wanted to," I said. "But I wasn't sure you'd want that."

"Yeah, Creigh, I'm gonna figure this out, I promise."

And she smiled at me.

It was on this day, this very moment, on the little beach just outside of Breton, when things started to change between me and Carin. She didn't say the words, but I knew I was more than just her friend. I don't know how my apology changed things, but somehow it was different after that. Maybe she'd needed to release the pain inside her. Or did she just need that conversation with me, letting me know what she was all about? I saw now what was underneath her black hoodie. She had small scars on her wrist that were usually hidden away, that I hadn't noticed before—her perfect body, everything about her, exposed for the first time.

CHAPTER 19

Schooner hadn't been coming around as much as usual. He hadn't stayed the night in a while. So, when he rolled up on his bike one August afternoon, just as I was heading outside to mow the lawn, I felt relieved.

"Where you been, buddy?" I asked, as Schooner made his way up the stairs toward me.

"Workin' lots, man, just workin'," he replied.

He plunked himself down on an empty chair beside Dad, who was reading the paper and having a smoke on the porch. I sat down as well.

"Schooner!" Dad said, folding his newspaper. "I've been thinking about you. Where you been hiding lately?"

"Busy, ya know. They need me lots at the rail yard," Schooner replied.

Both Dad and I knew that wasn't really the case. And even when Schooner did work, it never stopped him from staying the night at our place.

"Let me grab you a pop or something," Dad said, walking into the kitchen.

Schooner looked worn, tired. He brushed at the loose ashes that had fallen from Dad's cigarette onto the table. I noticed his long, untrimmed fingernails. His eyes darted around, scattered.

Dad kicked the porch door open with his foot, as he balanced an armful of cans. He threw a bag of chips in my direction, as the door swung shut behind him. He set the pops in front of us and cracked open his beer. I poured some chips on the table, and then slid the bag toward Schooner. I was surprised when he reached in to grab one.

"You staying over tonight?" I asked.

He shrugged.

Schooner bit a small corner off the chip and placed the remaining bit on the table in front of him.

"Maybe hit the river tomorrow?" Schooner replied, changing the subject. "You working, Creigh?" As he talked, I could see the soggy bit of chip on his tongue, a piece small enough to be swallowed without chewing at all.

"No, day off, since I gotta work the weekend."

"'K. Meet at the tracks then, before the ten train. You know?"

Schooner stood up, guzzled the remaining bit of pop from his can, and then crunched it with both hands.

"What'd you do to your lip?" Dad asked, looking up at Schooner.

He had some sort of welt, it seemed, maybe a sunburn that blistered, or a cold sore. The corners of his eyes were also packed with a yellowish gunk.

"Gotta run! Got lots of crap to do today," Schooner said.

He was in the same cut-off shorts he wore every day that summer. He barely had any hips, so the shorts were hanging way below his light blue underwear. Schooner wasn't wearing his T-shirt. It was pulled through one of the belt loops, weighing the jeans shorts down even further. His ribcage seemed to stick out more than usual. Every bone in his upper body looked like it was about to poke through his skin.

"Well, you come on back for dinner, if you like," Dad called. "We could barbecue something up, maybe? Gotta get some meat on those bones of yours."

"Yeah, we'll see," Schooner replied, as he climbed on his bike at the bottom of the staircase. "See how things go."

"Guess he doesn't like chips, either," Dad said, once Schooner rode off. "I was expecting him to talk my ear off." Dad turned back to his newspaper. "Kinda wish he had. He's a strange one—never sure I know what's up with him," he mumbled, staring down at the paper.

I waited at the tracks for Schooner, just like he'd asked me to the night before. I could hear the ten o'clock train approaching, but there was still no sign of him. Schooner was NEVER late, not once, except for the day he made my birthday tag. The ten o'clock train came and went. Schooner was not there to see it.

I didn't wait. I knew something was up. All the thoughts I had ignored.

I dropped my bike on Carin's lawn and knocked on the front door. Her mom called, "Come in!" Mrs. Reiner was reading a magazine at the counter and got up as I entered.

"Hi, Mrs. Reiner, Carin around?" I asked, as I walked into the kitchen.

"Creighton, you okay?" she said, as she leaned in to feel my forehead. "You're sweating. Let me grab you some water."

"I'm fine, thanks. Is Carin around?"

"Carin! Carin! Creigh's here for you," Mrs. Reiner yelled down the hall.

"What's up? Has something happened, Creighton? What is it?" her mom asked me. I was out of breath as well as sweating. I started shaking, like I always seemed to do in stressful moments.

"Creigh? What's the matter?" Carin asked, as she came out of her bedroom.

"Schooner. He didn't show today. He's never been late for the ten train. Something's up—we gotta check on him."

I didn't have to explain to Carin. Like me, she had been worrying, too. She phoned Ratchet, and he said he would stop what he was doing to help us out. We waited on the front steps for him to drive in from the dairy.

"I wonder what's up with him?" Carin said. "Seriously, does anyone know a thing about Schooner?"

"How will we figure out where he lives? You think Ratchet knows?" I asked.

"Ms. Hayworth would know. She has all that kind of information about us. We could stop by her place. I know where she lives. Mom cleans the house right beside her."

"He told me it's a forty-minute bike ride on a clear

day," I said. "That's far."

"You think this is all about school? He's freaking out about going back, maybe?" Carin asked.

"I was thinking that, too."

Ratchet, driving faster than usual, pulled up to the curb and squealed his brakes. Carin climbed into the truck and I followed behind. She was already telling Ratchet to drive to Ms. Hay's house.

We talked about the many strange things, the little changes we'd noticed about Schooner. The more we shared stories, the more we freaked out.

When we pulled up to Ms. Hay's driveway at the end of a cul-de-sac, Carin was already climbing across me to open the door of the truck. "Wait here," she said, as she frantically climbed over my lap. "I'll ask Ms. Hay where he lives."

We watched as a bearded man answered the door—Ms. Hay's husband, we figured. Then Ms. Hay appeared, pushing her way in front of the guy. She looked different. She was wearing black leggings and a T-shirt that pressed firmly against her enlarged belly. Her hair was down, not clipped into a bun at the back of her head like it normally was, and she was barefoot. We could see the smile on her face disappear as Carin explained what was happening.

Ms. Hay ran back inside to grab her keys and slipped on the flip-flops that were lying on the front steps.

"We're going to follow her," Carin said, as she climbed over top of me to get back into the middle of the truck.

We wound our way through the countryside, passing some small farms scattered with cows and horses. We turned off the highway onto a smaller paved road, meandering our way through a forested area, eventually turning down a long dirt road. The rows of pine trees made it feel secluded, dark, allowing very little sunlight to seep through the dense evergreens. No houses were in sight. A narrow driveway, barely visible from the dirt road, due to the overgrown brush, was in rough shape. Heavy rains had taken their toll, and Ratchet did his best to maneuver the old truck, dodging potholes and fallen branches.

We were impressed that Schooner biked so far to get to school, no matter what kind of weather it was. The narrow driveway curved steeply, leading up to an open field, with a single wide trailer sitting on one side. We all sat for a moment, staring, unsure of our next move, surprised at the sight in front of us.

The place looked a bit like a garbage dump. The beaten-up trailer was balancing on some temporary supports, and the long grass had overtaken the place. There was an old wooden barn, the roof caved in from years of heavy snowfalls. There were piles of garbage, swarming with flies, and rusted parts of old farming equipment and broken-down cars scattered everywhere. A fridge, lying on its side with its door hanging open, exposed many old jars and food containers left to rot. Paint was peeling off the sides of the white trailer, and the small front window was hanging by its last hinge. A black moldy residue coated the side of the structure, from where the gutters leaked onto the aluminum siding. There didn't seem to be much sign of life.

"Jesus Mercy!" Ratchet whispered under his breath. "Let's go," he said. We all clambered out of the truck and headed for Ms. Hay's car.

"I'll wait here," she said. "You go and see what's up. I don't want to cause him more distress by showing up at his front door. He was so unhappy his last week of school, I'm not sure he's ready to see me yet."

We could barely find the front steps, since tall weeds covered each plank, loosening them with their force.

"Watch where you walk," Ratchet said, as he pushed the grass aside. "There are some rusty nails sticking out of this wood."

The wooden boards were wiggly, so we made our way carefully up the few stairs to the landing. At the top, several boards were split, and some were completely missing. We inched our way toward the door, afraid we might fall through the deck. I leaned forward, tilting my head to the side, so I could peer into the small hole where a doorknob once was.

"Oh, my God!" I said.

"What, what is it, Creigh?" asked Carin.

"Let me see! Move over," demanded Ratchet, pushing me out of the way. "Holy crap!"

From corner to corner of what seemed to be the living room, there were boxes, dirty clothes, black garbage bags, loose papers and magazines, a fly swatter, pop cans. The coffee table was littered with dishes, and many were stacked on the floor below. There were cats. One was on the coffee table, licking the dirty plates, and another was curled tightly on the back of the couch. The litter box was overflowing, and the smell of cat pee was intense. Swarms of flies hovered over every surface.

Carin knocked but there was no response. She called Schooner's name, but nothing could be heard, other than a cat scratching in desperation to get out of the trailer. We walked around, noticing Schooner's bike propped up against a rail. Making our way through the waist-high grass, we all called his name.

Nothing.

"Shh! Shut up! Listen!" Carin said, backhanding us in the stomach.

"Did you hear that? Listen. I hear something," she repeated.

Both Ratchet and I looked at each other. We started to walk but Carin held us back.

"Did you hear it this time? Listen!"

Ratchet kept moving through the long grass.

"Just shut up! Stop moving. I hear him. I can hear Schooner," she said.

I couldn't hear a thing. Carin ran ahead, back to the front door. She pushed it open quite easily, since there was no knob to latch it. We followed her inside. Ratchet started gagging, pulling his shirt over his nose, and ran back out. The smell was overpowering. I wanted to follow him, but knew I couldn't leave Carin alone in there. I covered my nose. As we moved down the narrow hallway, she called out again, and this time, I could hear a sound, a whimpering.

"Schooner, it's Carin. Schooner? Where are you?"

The sound took us to the end of the hallway and into a

bedroom. There he was, sitting on the floor with his face tucked tightly between his knees, sobbing.

The stench in the bedroom was harsh, and Carin and I were both coughing, trying hard not to vomit. We made a pathway with our feet, pushing clothing and other items out of the way, as we moved toward Schooner.

Suddenly, Carin stopped.

She turned toward me, grabbing my shoulder with her hand, while holding her nose with the other. She stepped back, closer to me. And then I saw what she was looking at. We both froze.

There, in the middle of the room, was an old woman lying on the bed. Her gray body was lifeless, stiff, and her wide-open eyes stared toward the ceiling.

Carin swallowed hard and took a big breath, and then moved slowly toward Schooner.

"Schooner," she whispered. "Schooner, we're here now. It's okay."

She was so calm. He looked up. She put her hand on his shoulder and crouched down in front of him.

"We're here, Schooner. We've come to help you. It's going to be okay," she said reassuringly.

Schooner looked up at her, and then turned his head

toward me. He wiped his nose with his hand and stood up. He kicked some things out of his path. He kicked the corner of the bed and he walked past us.

"Just go! Get out of here. I don't want you. I don't need you guys. I don't need anybody!" He slammed the trailer's back door as he left.

I couldn't stop shaking. I couldn't stop looking at the body. Her eyes were bulging out of their sockets. Her tongue looked swollen and was sticking out through her lips. Her skin was covered in blisters. I gasped a little, trying to get some air. I could feel the inside of my cheeks start to water and I heaved, thinking I might puke. Carin grabbed my arm.

"Get it together!" she said. "He needs help, Creighton."

How was Carin so brave? Maybe she got her toughness from Ms. Hay. After she took that first breath, she held it all together. She seemed unaffected by the sickening stench and the presence of death in front of us.

We ran outside to Ratchet and Ms. Hay. We told them what we'd seen.

Immediately, Ms. Hay covered her mouth in shock. "Oh, gosh," she said. "His grandmother!"

Ms. Hay ran into the trailer and we followed.

"Down the hallway," Carin said. "In the bedroom at the end."

I saw Ms. Hay swallow. Her pace slowed down, as she covered her nose and mouth, obviously bothered by the smell, like us. She stopped suddenly at the door to the bedroom, turned back to look at us. Her face was white. She turned toward the bed again, taking a second look at the body. Even though the sight was terrifying, it was hard to look away.

She turned back toward us, pushing her way through the door, as though she was going to be sick. We followed her to the car.

"Are you okay?" she said, looking at the three of us. "Are you all okay?" She stood there for a moment, beside her car, as if she was unsure what to do. And then she opened the door, dug around for a bit, until she found her cell phone.

As Ms. Hay called 911, we all stood there, speechless. Ratchet finally interrupted the silence. "Where do you think he's hiding?"

We walked around, calling his name, while we waited for the police to arrive. His bike was still there. He had to be hiding somewhere. I couldn't help wondering when his grandmother had died. When he'd stopped by the night before, she must have been dead. Did he want to tell us? What would he do now? Where would he go? I couldn't stop shaking. I was embarrassed by my weakness, when strength was needed.

After a good forty minutes of waiting, we finally heard the sirens. And that's when Schooner bolted out from behind the trailer. He jumped on his bike and pedaled away. We explained to the police what was happening. Ratchet jumped in his truck to go after Schooner. The police radioed, sending a car to find him. The officer took a statement from us. Ms. Hay did the talking and, occasionally, Carin interrupted. Ms. Hay knew a lot more stuff about Schooner than we realized. When a second officer arrived, the two policemen went into the trailer together. They were in there for a long time, maybe an hour. And then a van pulled up. A young woman and an older man went inside the trailer.

"Who are they?" Carin asked.

"They must be here to do the removal," Ms. Hay replied.

We stood in the distance, as the body of Schooner's grandmother was removed from the home, like a scene from a movie. The tightly wrapped corpse was placed inside the van. The vehicle reversed and drove slowly down the dirt road, with the police car trailing behind. No lights, no sirens. There was no hurry. She was taken away, Schooner's only family.

CHAPTER 20

That night, we searched every place in Breton we thought Schooner could possibly be. Ratchet, Carin, and I did not sleep. Carin let her mom know we were trying to locate Schooner. Although Mrs. Reiner didn't like the idea of Carin being out all night, she seemed to understand. Ratchet walked along the river where Schooner loved to spend his days, and Carin and I checked the rail yard, looking inside every unlocked boxcar that we had access to. The three of us even did the fifteen-minute drive to the beach, but found nothing. The police had extra cars out, monitoring the streets, in case he was spotted. Ms. Hayworth also drove around late into the night, and even Dad searched until eleven, way past his bedtime. I imagined Schooner alone, hiding somewhere, afraid. He would be terrified for his future.

By 3 AM, Ratchet needed to get back to the farm for the early milking shift, and Carin and I sat on the couch back at my place, watching TV, not knowing what else to do. She sprawled out with her head on my lap, and I flipped through the channels, until we found something to watch. As I tucked strands of hair behind her ear, just as Mom had done for me each night, I tried to imagine my life without Carin. I didn't have that loneliness anymore, those moments when I wished I had a mom to talk to. Carin had changed that.

But Schooner had no one. I thought of his lonely days at the river before he met me. How awful, to go home each day to a sickly grandmother, who obviously couldn't care for him. I imagined him riding his bike in the rain to get to school. He probably couldn't wait to see Ms. Hay, to be cared for by someone. No wonder he felt angry about her leaving. School was all he had.

Hours went by and I was still wide awake. I could feel Carin's heavy breathing and knew she was deep in sleep. I slipped my legs out, slid a pillow underneath her head, and grabbed the quilt off my bed to cover her. I couldn't sit there any longer, doing nothing. My mind was spiraling with worry. I left a note beside her, making sure she knew where I was, and headed to the rail yard again. As I sat on the grassy bank, the place I had met Schooner a hundred times, I stared at the tracks. I knew we had searched the boxcars, and there was nothing more to check. A couple of guys pulled in just before eight, probably the CPR employees getting ready for the ten o'clock train. Maybe he'd hopped on the evening train in Breton, after he'd fled on his bike. The train would have traveled to Fairburn, staying there for the night to get reloaded. It would be back by ten in the morning. Schooner would know which boxcars were left empty for the night. It would be a place to sleep. This was the only option I could think of.

Carin showed up around 9:45.

"You didn't sleep, did you?" she asked.

"Thinking I wanna wait for the ten train and see if he jumped on that. He could have got the evening train out of here. The same one comes back this morning," I explained.

The train was late. We didn't hear the whistle in the distance until 10:15. I got up to be sure I could see every car go by. I'd sat on the bank with Schooner enough times to know the whole routine. The engine went by and its brakes screeched. It finally came to a stop. A few guys got out and talked with the men who had been working in the yard.

"What's that, Creigh?" Carin said, pointing down the line

of cars. "Can you see way down there? There's something sticking out of that boxcar," Carin said.

"It's a bike."

The bike flew out of the train and then Schooner's strawberry blond head poked out. He looked both ways and jumped.

"They saw him," Carin said. "That guy's pointing." Schooner picked up his bike and started pushing it over the loose gravel.

"Hey, kid, stop! Where do you think you're going?" a guy called out as he approached Schooner, who was about ten cars away.

Schooner put one foot on the pedal, attempting to jump on, while running full speed. But the bike slipped from under him. Schooner lay on top of it as the man got closer, still yelling. We ran, too. Schooner panicked—he struggled to jump on his bike to make a getaway, but the tires were sinking in the fine rubble.

"Leave him!" Carin shouted at the men.

We began running along the top of the bank.

Each time Schooner tried to raise his bike, his leg slipped on the loose gravel. The man was gaining speed, still yelling at Schooner to stop. Schooner looked frantically behind him, his face red.

The man reached out to grab Schooner's shirt as he attempted, yet again, to get up. Then the man fell too, tripping over the rocks that lined the tracks. He pulled at Schooner's pant leg and they both went down, Schooner sprawled on top of his bike. He kicked the rocks toward the man, yelling at him. He managed to maneuver the bike between them.

"Leave him," Carin yelled again. This time we were close enough, and the guy looked up.

"It's Schooner!" I added, hoping the man would realize this, since they must have known each other.

"What the hell you think you're doing, riding the train?" the man said, finally recognizing Schooner, the kid who worked in the rail yard.

Schooner did not respond. In fact, his kicking became more aggressive, and he started to throw loose rocks at the man's face.

"Slow down, kid—stop, stop!" the man said, as he blocked the flying debris with his forearm.

"Get away! Don't touch me! I'm warning you, don't touch me," Schooner screamed.

The man held his hands up, slowly moving into a standing position while backing up. "It's okay. Calm down.

I ain't gonna touch you. Calm down, fella."

Schooner gave one last kick, and tossed a handful of rocks in the man's direction. Without taking his eyes off him, Schooner raised his bike. "Don't ever touch me! Don't ever touch me again!"

I don't know who was more scared, the man or Schooner, but they both backed away from each other. Schooner climbed on his bike and rode away.

For that whole last week of summer holidays, Schooner avoided everyone. He was continually spotted all over town, and the police did their best to make contact. I guess if he wasn't causing any harm, what could they do? He saw us many times, but ran when anyone approached him. Ms. Hay, Dad, and all three of us did our best to try to talk to him. But Schooner wanted no part of it. A couple of social workers tried, too. They even stopped to talk to Dad, to see if Schooner was at our place. They tried to connect with him, to make sure he had a safe place to go, but he made sure he stayed away.

It was my last evening of summer holidays. I'd hated this night my whole life. I always felt nervous, worrying about the new school I'd be attending. This year, my mind was preoccupied by Schooner and his whereabouts. School was the last thing on my mind.

Carin and I met the next morning, like we always did before school. She was starting Grade 11, and Ratchet would be in his final year. I'd be entering Grade 9, even though I was the same age as Schooner, and only a year younger than Carin.

"Think he'll be sitting there?" Carin asked.

"He's not gonna show up. Not without Ms. Hayworth."

We had dreaded meeting our new teacher for the first time, but since we had so much on our minds, it wasn't such a big deal. We walked in and Schooner, no surprise, wasn't there.

The room looked empty. There was no colored paper on the bulletin boards, neatly trimmed with borders. The list of frequently misspelled words that Ms. Hay added to each day was gone. How would Schooner write anything? He depended on that wall. There were no plants, and our mugs were not hanging on the hooks above the sink. The pillows that Carin burrowed into each morning were no longer piled on the carpet. The microwave was also missing. How would Will heat up his noodle soup each day for lunch? There was a new sign above the door that read: RESPECT IS EARNED. The basket of fidget toys was not sitting on the back table, and the crib boards were no longer on the shelf. It didn't look like our classroom at all.

A man sat at Ms. Hay's desk, which had been moved to the front of the classroom, directly in the center. He was reading something and seemed unaware of our presence. Carin slammed her backpack on an empty desk, maybe in an effort to startle him, but more likely to show the new teacher where she stood.

"Well, good morning," the man said, looking up from his work.

He did not get up to welcome us.

"I'm Mr. Stewart. You must be Karen? The only girl on the list."

"It's CAR – IN! My name is Carin, not Karen," she replied. He had made his first mistake already, getting her name wrong.

"I figured, you being the only girl in this program, you'd be a challenge. I can see I thought correctly," the man said, scanning her body up and down, still making no effort to get up.

"I'm Creighton," I said, interrupting before Carin could

respond. I walked to his desk with my hand extended, thinking we should at least shake. He didn't put his hand out. Instead, he looked down at his small class list searching for my name.

"Creighton Fischer? Grade 9?" he said, still looking down at the list.

"Yes."

"Did you fail somewhere along the way? Seems you should be in Grade 10, according to your age."

"No sir, I started school a year later, that's all."

"Good, so you'll be extra smart, then, I expect." I didn't know how to reply. Carin was already giving him a death glare. Just then, the back door crashed open. It was Ratchet, pushing his bike through, while balancing a pop in one hand and a breakfast sandwich in the other.

"Hey, hey, hey!" Mr. Stewart shouted, getting up from his seat and walking toward the scene. "What are you doing? You can't bring a bike into this classroom," he said to Ratchet.

"Where's the truck?" Carin interrupted.

"No insurance. Boss said I can't use it till I pay for some. Next month maybe. Before winter, for sure."

Ratchet ignored Mr. Stewart and kept talking to us.

"What's your name?" Mr. Stewart demanded.

"Ratchet! Name's Ratchet!" he replied.

"Well, there's no Ratchet on this list, so you need to leave with your bike," Mr. Stewart continued.

Ratchet leaned the bike against the wall at the back of the class. "I ain't leaving my bike outside without a lock, man." He continued to eat his sandwich and drink his pop, ensuring he made loud slurping sounds through the straw, probably to rattle the guy.

"His name's Matt. Matt Radcliff," I said. "He's in this class, been here four years."

"Hmm ... Matt Radcliff. Maybe you want to go back out and start the morning over, Matt. Why don't you push your bike out that back door, finish your food, and enter through the main entrance like all students are expected to?"

There was a silence. Ratchet stopped chewing and held his drink still. He was sitting on top of an empty desk at the back of the class. He stared at Mr. Stewart, motionless. Then he started to chew slowly, his eyes firmly locked on Mr. Stewart's. He held his sandwich up to his mouth and took another, extra-large, exaggerated bite. Without moving his eyes, he put the straw in his mouth and slurped the drink. Then Ratchet stood up and walked toward the garbage can, still staring at the new teacher. He crunched the sandwich wrapper into his hand and squeezed the paper cup flat, before dropping it in the garbage can. He looked down at his hands and wiped them on his jeans. Ratchet glanced around at the bare classroom, noticing all of the changes. He stared at the sign above the door—RESPECT IS EARNED—and turned back to Mr. Stewart, who was standing, watching.

"Maybe you should check out that sign you put up!" Ratchet said, as he walked into the hallway, leaving his bike at the back of the class.

The others started to arrive, and the classroom's chaos began, just as it had with Ms. Hay at the beginning of each day. Mr. Stewart didn't know what to do. It was clear he was unprepared to deal with the challenge of Lane Oslo students. Carin had figured we'd get a bad teacher. There weren't too many Ms. Hays who'd want the job. He was probably the only guy who'd applied, 'cause he couldn't get a job anywhere else.

Ronnie walked around in a circle. His desk was not in the same spot as it had been. He knew which one belonged to him, even though they were empty, because he'd memorized the location of each cut and groove that was scraped into the surface before his time. His arms flapped, as he noticed the changes in the room.

"I'm gonna move this desk for Ronnie," Carin said lifting it up.

"That's not necessary. He can sit right there or choose another one," Mr. Stewart replied.

"No, that's not going to work out too well—I'm just going to put it where it needs to be. He doesn't do so well with change," Carin said, as she placed the desk right where it had stood for years.

Then Carcass walked in, and plunked himself heavily into an empty seat at the back, just as Hamilton and Mrs. Scarlet appeared at the door. Carin immediately went toward them.

"Hamilton, how was your summer?" she said sincerely.

"I got a new teacher," Hamilton said. "No Ms. Hayworth, no Ms. Hayworth. I got a new teacher. My new teacher is a man. No Ms. Hayworth. Ms. Hayworth isn't here today, but I got a new teacher," he continued to mumble as he walked around the room. Mrs. Scarlet had obviously prepared him.

"Yes, Hamilton, this is Mr. Stewart," Carin said, walking Hamilton up to his desk. "Mr. Stewart, this is Hamilton."

"Hello," Hamilton said, extending his hand to shake,

just as he had been taught to do. "Hello, Mr. Stewart."

Mr. Stewart did not shake in return. He focused on Mrs. Scarlet and said, "Nice to meet you. You can help him get organized at a desk." He didn't say anything to Hamilton, who stood facing his new teacher ... still waiting.

"I'm Audrey Scarlet," she said. "And I think Hamilton really wants to shake your hand."

"Well, good thing there's some support in this room. Seems as though it's needed," said Mr. Stewart, shaking Hamilton's hand.

Mrs. Scarlet led Hamilton to the desk beside me.

"Hello, Creighton, I have a new teacher. My new teacher's name is Mr. Stewart. Ms. Hayworth is gone today, and my new teacher is a man. His name is Mr. Stewart," Hamilton chattered.

"Yeah, we do have a new teacher. How was your summer, Hamilton?" I asked, trying to get him onto a new topic.

Ratchet returned to the classroom, and chose one of the two desks that were left, the one directly in front of Mr. Stewart's desk.

"So, who is missing then?" Mr. Stewart asked. "One desk left."

"Schooner," Carin said. She moved toward Mr. Stewart.

Then she leaned in, and pointed toward a name on the class list.

"Ha, what is it with this class? None of you use your own names?" the new teacher said, chuckling to himself. "Well, let's get things started. Can you all unload and organize your supplies?"

No one had supplies, except Ronnie and Hamilton. Ms. Hay had always made sure we had everything we needed. Probably because she knew there was no hope of us bringing a thing.

"Since you're all in different grades, I made up some packages to see where you're at. You're going to work through these assignments and hand them in at the end of the day. A finished booklet is your ticket out the door. Karen, why don't you hand these out to everyone."

"It's CAR–IN!" she said in frustration, as she got up to distribute the work packages, slamming them on each desk.

"Watch the attitude with me, young woman," Mr. Stewart snapped.

Carin slapped the packages down even harder.

The booklets were heavy. Pages and pages of math and maps, and fill-in-the-blank sentences. So much reading, most of us would never get through a single page.

"What the h ...?" Ratchet started to say, as he skimmed through the book in amazement. "This is crap, man. I ain't doing all this work." Ratchet stood up, walked toward the garbage can, and threw the stapled package in. He continued to the back door, where his bike leaned against the wall. He tipped his hat toward Mr. Stewart, saying, "Thanks for coming out, man! Have fun, guys," and he left the building.

Mr. Stewart didn't explain any of the pages or check in to see our progress. Mrs. Scarlet did her best to circulate, but no one was working. Ronnie sorted his school supplies and Carin rushed around, trying to help people, just as Ms. Hay had done. Will used his penknife to dig a hole deep into the front of his desk. Carcass was unusually quiet, maybe because the teacher was a man.

It was not good. School would never be the same without Ms. Hayworth.

Two weeks passed and Schooner still had not showed up for school, and Ratchet hadn't returned. But we were excited, because Carin let us know that Ms. Hay had a baby girl. She'd bring her in for a visit next week, once she got into more of a routine. We called Ratchet after the baby was born, letting him know the news, and we planned to drive out to Schooner's, to check if he'd gone back to his trailer. We also wanted Schooner to know Ms. Hay was coming for a visit with the baby. If we could somehow give him the message, maybe he'd come back to school.

It was Monday, our third week of school, and Ratchet met us in the parking lot at three. We made our way around the final bend of the long dirt driveway, and were shocked to discover the charred remnants of what was once Schooner's trailer. Everything in the yard was burned and piles of ash were still smoking. Only the rotting charred steps remained. A loaded pickup truck was parked in the corner, and we could see the filled garbage bags piled in the back, along with an old mattress, springs protruding. More heaps of junk rested in various parts of the yard, amongst the burn piles: broken lawn chairs, a TV, an old refrigerator, hundreds of filled canning jars. The three of us slowly got out of the truck, staring in disbelief at the remaining evidence of Schooner's home.

A man was mowing the long grass with a tractor and stopped to speak with us. He said he was hired to clean up the property, burn the place down—unfit for human habitation, as far as he knew.

"The boy got sent to some group home, from what I heard, in town someplace."

Ratchet's face lit up. In a town the size of Breton, there wasn't going to be more than one home for runaway or abandoned teens.

"I seen him come 'round here couple times now. He rummages through things ..." the man continued, pointing his head at the piles of garbage. "Tried to talk to the kid a few times, but he seems real angry. Doesn't say too much. But, hey, I was just hired by the town to clean up the place."

We made our way back into town. Ratchet knew exactly where the group home was, since he'd lived there for years himself. Schooner would not come to the door when we arrived, so Carin wrote a note. Ratchet asked his buddy to take it to Schooner. He told the guy he'd have to read it aloud to him. It said:

Missing you, Schooner buddy!
Ms. Hay is coming to visit on Friday
with her baby, so you should come to school.

There was nothing else we could do.

CHAPTER 21

On the Friday that Ms. Hayworth had arranged to bring her baby to school, every student was in attendance, except Schooner and Ratchet. I was disappointed that Carcass showed up. I didn't want him to ruin the special day.

Carin had things totally planned out. She wanted the classroom to look perfect. Since the beginning of school, the room had deteriorated, even though Carin did her best to take care of everything. She tried to keep some of Ms. Hayworth's special routines, but it seemed like an impossible task. On this particular morning, Carin assigned jobs. Ronnie lined up all the books on the shelves. Gabe and Cass sorted the mixed-up piles of paper onto the art shelf. Devon washed the whiteboards and organized the magnets, just the way Ms. Hay would have liked them to be. Will cleaned out his desk, because it was exploding with wood shavings. Carin gave Hamilton a sponge and some soapy water in a bucket to wash the desks, something to distract him. He fixated on squeezing the sponge and watching the water drizzle back into the bucket. Suddenly, I heard Carcass say, "What am I supposed to do? Just sit here?"

"Do you want a job?" Carin asked, surprised.

"Well, isn't that what you said? We all need jobs."

"Well, could you organize the boxes of games and put all the pieces back in the right places?"

I re-attached some shelving that had broken off the wall, wishing Ratchet were here to help. I also re-fastened the paper towel dispenser, which was hanging by one screw, after Will and Devon had knocked it off during a wrestling match. Carin had made a cake and had a card for all of us to sign. She had flowers, the stems wrapped in moist paper towels, to give Ms. Hay. It was clear Carin had been thinking about this day for some time, hoping, like me, things would go smoothly. We helped her string decorations around the room. Everyone struggled to stay focused on our assigned jobs, but we were nervous about Ms. Hay's brief return.

Mr. Stewart didn't get involved at all. He stayed busy at his desk and let Carin take charge.

Everyone was on edge. After Ronnie straightened the books, he stood back and tilted his head sideways, checking to see that the tops were aligned. Carcass knew about his need for perfection, and pulled a book off the shelf, laughing. Ronnie flapped his arms, replaced the book, and stood back to view his work again. Carcass always took pleasure in aggravating Ronnie's need for order. Hamilton plugged his ears and squealed. He couldn't handle the change in routine, and the novelty of the dripping sponge wore off fast. I tried to distract him by having him hold the screws for me, but he finally curled into a tight ball on the floor with his eyes closed, squeezed his ears, and hummed. We all wanted the same thing, to make Ms. Hay happy, yet it was turning into a gong show.

When Ms. Hay appeared in the window, everyone scrambled to open the door. Mr. Stewart made no attempt to control the class. Carin sat on top of her desk, looking across at me, shaking her head in frustration.

Ms. Hay was bombarded. She lifted the baby from her car seat, turning her body around to face us. "Meet Camille," she said, beaming. And then she looked at Mr.

Stewart. Ms. Hay walked to his desk. Holding Camille over her shoulder with one arm, she reached out her other hand toward him. "I'm sorry, I know we've spoken on the phone a few times, but I should officially introduce myself. Elizabeth Hayworth."

"So, you're the famous lady! Good to put a face to the name. Bet you're soaking up the maternity leave, having a good breather from this bunch." He laughed.

Ms. Hay put her hand back on Camille, rocking her as she turned toward us. "It's been hard to be away," she said. "Exciting to be a mom, but so hard for me to leave my students."

Carin rubbed her fingers together. I could tell she was anxiously waiting her turn to talk to Ms. Hay and see the baby. Hamilton unwrapped his body from the cocoon-like state when he saw Ms. Hay. At the sight of the baby, his stream of thoughts started up.

"Look at her fingers. She has little baby fingers. See her fingers? The baby has so many fingers. I like her hair. She has pretty hair," Hamilton continued.

Then Frasier shouted, "There's Schooner!"

Schooner peeked through the back window. I ran to the back door, hoping to let him in, but he was gone. I circled the school. I couldn't find him, but his bike leaned against the side of the building. He must have got our message. Why did he have to be so difficult? Couldn't he just enjoy the visit like everyone else? I called his name but knew there was no point. He would never come in. Why'd he show up at all?

"He took off again," I said as I came through the back door. "His bike's still here, so he must be kicking around somewhere."

"Poor Schooner," Ms. Hay said, shaking her head. "Such a hard time for him."

Hamilton had his comb and gel out, trying to style Camille's blond mop of hair.

"We'll just look at the little baby, Hamilton. She's a bit small to have her hair combed yet. You can hold her hand, though," Ms. Hay said, protecting Camille from the purple comb that was very close to her baby's face.

Just then, Ms. Hay noticed Carin standing back, and slid baby Camille out from under Hamilton's reach. Ms. Hay smiled and walked over to Carin. "How's my girl?" she said. "You did all of this, didn't you?" She admired the decorations. "You're so kind and thoughtful. You doing okay? Your mom okay?"

"It's not the same without you, Ms. Hay."

Carin didn't need to explain. Ms. Hay could see that things were different. Occasionally, she would glance at Mr. Stewart. I could tell she was shocked. Shocked at what her classroom had become.

"Are you okay with all this?" Ms. Hay said, turning to Mr. Stewart. "I was afraid I might be disrupting your whole afternoon, when I asked if I could come for a quick visit."

Mr. Stewart looked up. "All good," he said. "It's a pretty relaxed day. They really get no work done, anyway," he said, raising his eyebrows. "Stay as long as you like. Come back whenever you want."

We all sat on top of the desks and enjoyed the cake Carin had made. Ms. Hay asked about our lives, and everyone talked at once. When Camille started to fuss, Carin lifted her from Ms. Hay's arms. "Here, I'll walk her around for you," she said. Carin held the baby against her body, swaying gently, humming. Behind the dark makeup, piercings, and dread knots, she seemed like a mom. The chaos had ended. Even though everyone spoke at once and interrupted one another, her voice calmed us.

"Where's Ratchet?" Ms. Hay asked.

"He quit the first day," I answered.

Ms. Hay swallowed.

She spent the rest of the afternoon in our classroom. Although her intention was to "pop in for a quick visit," it seemed she really missed us. Carin rocked the baby to sleep, and Ms. Hay gently placed her back in the car seat. As Camille was safely buckled in, the bell rang. Cass and Gabe were the first to leave, as they caught the early bus. Others hung back, staying with Ms. Hay as long as possible.

She began to gather her things, which were scattered throughout the room. She reread the card we'd signed. Her eyes watered a little. She dropped the soother in the car seat beside Camille, picked the blanket off the floor, and placed it over her baby, tucking the edges in tightly over top of the straps of the seatbelt. She put a pink woolen toque on Camille's tiny head, even though it was a warm September afternoon. She slipped the wrapped flower arrangement gently into her bag, so the petals delicately hung over the top. Just as Ms. Hayworth picked up the car seat, Carin interjected, "Ms. Hay, we forgot to show you the totem Will finished carving. Come!"

The others had left. Mr. Stewart stood with his backpack on, waiting for the final bus bell so he could make his exit.

"Oh, gosh!" she said, placing her bag and the car seat back down on the classroom floor, "you're right."

"Come!" Carin said, leading Ms. Hay to the door. Will and I followed them to the cabinet that stood in the hallway, just outside the classroom, inside the front entrance of the school. There it was, the miniature totem, about a meter tall. Will had fixed the animals after destroying them with the blade of his knife, when Ms. Hay had given us the news of her pregnancy.

"Oh, my, Will, it's amazing," she said.

"That's you," he said, pointing to the hawk at the top. "You are the protector, the leader who kept us on the right path."

I could see Ms. Hay's eyes fill with water again.

"And the butterfly? The butterfly must be Carin?" she asked.

"Yeah, that's me," Carin replied.

"Means transformation," Will added. "Rebirth."

"And let me guess, Creighton must be the deer? Am I right?" Ms. Hay asked. "He's our sensitive guy, filled with intuition," she added, winking at me.

Ms. Hay was right. I was the deer, according to Will.

Will continued to tell the story of each spirit animal, and the person it represented in the class. Ms. Hay looked proud. She took a picture of Will standing beside the cabinet.

Will walked out the front door after saying goodbye, and I could see the grin stretching across his face. Ms. Hay knew how to make us feel good, when nothing else in our lives was working. The three of us walked back to the classroom.

"Will you come back each week?" Carin asked.

"Well, I'm not sure how productive that would be," Ms. Hay laughed. "Nobody got a thing done this afternoon with me and Camille around."

"Nobody gets anything done when you aren't around, either," Carin replied.

Ms. Hay glanced around the empty room, noticing the many changes. "Schooner will come around," she said. "He'll slowly become himself again. Look how he checked in today. He wanted to come, just wasn't quite there yet," she said. Ms. Hay picked up her bag, being careful not to disturb the flowers that hung delicately over the edge. "You need to be patient with Schooner. He takes a lot of time to process things," Ms. Hay continued, looking at Carin and me.

If there was anyone who understood Schooner, it was Ms. Hay. I felt reassured by her words. She basically said the same thing as Dad.

I leaned in to give Ms. Hay a hug, to make my exit, since I knew she'd want some time with Carin. And then I walked to the back of the classroom, where my bike was waiting outside. As I opened the door, I turned toward Carin and Ms. Hay. I was going to let Carin know I'd wait outside till she was done, when I noticed the panic on Ms. Hay's face.

CHAPTER 22

"Camille! Didn't I set her down right here? Carin, did you move her?" Ms. Hay asked, as she stared at the empty spot on the classroom floor—the spot where she had set the car seat down, before checking Will's totem in the hallway.

"No, I didn't move her. You buckled her in right here, beside your bag ..." Carin said, glancing quickly around the room, "... when we went to look at Will's totem."

"Are you sure, Carin? I thought I set her right here, too." Ms. Hay put her hand over her mouth. She looked panicked. Her eyes scanned the room. "Oh, oh!" she gasped. "Jesus!" I heard her whisper. "Why didn't I bring her with us? What was I thinking?"

"Creighton?" Ms. Hay said, turning toward me. "Did you see Camille here, too? Wasn't the seat sitting on the floor right here, when we walked out to see Will's totem?" She was staring at the empty spot on the floor. She slid her hand through her hair and, as she pulled it out, half her bun loosened. She ripped the elastic out and threw it on an empty desk.

"Yeah, I'm sure she was right there." I moved in closer. "We were only gone a minute, Ms. Hay; we were close by the whole time. If someone came in, they would have walked past us. This is so weird," I said, looking around.

"The back door!" Ms. Hay said, turning toward the back of the room. She rushed to the windows.

"Creighton, check outside! Hurry, go look; she's not in here."

Carin's eyes became intense.

I ran out the back door. Ms. Hay followed. She stood there, her hand rubbing her face, hair completely unraveled.

"I'll go," I said to her. "You stay here." I ran around the high school, looked at the parking lot to see if there were any strange cars. By the time I returned, Carin and Ms. Hay had already looked through the rest of the two-room school. They had checked the short hallway, the second classroom, the bathrooms, and the entrance area where the cabinet stood. Ms. Hay moved like a whirlwind through Lane Oslo.

"There's nothing, no one outside our school. Buses are gone. I ran all around it," I said. "Even Mr. Stewart's car is gone."

Ms. Hay ran to the intercom to contact the high school, asking for help. Her voice cracked as she held her stomach.

"Get Mr. Roland! Send him next door to Lane Oslo. I need help, there's an emergency!" she yelled. "It's Elizabeth Hayworth. I was visiting with the baby. Call the police!"

Someone, probably the secretary, was asking questions, and Ms. Hay became frustrated. "I don't know!" she continued sharply. "Just send someone. It's my baby. My baby is missing."

When Mr. Roland arrived, Ms. Hay started to cry. Carin teared up as well. Neither of them could talk coherently, so I told Mr. Roland the series of events. He paced the floor nervously, while waiting for the police, playing with the change in his pocket, looking all around the room for the car seat himself. He seemed to think we had misplaced it. He called the high school, asking all the remaining staff to help search.

Mr. Roland told Ms. Hay to stay put. The police didn't want her to leave the classroom until they arrived. She sat at one of the desks, holding her head down. Sometimes she stood up, walked in a circle, and then sat back down. Carin brought her a box of tissues, but she didn't seem to care. Finally, Ms. Hay reached into her pocket for her cellphone and, shaking, called her husband. Her voice was frantic.

"You need to come. It's Camille—she's been taken," she said into her phone. We could hear a muffled voice on the other end.

"Not now, please, just come. I need you here. I don't know how, but something's happened." And she hung up her phone.

I went outside again to search around Breton Secondary. Many teachers were searching, too. Even the custodian was out.

Finally, the police arrived and asked Ms. Hay for a description of Camille. They needed the most recent picture. Ms. Hay called her husband back, asking him to bring a photo. She tried to answer the questions that were being fired at her by one of the officers.

"She's only two and a half weeks old," Ms. Hay cried.

"I just sat her down for a minute. We were all right here. I shouldn't have left her."

"Excuse me, Elizabeth, can you carry on describing her?" the man continued.

"Sorry. She has blue eyes. She is very blond, a lot of hair, kind of going in all directions. It's almost white. Um ... she was in a little jumper ... yellow ... light yellow."

Another officer asked me and Carin to list all of the students who were in attendance that day.

Ms. Hay's husband arrived. He ran in, his eyes staring at the commotion, as he scanned the classroom for Ms. Hay. He looked angry, upset.

"What's going on?" he said as he approached Ms. Hay.

Ms. Hay buried her head in his chest and cried louder. He grabbed onto her shoulders, then straightened his arms so that he could look at her face and ask questions.

"What do you mean, she's gone? How is she gone?" he asked. "I told you not to bring her. It's not a place for a baby. These guys are a bunch of hoodlums. I've told you that." He kept repeating, "You never listen to me. I was right about these kids. But you never, ever listen!" Ms. Hay turned away from him.

By now, there were many police cars, two dogs, and a

lot of staff from the high school, moving in and out of the room. Mr. Stewart returned and was being interviewed by an officer; so was Mrs. Scarlet. Ms. Hay was still being questioned. We were told to wait, because they needed to speak with both me and Carin. The room was filling with adults, some in uniform, some not. A Trauma Response Team had arrived. They were rapidly coordinating a search. People were on their phones and jobs were being assigned. The Search and Rescue team was also called. I even heard them ask for divers, to check the river that ran through town. The counselor from the high school had arrived. She was sitting with Ms. Hay and her husband, who still seemed to be ranting at his wife for losing their baby girl.

As the room transformed into the command post for a missing person, with radio static, phones ringing, background chatter, and confusion, Ms. Hay stared blankly at a wall. In my one year with her as my teacher, she had been our strength. She seemed to cope in every challenging moment. Now I saw a different Ms. Hay. She looked helpless.

After two and a half hours, there was no trace of little Camille. She had simply vanished from our classroom at the end of the day. A counselor from Fairburn was brought in, too. She created a waiting area in the hallway, and only those directly involved in the search were allowed inside the classroom. Carin and I sat on the carefully arranged chairs, waiting our turn.

We were interviewed separately. We were asked if there had been any unusual behavior among the students that day. With Ms. Hay around, everyone had been calm and happy. The police wondered if anyone else had been in the room, any adults, aside from the teacher and Mrs. Scarlet, of course, but no one different had been around.

When my interview finished, I waited for Carin back in the hallway. I couldn't believe the flurry of people who had taken over our small space. The whole thing seemed crazy. How could this great afternoon turn into this kind of disaster? Why would a student or teacher take Camille? The possibility of a stranger walking into the room at the end of the day to snatch a baby seemed unlikely. I did have one thought, though, something I'd never shared during the interview.

When Carin was done, we were given posters to put up around the school. The secretary from Breton Secondary had a huge pile she had photocopied. We wanted to stay, to be part of the action, but they were getting people out fast. We left, feeling sick. As Carin and I walked through the front doors, we could see a canopy over some tables that held muffins and bottles of water. The Trauma Response Team was setting up a second one. We could hear them planning a community search. We realized news had spread throughout Breton. Roads were closed, media circulated around both schools, and we could see, as we left the parking lot, that a great many people had gathered. Cell phones were out, neighbors chatted with each other on the street, and people peered out from their windows. Behind the barricades, across the road from the school, were hordes of students. Our tiny Lane Oslo building, which many people didn't know existed, was now the focus of our small town.

I walked my bike beside Carin. It didn't seem right, just walking home, abandoning Ms. Hay. We put up all the posters we had been given.

"You know what I was thinking?" I said to Carin. "Carcass! Where was he after school?"

We both figured it was odd that he'd made it through the entire afternoon's visit without a challenge. He hadn't annoyed any student, other than Ronnie. He hadn't made rude comments or hurt Ms. Hayworth with horrible words. Although he'd showed no interest in the baby, he wasn't rude about her, either. In the busyness of the day, neither of us had noticed when he left. Cass and Gabe had rushed out to catch the bus. Ronnie and Frasier left just after. Devon rode his bike home. Hamilton and Mrs. Scarlet packed up and exited through the back door. Will continued out the front of the school, once he'd showed his totem pole to Ms. Hay. Schooner had made an appearance in the window, but it was early in the afternoon, shortly after Ms. Hay arrived. But when— in all of those departures—had Carcass made his exit? In June, when Ms. Hay was saying her goodbyes, he'd waited for a hug, and then abruptly pulled away, just as Ms. Hay had reached her arms toward him. Where was he this time during the goodbyes? Had he still been in the classroom, when the four of us went to the front doors to look at Will's totem? Neither of us had noticed, which was strange, since Carcass was *always* noticeable.

We turned around, walked back to the school, and begged to speak with a police officer again. We couldn't tell whether our information was important or not. But it was all we could offer.

It was now 6:30, a hot September evening, and Carin and I stretched out on the lawn behind our house. Dad wasn't home, probably still on a delivery somewhere. Carin leaned back, resting her head on my lap as she chewed on the end of a long piece of grass. "I don't get it, Creigh. Why does stuff like this happen to people like Ms. Hay? She's such a good person. I just don't get it."

She stopped talking for a bit.

"And why did I ask her to see Will's totem? She was on her way out the back door. It was me who wanted her to check it out. That's when it happened. We left Camille in her car seat all alone in the classroom. We shouldn't have done that."

"Don't blame yourself, Carin. Ms. Hay would have wanted to see the totem. She thought of that project to keep Will coming to school each day," I said.

"We should have taken the car seat. Why did we leave it in the classroom?"

"Carin, it's a tiny two-room school. It's not liked we abandoned a baby somewhere. Camille was asleep. We weren't away long. We literally walked to the entrance, which is basically right outside the classroom."

"This whole thing is so messed up. I seriously don't

understand why stuff like this happens to people," she continued. "Look at Schooner; look at Ratchet. What did they do to deserve all the crap they've been through? Look at you, Creighton. I mean, you were five. You had no control over what happened to you."

I knew Carin was thinking about herself, too, the assault. "And you, Carin ... you didn't deserve it, either. You're a good person. Yet look what you had to go through."

"Yeah," she said looking up at the sky. She stopped talking. We sat quietly.

"I wasn't afraid before, you know, Creigh," she continued. "I remember liking the dark. I loved the night sky, its peacefulness. He took that from me."

The last time, Carin was in a rage when she talked about her assault, telling me I would never understand what she went through. She sounded so peaceful now. She sat up, tossing a handful of grass beside her, turning to face me. She leaned back on her hands and touched my bare feet with hers. "You know what really makes me mad, Creighton? It was Canada Day when he did that, July 1st. He took something away from me that night. The moon was full and the sky so perfectly clear. I felt happy, free. It was the first week of summer holidays. I had just finished elementary school."

She paused, picking up more grass with her hands and tossing the pieces back down, while shaking her head.

"I was starting high school in the fall; I was thirteen, so naïve," she said quietly, shaking her head. "I never imagined something could go so wrong that night, not on Canada's birthday. It's supposed to be a country known for peace, a small town where nothing goes wrong. And it was the first time I had been to a party. I couldn't believe Mom actually let me go."

I rubbed her feet with mine. I didn't say anything.

"I believed in the goodness of people back then, just like Ms. Hay does."

Carin was silent again. I still didn't say anything. I figured I needed to keep quiet. She wasn't done.

"I don't know, this may seem weird to you, Creighton, but sometimes now, I'm glad it happened."

"What do you mean?" I asked. "Why would you be glad you got assaulted?"

"I know, it seems dumb. I'm glad I experienced some kind of pain in my life and survived."

"Why would you want pain?"

"'Cause look at all this stuff that's happened, Creigh. I can't stop thinking about Schooner, and what he was probably dealing with all the time. Ratchet was raised in a closet, Creighton, a closet! What kid goes through that and comes out somewhat normal? He doesn't even have a family now."

"So, it makes you feel better that you had pain like them?"

"No, I just get it more. I understand pain. If I hadn't had a really bad experience, I wouldn't have become friends with any of you. I wouldn't have hung out with guys like you. Sorry, but that's the truth."

I started to laugh. "Guys like us? Hah. So, what are 'us guys' like?"

"Well, you have your crap, Creighton, like all the stuff with your mom. You know what I mean; we're all in that school for a reason. Once I started Grade 8, I was brutal. That grandpa of yours messed me right up. I stopped caring. I hated everyone. That didn't work out so well for me in high school, so they sent me to Ms. Hay. Sometimes I think she must have a story, too. I don't think she could understand all of us so well if she didn't."

Everything Carin said made sense, although I'd never thought about it before. Had I been raised with two parents in a really good home, I probably wouldn't understand people like Schooner and Ratchet, either.

Dad's truck pulled into the driveway, and he leapt out faster than normal.

"What's going on? You didn't answer the phone, Creighton. It's all over the radio. That's all they talked about since I left Fairburn. I can't believe you're both sitting here," Dad said, walking toward us. "Who took the kid?" he continued.

"Don't know, Dad—weird situation. She just disappeared from the classroom at the end of the day. We've searched all over, put up posters."

We told Dad the story. He stood there, shaking his head.

"Well, it's not right we just sit here. Don't you think we should be looking, or doing something? This is Ms. Hayworth we're talking about."

Dad was the strangest guy. He'd never even met Ms. Hay, just heard us talking about her once in a while. He never seemed interested in anything about school.

"Come on, get in the truck!" he shouted as he climbed in.

"Dad, they won't let us help. They said we have to be eighteen. And there's roadblocks around the school, barricades keeping people out of the whole area."

"Well, we gotta drive around, check out some places,

at least, do our part," he said, starting the engine. And that's what we did. The three of us drove aimlessly around Breton. Like everyone else, we needed something to do, to feel like we were doing our part.

We pulled back into the driveway after two hours of searching. Ratchet was sitting on the front step. He'd got our messages after work and come into town right away. We told him the story. He'd listened to the radio on his way in. He had a thousand questions. Dad ordered pizza and we gathered around the TV, anxiously waiting for the news to start. It was strange to see the little town of Breton on the screen, our school, and so many people we knew. The photo of Camille that Ms. Hay's husband brought in, was flashing every few minutes.

We had wanted Ms. Hay's visit to go well. We'd hoped everyone would cooperate and hold things together. Instead, our good intentions had turned into a living nightmare.

CHAPTER 23

It had been sixteen hours since Camille had vanished on Friday afternoon. The small community of Breton was shaken. The town banded together, as the search expanded rapidly across the country. People contributed in whichever way they could.

Rumors floated around town, and almost all of them pointed toward Carcass. After all, Carlos Gromson had worked hard to make a name for himself wherever he went.

We knew that Carcass had been interviewed, like every other student who attended the alternate school. We also knew that, throughout his life, he'd managed to talk his way out of every negative situation. Maybe we were wrong. Maybe he'd had nothing to do with the abduction of Baby Camille. But our instincts told us otherwise.

We stayed glued to the television set that Saturday, waiting for the twelve o'clock news, hoping to hear new information. Ratchet came back after the morning milking shift, because he didn't have cable in his shack. Everyone was still in shock. Everyone was waiting. Ratchet sat on the couch, holding a cushion. Carin knelt on the floor. I sat in Dad's recliner, since he had rushed to work after the early morning news.

During a commercial, Ratchet tossed a couch cushion toward me. "Catch this!" he shouted, as it hit me in the face. I threw one back, laughing.

"Shut up! It's on," Carin yelled. The twelve o'clock news had started.

"Ground-breaking news in the small community of Breton," the anchorwoman began.

We stopped. Both Ratchet and I held the cushions on our laps, staring at the TV.

"Baby Camille has been located!"

"Oh, my God," Carin said, getting up to walk closer to the TV.

"Although hungry, the infant seems unharmed and has been safely returned to her parents, following medical examination," the announcement continued.

"The two-and-a-half-week-old infant, who went missing at approximately 3:15 PM on Friday, September 17, from Lane Oslo School of Educational Reform, was located in an empty freight car in the rail yard in the small community of Breton, fifty kilometers outside of Fairburn. The rail crew was preparing to load the bulk freight, when they heard the infant crying inside the car. Breton RCMP were called to the scene at 10:35 AM on Saturday, September 18, and immediately activated an emergency medical response. Jane Coleman, an emeritus professor of pediatrics at the University of Valemont, said healthy babies are born with enough fluid to help them survive for some time without feeding," the anchorwoman continued.

Then the screen flashed to Jane Coleman herself: "Fortunately, Camille was a full-term baby, which means she had enough fluid on board to keep her going for the nineteen hours she was missing. Healthy new babies have a good amount of fluid storage, and extra glucose stored in their liver, as well."

Back to the anchorwoman: "Baby Camille was wrapped in a blanket, and safely buckled in her car seat when found, leading authorities to question the motive of this unusual kidnapping."

We were silent, not wanting to miss a word.

"Murray Corruso, supervisor of the Breton rail yard, says the baby must have been on board before the 5 PM train on Friday, which traveled to Fairburn, remaining there for the night," the announcer continued.

"'Unfortunately, the freight car the baby was placed in yesterday did not get loaded until the train returned to Breton this morning at ten o'clock, when we found her shortly after. It's real lucky this trip was a short one,' Corruso said. 'It would be hard to hear a little one crying from a freight car if the door wasn't opened.'"

"A suspect has been taken into custody for questioning. Although a name cannot be released, due to the Young Offenders Act, the youth is said to be cooperating with the investigation."

"Oh, my God!" Carin said. "What if it was Schooner? I mean, seriously, Camille was found in the rail yard?"

"No way, he'd never do that. Not to Ms. Hay," I said.

"But he was at the school that day. Frasier saw him, right?" Carin asked. "Right, Creigh?"

"Jeez, I forgot all about that."

"When you went outside to look for Camille, was his bike still there?" Carin was pressing hard. "I remember when you went out to find him, you said his bike was outside the building—was it still there when you went back out later to look for Camille?"

"Holy crap! Was the bike still there, man?" Ratchet cut in. "You guys never told me Schooner showed up."

"Well, he never came in," I said to Ratchet. "Frasier just noticed him at the window. When I went to the door, he took off, probably hid somewhere, scared to come in, after not talking to anyone for so long."

Carin said slowly, holding onto my shoulders. "Later ... when you went outside the second time ... to look for the baby ... was ... the bike ... still there?" She was staring into my eyes, trying to get me to focus.

"No," I said. "I would have noticed the bike when I went out again. But I wasn't thinking about Schooner when I went to look for the baby. I'm sure he was just hiding, the first time I checked. Probably embarrassed with everything. Nervous to see Ms. Hay, since he didn't even say goodbye on the last day of school. He probably took off as soon as I stopped looking for him."

"No, man!" Ratchet said as he got off the couch. "This ain't Schooner," he said, pointing to the TV. "It's that bastard Carcass. He'd do something like this and make it look like Schooner did it." Ratchet stood up, punching his fist into his hand. "I hate that kid. Bets Carcass did this, guys. I want to kick his ass right now!" Ratchet shouted, as he punched the corner of the coffee table, while throwing the pillow at the wall. "If I ever see that kid, I will kill him. Seriously, don't ever let me near him, or I will beat him till he can't walk again. He framed him. I know it. He's trying to corner Schooner."

Ratchet made sense. He had to be right. We all agreed, there was no way Schooner could commit this type of crime.

"Hopefully, no one told the police Schooner was at the school that day. It would look so bad if they knew he was hanging around during Ms. Hay's visit," Carin said

"Well, at least if it's Carcass, he'll go to Juvy and be out of here; we won't ever have to look at him again," I added.

"Whatever! He won't stay in there. You know Carcass. He'll be out before you know it. He'll just talk his way out, like he did for everything else he's done," Carin said, pacing the room. "I wish I could see Ms. Hay. What would she say to him after this? I wonder if she'd still believe he was fixable. I hate him! I'll help you kill him, Ratchet. I just want to go there and rip his face off."

We didn't know what to do with ourselves for the rest

of the day. It seemed like we were such a big part of the event—yet, really, we were nothing. We wanted to know the details. Was it Carcass? Was he at the police station? Had he already been transferred to a juvenile detention center? We walked back to the high school to be part of the action. At least, standing across the road amongst the crowds of people, we could hear what was happening.

The three of us waited behind the barricade. Ratchet had a couple of cigarettes. Lots of other kids from the high school were also gathered around, even though it was a Saturday. Then Ratchet turned toward the empty road in front of the school. His eyes squinted as he tried to make something out in the distance.

"What the ...?" He tossed his cigarette down, only half-finished, and stepped on it with his foot. He ran and we turned to watch. He yelled something as he headed up the road, past the barricade. We could see a kid on a skateboard in the distance on the closed road, heading toward the school. Ratchet ran toward him, grabbed the kid's shirt, pulled him off the skateboard. The guy tripped, stumbled to the ground with Ratchet's body on top. Ratchet was straddled over him, punching his face. I jumped the barricade, worried, trying to get closer.

"Ratchet! Stop!" I yelled.

The crowd started to follow. The community volunteers, who manned the barricades in bright yellow vests, were ignored. They had their radios out, calling for backup. As Ratchet hit the guy, a pool of blood formed on the uneven pavement. The kid attempted to get up. For a moment, Ratchet let him try, but Ratchet was blocking our view. Then we saw the kid's fist take a swing. Ratchet took a blow to his own head, falling backwards. And then we saw ...

"It's Carcass!" Carin shouted.

"Why the hell would he ride down this road on his skateboard? Why is he even loose?" I said.

"'Cause that's exactly what Carcass does! He rubs it in our faces that he got away with something."

Ratchet stumbled to his feet, swaying from side to side.

Carcass pushed Ratchet down and pinned him to the ground, straddling his body, just as Ratchet had done to him.

And then Carcass pulled a knife from his back pocket. I moved in just as Carcass flicked the switchblade open with a fast snap of his wrist. Ratchet couldn't see it. Carcass raised the blade, almost in slow motion, still straddled over Ratchet, staring into his face. I ran in behind Carcass and grabbed his arm. He yanked it away, pulling the knife back into position, and stabbed, just missing Ratchet's neck, but piercing his right shoulder. Ratchet clutched the wound and attempted to pull himself up.

But Carcass was going in for a second stab. This time I threw myself on his back and wrestled him off Ratchet. Kids circled us, encouraging the fight. And then I heard Carin.

"Stop!" she screamed. "No, Creighton, leave them."

Blood was oozing from Ratchet's shoulder. He held it with his hand and used his feet to kick at Carcass, who was trying to get back over top of him. Ratchet pushed himself backward, away from the approaching blade. I was on Carcass's back, restraining his arm, preventing it from making another slice into Ratchet.

The cops had come out of Lane Oslo, and sirens howled in the distance.

Carcass swung his elbow back, shoved me onto the ground. I stumbled my way up, reaching toward the blade again, which was aimed at Ratchet's neck. I couldn't grab it. Carcass held it in his fist, whispering words I couldn't hear. All I could reach was Carcass's sleeve.

Just as Carcass went for his neck, Ratchet turned his head, and the knife went through his left cheek. Ratchet shrieked, a sound I'd never heard him make before. He grabbed onto his face and I could see the blood ooze between his fingers. I shoved Carcass to the side, as he climbed off Ratchet. People gasped. The crowd started to move in, closer, to see if he was alive.

"Ratch? Ratch?" I said. "Ratchet!" I leaned in.

His eyes rolled back. His white T-shirt was soaked red. Blood poured from his shoulder and face. Carcass stood there and watched. He wiped the bloodstained knife on his jeans and then flipped the blade closed with a quick snap of his wrist on the side of his leg. He smiled, looked at the audience.

A police officer grabbed me. "Don't move!" he said. "Walk to the car. Don't talk, just walk," he continued, as he handcuffed me from behind.

"But Ratchet ...?" I said, turning back.

"Ambulance is on its way," the officer said. "Just keep walking, don't worry about the crowd."

"No, Creighton!" I heard Carin call. "Don't take him!" she shouted again.

As the officer led me toward the car, I looked back. Ratchet lay motionless, the puddle of blood widening. Carin knelt beside him, crying. Another policeman was handcuffing Carcass. I could see his hands in the air, as he was escorted to a different police car. I could hear the ambulance.

As I sat alone in the police office, waiting, I felt empty. I didn't care if they locked me up. Everything was such a mess. Schooner's life was ruined by the death of his grandma. We'd lost Ms. Hay as a teacher, and now school was a waste of time. And Ratchet—I wasn't sure if he was even alive.

My thoughts were interrupted by a knock on the door. It was Dad, standing with the officer. I put my head down between my knees, and started to cry. They both came in. The officer sat in the chair across from me. Dad didn't say a thing. He put his hand on my neck, rubbed it. I started to shake.

"Dad, did he kill Ratchet?" I asked.

Dad shook his head. "Shh! Shh!" he said. "Take a breath, son."

"I was trying to protect Ratchet," I said, crying.

Dad put his hand out to stop me from talking. He didn't need to know the story. "I know, son. Leave it!" he said.

"Why was Carcass loose, Dad? What was he doing on that road? Why wasn't he arrested for the abduction?"

The constable interrupted. "It wasn't Carlos who was brought in, Creighton. Another youth was taken into custody."

"Who else would have taken Ms. Hay's baby? It was him. No one else would want to hurt Ms. Hay. I don't get it."

"I'm not in a position to release a name, but I am sure you will hear the details soon enough," the officer continued. "So, Creighton, I spoke with your dad earlier, and we'd like you three boys to go through a process of Restorative Justice. Our job is to ensure everyone in the community is safe, and when a fight occurs that involves a weapon, an investigation must take place. We also have to feel satisfied that you boys are safe from one another. The outcome may involve community service, or some other form of restitution. Today, you're going home with your dad, and he knows that it is important for you to remain in his presence until the process is initiated, probably in the next day or two. Do you have any questions?"

I tuned out most of what the officer said. My mind was churning. If it wasn't Carcass, then who took the baby? Something wasn't right.

As Dad and I left the station, he turned to me and said, "Creigh, it was Schooner who was taken into custody today. They figure he put the baby in the boxcar."

I stopped walking toward the truck. "No, Dad! Not Schooner. Schooner wouldn't do that. He loved Ms. Hay. She was so good to him."

"Well, son, apparently he'd been slinking around the school yesterday afternoon. So, what do you figure he was doing? Had some kinda plan brewing, I guess. He was pretty upset with Ms. Hayworth for leaving—you told me yourself."

"Schooner was scared, that's all. He didn't come in, because he hadn't talked with any of us for so long. We knew he wanted to see Ms. Hay and her baby. He just didn't have the courage to make the entrance. That's how he is, Dad."

"Well, his obsession with trains? You've talked about that before. He knows that rail yard like the back of his hand. Would have been easy for him to slip that baby into a boxcar, as the train came through that evening. Who else would have the schedule memorized? Maybe Schooner was more messed up than we thought. You told me yourself how bad he's been doing since his grandma died. Heck, I heard he's been shoplifting, too. Got caught a couple times for that. Was a matter of time before he got himself in some kinda trouble. He's hardly come around our place at all. You know how strange that is."

I stopped listening. Everything he said made me angry, even though it was true

When we arrived home, I was ready to bolt to Carin's. She would know how Ratchet was doing. She would have heard the news of Schooner's arrest. She would want to know what was happening with me. I grabbed my bike off the front lawn, ready to ride away, when Dad stopped me. "Not so fast! Did you hear what the cop said? You ain't going nowhere, son. You're housebound for a bit, remember?"

This was stupid. I stopped Carcass from stabbing my buddy through the throat, and I'm in trouble?

I called Carin and she came over right away. Her face was blotchy and swollen from crying. Dad and I were sitting on the front steps while he had his cigarette. She didn't hesitate; despite his presence, she threw herself at me in relief.

"Creigh, I figured they were taking you away, locking you up somewhere."

"Well, he is kinda in lockup, Carin. Afraid he can't be leaving the house until the three boys have gone through some sort of process."

Carin and I went into my room. We needed some time. I'd grabbed a box of soda crackers from the cupboard on my way. Suddenly, I was starving. We sat on the edge of the bed, and I tried to put a cracker in her mouth. She pushed it away, irritated.

"So, what the hell, Creighton? What are we going to do? They took Schooner. Carcass is probably riding his skateboard around town, smirking like he does. He kidnapped a baby, almost killed Ratchet, and he's just riding around."

"Well, he was in the station, too. I could hear them talking. But I'm sure he got released like me. The police say we have to do some sort of Justice thing. What's the scoop on Ratchet?"

"His face is pretty mangled. The blade went straight through, even cut his tongue," she said. "Poor Schooner, Creigh. I bet he's so scared. He probably has no clue what's going on."

I nodded. The whole thing seemed crazy. We knew there was no way Schooner was guilty, yet he would have guilt written all over his face. Carin lay down on the bed and I curled up beside her.

"I can't even go see Ratchet in the hospital. Not allowed to be near him till they do an investigation," I said quietly.

Life seemed to be all about loss. I pulled Carin in closer

to feel her breathing against my body. Her eyes closed. Even though everything felt so painful, I knew in this moment, I had something. I kissed her on the forehead.

CHAPTER 24

Schooner was charged with the abduction of Baby Camille, because they had enough evidence pointing to him.

Dad showed me the story in the newspaper:

"Following a review of the report prepared by Breton RCMP, Crown Counsel approved the charges, given the youth's prior history, including a conviction for mischief under $5000 due to the intentional damage and destruction of property. At his court appearance, the fifteen-year-old youth pleaded not guilty to his current charge of abduction, and will be placed in custody until his scheduled trial in Youth Justice Court."

Schooner had been convicted for the damage done to

the boxcar when he'd painted my tag. He'd served a lot of community hours for that offense. Although his identity was supposed to be protected because he was a minor, Breton was a tiny place, and everyone knew everything. That's all the community talked about: one of the bad kids from the Reform School had kidnapped the teacher's baby.

Carcass, Ratchet, and I went through Restorative Justice about a week after the fight. We were brought together in a room to talk in a large circle. There was a lady, the facilitator, who coached us through. She had a talking stick that we passed around, so only one of us could speak at a time. It was wooden, sanded down really nicely, with feathers and beads dangling from the end. I knew it was something Will would have liked, something he would have made himself. The point of the meeting was to make sure none of us killed each other in the future. It was supposed to give us "healing and understanding." The police needed to know we weren't a threat to the community or to anyone else.

We had to attend with a family member. Dad came with me, of course, and so did Carcass's mother. It was the first time any of us had met her. Ratchet didn't have a family member to bring, so a social worker came, someone he'd worked with when he lived at the group home.

Ratchet wanted revenge. He wasn't sorry, and he would never forgive Carcass for framing Schooner. He would also never forgive him for the two stab wounds. But he talked the talk. He said what they needed him to say, reassuring the team that he was filled with remorse for his actions.

Carcass was also smooth. He was always smooth when he was in trouble. And his mother made him out to be a saint. She defended him, her child, who had never done wrong. He was an innocent victim, "bullied all through school," she claimed. He only carried the knife to protect himself from guys like Ratchet.

"I was just going for a skateboard ride, minding my own business, heading to the park that Saturday afternoon. He came out of nowhere. Just grabbed me right off my board, started pounding me in the face. I didn't even know what was up," Carcass said calmly. "Luckily, I had a knife, or I don't think I would have made it."

"Can you add to that, Matt?" the facilitator said to Ratchet. "Is there anything you want to share?"

"No, man," Ratchet said, looking down between his knees. "I was just real angry because I thought he took Ms. Hay's baby," Ratchet continued.

And then Ratchet turned toward Carcass. He paused for a moment. "I'm sorry for catching you off guard like that. I guess it wasn't you, after all." I knew Ratchet was not serious. He was mad—really, really mad. He was not sorry. And he wasn't done with Carcass.

The facilitator asked about our backgrounds, but she said we only had to share what we were comfortable with, so none of us really shared at all. At the end of the circle talk, we went around and said how we felt. She wanted to know if we had gained more understanding for one another. The facilitator was reassured we had closure. I guess we were healed.

The following day, I got a letter of warning, but Ratchet and Carcass were referred for a Community Accountability Program. They could not be in close proximity to one another until a follow-up session occurred in one month. Even though Carcass was the one who'd pulled a knife, it was determined that "he did so in self-defense, following an aggravated assault." None of us had any prior criminal history. Even though Ms. Hay could have pressed charges for Carcass's mice guts incident, we figured she never did.

With all that had happened, and a teacher who didn't care, attendance at Lane Oslo School of Educational

Reform rapidly declined. The school had become a national focus, due to the publicity about the missing baby. The purpose of the alternate program was questioned, and media people argued back and forth whether "segregating students with diverse needs" was "educationally sound." People in Breton seemed to think having all the bad kids together in one room made us do bad things, like steal babies. Just like Ms. Hayworth's husband, most people didn't have a clue what it was about. They had no idea that being together had been the only thing saving us all, thanks to Ms. Hayworth.

By the beginning of October, they closed its doors permanently. The kids that continued to attend, like Hamilton and Ronnie, were integrated back into the high school. Carin forced me to sign up for a Distance Education program with her. It was basically home school! We'd check into an office each week, get our books and assignments, and then work on our own at home. She figured we had to graduate somehow. Carcass? None of us knew what he was up to. We never saw him around town at all.

On October 17, Schooner was scheduled to appear in Youth Justice Court for his trial. Even though he pleaded not guilty at his first appearance, it sounded like there was enough evidence to prosecute. We waited anxiously for this day. We wanted to be there for Schooner.

Out of respect for him, Carin and I made a point of sitting on the hill in front of the tracks, to see the ten o'clock train come through town, whenever we weren't working. Occasionally, my VENUS car would pass through and I'd get all choked up.

On a cold October morning, with Carin cuddled up beside me on the bank, we waited for Schooner's train to arrive. On this particular day, I noticed a tag. I had seen it before, but hadn't given it a second thought. *DALLAS*. The word was familiar; the way the letters were formed reminded me of something. Then I remembered my first day in Mrs. Fitzgerald's class back in Fairburn, tracing the name carved on the small wooden desk. Here it was again, the same graffiti. It seemed puzzling. It must have been the same kid 'cause, really, there weren't too many Dallases kicking around. I didn't share my thought with Carin. It wasn't important at all, until October 17, when it all made sense.

Carin, Ratchet, and I arrived at the courthouse early. We could see Ms. Hay sitting on a bench at the other end of the hallway, beside her husband. She smiled at us. Her husband whispered something to her when he noticed us, shaking his head. I could also see the police officer who'd interviewed me and Carin on the day of the abduction. He was sitting on a hallway bench across from them. We were told to sit and wait until the doors were open to the public. I thought of Schooner being called up to the stand. Would he tell the truth or would fear get the best of him? I wondered if Ms. Hayworth was a witness, since they had her sitting down the hall across from the officer.

The door opened, and the three of us were directed to the back of the courtroom, the first to enter. Ms. Hay's husband came in behind us and sat in a different row. After a few minutes, another guy entered and sat in front of us. Ratchet seemed to recognize him, because they nodded at each other.

"Who is that?" I whispered.

"Social worker!" Ratch said. "He wasn't mine, but I saw him at the group home a bunch."

Most of the gallery seats remained empty, except for two other men at the front, who were wearing suits—lawyers or something.

When the clerk called the court to order, we stood up. We were supposed to remain standing until the judge entered. After we all sat down, the judge asked for the accused to be brought in. Following the sheriff was Schooner, handcuffed and head down. His skin looked pale. Maybe it was the yellow coveralls so near to his blond hair. Once Schooner was seated, the handcuffs were removed. The judge looked at Schooner, and then turned toward the few of us who were seated in the gallery:

"We're here for the trial of Dallas Prairie, who has been charged with the abduction of Camille Roslyn Hayworth. Is the Crown prepared to proceed?"

"We are, your honor," said the lawyer.

"Who did they say was charged?" I whispered to Carin.

"Shh! They just used Schooner's real name," she snapped.

I realized I didn't even know Schooner's real name. No one had ever used it before. Even adults referred to him as "Schooner."

"Then let's begin," the judge continued.

When Crown Counsel called the police officer to the stand, everything he said about Schooner made him appear guilty. He talked about the anger Schooner displayed toward Ms. Hay when she announced her maternity leave. He had even shattered the classroom window with his fist.

When his grandmother died and he went missing, he took refuge in a boxcar for the night. I forgot that, too. He spoke of the mischief-under-$5,000 conviction for spray-painting a freight car, my VENUS sign that he'd pleaded guilty to in the past. He was spotted on the school grounds during Ms. Hay's visit that Friday afternoon. His bike was unattended outside of the school, and Schooner could not be found. Someone must have told the police. And the shop-lifting from grocery stores, probably right after his grandma died, when he'd refused to accept help from anyone.

When it was Schooner's turn on the stand. Carin nudged me. "See him shivering," she whispered.

The court clerk asked him whether he wanted to swear on the Bible or affirm the truth. Schooner was stumped by the question. He scratched his head, confused, and became more flustered.

"Would you like to swear on a holy book? You know, a Bible? Would you like to swear on the Bible or just affirm the truth?" the lady repeated, to clarify.

"The truth. I will tell the truth," Schooner said quickly. The lady looked at the judge and he nodded.

"Can you please state your full name and address," she continued.

"Schooner ... my name is ... um ... I mean Dallas. Dallas Prairie," he replied.

I froze, repeating his full name several times in my head. I thought that's what the judge had said, but I figured I heard it wrong. The name was familiar. It's what I saw tagged on the boxcar. And the desk back in Fairburn, the name DALLAS was carved on the top. Ms. Hay had always addressed him as "Schooner," never saying his real name, even though she would have had it on the class list.

"And your address?" the lady said, still waiting for Schooner to finish his response.

Schooner scratched his head again. His feet shuffled uncomfortably. "I don't know ... um ..."

"Your address!" she repeated in frustration. "You just need to state your home address," she said, looking at Schooner, then toward the judge. "Where you live!" she continued, slowly.

I could see Schooner's fists tighten on the table in front of him, his knuckles whitened as he squeezed. His face looked hot.

"Juvy," Schooner said, his voice cracking. "I live at Juvy."

The lady looked at the judge. He nodded.

Schooner was asked about his history. He couldn't look

the judge in the eyes. He seemed frozen, trembling. His lawyer interjected—he seemed like a genuine sort of man, "Your honor, due to the age of my client and his current mental state, I will provide his background history."

"Please proceed," the judge replied.

"My client was born in Fairburn, British Columbia, on April 8, 1984," the lawyer began.

"Fairburn?" I thought. On our road trip to Strasville, Schooner had said Fairburn was the only place he'd been. I didn't know he'd lived there, though.

"His birth mother was struggling with addiction at the time, and the identity of his father was unknown," the lawyer continued. "Therefore, he was placed in foster care shortly after his birth, becoming a ward of the province of British Columbia. At age eleven, the family who had cared for Dallas since his birth experienced a personal tragedy and gave up custody." Schooner's head was down. We didn't know any of this, the fact that he was given away after eleven years with the same family.

The lawyer continued. "His maternal grandmother and grandfather, who formerly resided here in Breton, took over guardianship at this time. His grandfather passed away when Dallas was thirteen. Following his death,

Dallas's grandmother struggled with her own health, and passed away in late August of this year. Dallas has been placed back in care. He was living at the Rocky Mountain Group Home for Youth, until being transferred to Youth Custody, where he currently resides. Dallas, I'm going to ask you a few questions," his lawyer said quietly. "Just answer as honestly as you can. All right?"

Schooner nodded, looking down.

"How many years was Ms. Hayworth your teacher?"

Schooner held up two fingers.

"She taught you for two years. Grade 8 and Grade 9? Correct?"

Schooner nodded.

"Yes? That's a yes?"

"Yes," Schooner mumbled.

"Did you like your teacher, Ms. Hayworth?

"Yes."

The lawyer asked Schooner questions about school. He mumbled short answers back, not saying much of anything. Finally, his lawyer asked, "Dallas, did you abduct Ms. Hayworth's baby?"

"No," Schooner replied, shaking his head.

"Well, you were on the school grounds that afternoon.

Your classmates saw you looking in the window, yet you never went inside the classroom. When did you leave the school?"

"Maybe two. I dunno."

"Was it before the bell rang?"

"Yes."

"Where did you go after you left the school around two?"

"Home."

"The group home?"

"My old home."

"But your home was burned down. There was nothing left of your home. Why would you go there?"

Schooner shrugged.

"I have no further questions, your honor," and the lawyer sat down.

Schooner was cross-examined by Crown Counsel. He was asked many questions about his whereabouts on the day of Camille's abduction. Schooner did a lot of mumbling. He admitted that he was outside the school for some time. When asked about his location, when the bike was found near the backdoor of the classroom, during Ms. Hay's visit, Schooner said he couldn't remember. And then he blurted out angrily, "I was behind the dumpster. I was just sittin' behind the dumpster, man. I mean, your honor."

When he answered that question, he looked like he was going to explode. Anyone who didn't know Schooner at all could see his rage. There was no doubt he had a temper.

"So, you were sitting behind the dumpster when your class was having a party? The teacher, whom you said you liked, had brought her baby to visit, and you chose to sit behind a dumpster instead?" the guy asked.

"Yeah!" Schooner shouted as he ran his fingers through his hair. "So what? So, I sat behind a dumpster. Is there a problem with that?"

"You were *waiting* behind the dumpster? Were you waiting for the end of the day, Dallas? Waiting for the other students to leave? Waiting for an opportunity to take the baby?" he asked.

Schooner stood up. "No!" he yelled.

"Objection, your honor, counsel is badgering my client.

"Please be seated, Dallas," the judge replied. "Objection overruled."

"Did that baby take your teacher away from you, Dallas? Ms. Hayworth had to stop teaching once Camille was born, and you didn't like that, did you? Because Ms.

Hayworth was really all you had, isn't that right?"

Schooner did not reply.

"Your honor, I have no further questions."

I think he had provoked Schooner enough to make him look guilty. Things were not looking good. No one could back up those answers.

And then Schooner's lawyer called someone in as a witness. It was the man we saw cleaning up Schooner's property.

Once the guy was sworn in, Schooner's lawyer asked him a bunch of questions. Why he was at the property; how long he'd been working there; and then he pointed to Schooner, "Have you ever met Dallas Prairie?"

"Yes, I have. Seen him around the place a few times."

"So, you talked to Dallas?"

"Well, Dallas seemed a little put out that I was cleaning up the place. I mean, it was his home, after all. He kept his distance, just did his own thing, really. I did ask him if I could help him find something, since he seemed to be searchin'. I'd cleared some of the salvageable stuff out, you know. Thought maybe I could help him."

"Did he say what he was looking for?

"He did, finally. Said he was looking for a little wagon

he had. I had saved a bunch of the ornamental stuff. I'd seen a wooden wagon in the clean-up, showed him the shed where I'd stacked that kind of stuff. He was happy when he found it. Didn't take much, really."

"On September 17, 1999, were you working on the property?"

"I was, sir. Started working there mid-September; took about a week to clear the place."

"Can you recall if you saw Dallas Prairie on the property that 17th day of September?"

"Yes, I did. He rolled up in the afternoon on his bike, shortly after three. Long bike ride for the boy—guess he was used to it, though. I asked him how he got out there so fast after school. He said he hadn't been going to school anymore. So, I tried to talk to him about that. He didn't really say too much."

"Can you recall how long Dallas was at the property that afternoon?"

"Hmm ... well, I packed her in about 5:30. His bike was still kicking around. I knew he was sitting in the trees somewhere. He did that sometimes. Felt kinda bad for the boy."

"I have no further questions for my witness."

Then Ms. Hayworth was called into the court room by Schooner's lawyer, as a second witness. She was asked many questions. It was clear she did not believe Schooner was guilty of the abduction. She talked about his history in her class. She was asked about his anger. She seemed to have a good reason for every bad thing he did. She even made the spray-painting of my boxcar sound like an act of kindness, which it was. Ms. Hay had a way of bringing out the best in people. I could tell the judge was listening. How could someone not have empathy for Schooner when Ms. Hay told his story?

"Elizabeth Hayworth," Schooner's lawyer finally asked, "do you believe Dallas Prairie, sometimes known as Schooner, abducted your two-and-a-half-week-old infant, Camille Roslyn Hayworth, on September 17, 1999?"

Ms. Hayworth was confident. Her words were clear and her voice calm, just as we knew them to be. "Schooner ... I mean, Dallas ... is not guilty of this crime. I know Schooner. I was his teacher for two years. He did not hurt my baby or me. He was struggling with grief, over many, many losses in his life ..." She paused, took a breath, and her eyes filled with tears as she swallowed. And then she looked directly at Schooner. "You have the wrong person."

The room was silent, except for Ratchet, who stood, clapping. Carin yanked him down. "Shh! You can't do that here," she whispered.

The Crown and defense counsel were asked to make their final statements, and then there was a break.

We couldn't believe what Schooner had experienced. Again, little Isabella flashed through my head. I could see her wobbling, as she balanced on the eraser at the end of Schooner's pencil. I thought of us standing in the circle, burying the tiny caterpillar in Carin's small box, and his deep, deep sadness over her death.

We stopped talking when the judge re-entered.

"After listening to the evidence regarding the abduction of Camille Roslyn Hayworth on September 17, 1999, I do not find, beyond a reasonable doubt, that Dallas Prairie, the accused, is guilty of abduction. Dallas ..." the judge said turning to face Schooner directly, "you have been acquitted of these charges. This means you have been found not guilty."

Schooner did not move. The room stayed quiet. He stared back at the judge, tilting his head slightly to the side.

"You are free to go home, young man," the judge said. "Court is adjourned."

We could not hold Ratchet down this time. He jumped up and hollered loudly. Ms. Hay's husband stood up, turned around, and glared at Ratchet, shaking his head as he gathered his coat and Ms. Hayworth's purse. She smiled at Schooner, gave him two thumbs up.

We waited outside the building, hoping Schooner would appear. We didn't know what to expect. Would he run from us, as he had so many times since the death of his grandma?

"He doesn't even have a home," Carin said. "Why would the judge tell him he's free to go home?"

Finally, after what seemed like ages, Schooner walked out with a young man, the social worker who had been sitting on the bench ahead of us.

Carin did not hold back. "Schooner!" she said, wrapping her arms tightly around him, "We've missed you." She didn't give him the chance to reject us.

I could see a small smile on his face. I followed closely behind. I put my fist out. Schooner shook his head, still smiling, and gave me a fist bump.

Ratchet snuck up from behind, grabbed Schooner around the waist, and swung him into the air, squealing. Schooner's face lit up. The giant smile we used to see spread across his face. He was going to be okay, just as Ms. Hay told us he would eventually be.

"You're back," I said. "We missed you, buddy."

"You must be Creighton," the young man said, reaching out to shake my hand. "I'm Bruce, Schooner's social worker. Is it Corinne?" he said, turning toward Carin. "Schooner's talked so much about you all."

"*Car-in*, I'm Carin. Nice to meet you," she said.

"And I'm Ratchet," he interrupted, cutting in to shake the guy's hand.

At that moment, we got our Schooner back. He started talking and didn't stop. With barely a breath between words, he told us everything. His month-long stay in the corrections facility was filled with stories and events that he could talk about forever, even if they weren't true at all.

Suddenly, he turned to Bruce and said, "I'm gonna stay at Creigh's tonight. Or … is that okay with you?"

Bruce laughed. "Well, let's make a stop at the group home and chat about plans. Maybe we can figure out some sort of check-in. Sounds like you four have lots to catch up on."

"Oh, man!" Schooner said, shaking his head and laughing. Then he looked up toward the sky and let out a giant howl. "I'm home, ha-ha! I'm actually home." After three stressful hours in court that day—October 17, 1999—Schooner looked free.

I guess after his grandma died, he was scared. And when Schooner was scared, he ran. He always bolted when he was afraid. I wasn't sure why he didn't come stay with Dad and me after her passing, since he spent so much time at our house, anyway. Maybe he just needed to not need anyone. Or was he searching for whatever it was Ms. Hay said we're all looking for?

I thought about what she'd told Schooner when Isabella died. "Caterpillars are very solitary, Schooner. In times like this, they prefer aloneness."

CHAPTER 25

Schooner arrived at my front door sooner than expected. The social worker had called Dad to ask about him staying the night, making sure he was okay with the plan. Of course, Dad didn't care at all. He'd be happy to have Schooner around again. We had lots to talk about, since Schooner hadn't really been part of our world since August.

"Guys!" he hollered, barging in the front door, as if he hadn't missed a single day of visiting.

Carin and I were sitting at the kitchen table. I was eating a bowl of cereal for supper.

"Wow! You were fast," Carin said. "Did you even stop at the group home to tell them what you're up to?"

"Sure did," Schooner said. His voice was full. He didn't seem so frail.

"So, what do you want to do tonight?" I asked. "It's your first night back in town. Ratchet said he'd be here soon."

"I just wanna go to the river. That's what I missed the most. The river," Schooner said.

The three of us waited for Ratchet on the front step. He had put in a couple of hours on the farm after court, doing some light duties.

When Ratchet arrived, he winced as he climbed out of the truck, grabbing his shoulder. He obviously still had pain. He also had a long scar on his cheek in the shape of a checkmark, a constant reminder of Carcass. Even though it had been a month since the fight, the shoulder injury limited what he could do. Heavy lifting was a big part of his farm work, but now his damaged shoulder put him out of commission for many things. We didn't bring up Carcass's name, because we knew it was all Ratchet thought about. I wondered what the outcome would be, now that Schooner's charges were dismissed. We all wanted justice but were afraid of how Ratchet would make it happen.

"Got a surprise for you," Ratchet called out, smiling. He pointed at Schooner as he walked to the back of his pick-up. "Come see."

Schooner got up, excited. "For me?" he said.

"Check out that cardboard box," Ratchet said. He winked, looking pretty proud of himself. Carin and I got up, curious to see what Ratchet had brought.

Schooner climbed right into the back of the pick-up in order to reach the box. He lifted the cardboard flaps open and his jaw dropped.

"Last little guy left at the farm; boss said he's mine if I wanted him. But I figure he's supposed to be yours. The runt. Sorta thought you'd be perfect to take this dude on," Ratchet said. "He's a scared little fella, though, away from his mom and all. You'll have to take it easy on him for a bit,"

Schooner lifted a tiny yellow lab puppy from the box. He held it up; its little back legs dangled in the air. He turned it toward himself. We could see the large grin on his face.

"He's mine, Ratch? He's for me to keep?" Schooner said, glancing at Ratchet, then back to the pup.

"If you want the little guy, he's yours. Figured you could both do with each other, after all that's happened."

"Is he really the last one?" Carin asked. "He is adorable."

Schooner climbed out of the back, pulling the puppy closer into his body as he jumped off the tailgate.

"I will officially be his babysitter whenever you want, Schooner. Look at his ears," Carin said, rubbing them gently. "They are so soft. He is seriously the cutest thing ever."

The puppy was the cutest thing—Carin was right. And Ratchet. Well, he was the kindest guy—yet we were the only people who knew it.

"Gotcha some food—enough to get you started, anyway," Ratchet said, reaching into the passenger side of the truck.

The puppy started to whimper. He wiggled and squirmed to be put down. Schooner set him on the grass. He sniffed around cautiously, not venturing too far from Schooner's large boots. "Ratchet, you're the best," Schooner said, as he reached out to give his arm a punch. "Best thing ever." Ratchet flinched, protecting his sore shoulder.

The four of us sat on the back steps, and we heard Schooner repeat most of the stories he'd shared with us outside the courthouse, while he playfully tussled the pup back and forth. Just then, Dad pulled into the driveway. Schooner leapt up, grabbing the pup off the grass, and ran toward the truck.

"Well, hey, look who's back," Dad said with a smile as he climbed out. He gave Schooner a pat on his shoulder.

"Check this guy out," Schooner said, as he held the pup under its legs, dangling him in front of Dad's face.

We all laughed, shaking our heads.

"Well, would you look at that," Dad said, putting his thermos down on the grass to grab the puppy from Schooner's hands. "You got yourself a little pal?"

"Ratchet got him for me. It was a surprise," Schooner said, looking back at Ratchet with a giant smile.

When Dad held the baby lab, it started to whimper.

"Here, here, I better take him back; he's a bit scared," Schooner said. "He's a little afraid of strangers."

We couldn't stop chuckling. Schooner was completely attached to the puppy, and it had been less than an hour since he took ownership. He pulled the dog in toward his chest and whispered softly, "It's okay, little boy, Daddy's got you. No one's gonna hurt you." The puppy settled into his arms and didn't stir. Schooner kept kissing its small head, rubbing his face along its soft coat.

We stopped at the gas station to grab some hotdogs. I wondered what Carin was thinking, since she'd never been to the river since the assault. It was a place she had avoided for three years.

Schooner didn't ask to stop at the tracks, which surprised us.

We crammed into the cab of Ratchet's truck, and now we had a puppy crawling around, too. We pulled up on the side of the road, in front of the bridge where Schooner and I first met. Carin opened the door, to stretch, since she had been bent awkwardly, while half-sitting on my lap. Ratchet glanced over at me. I could see we were thinking the same thing, wondering how Carin would handle things. I felt bad that we'd brought her to the river.

I led Carin down the narrow, grass-trimmed path of the riverbank to the rocky beach below. It was the same path she had staggered up to find help along the highway after her assault. Ratchet was already at the bottom. He started to throw driftwood in a pile, preparing to make a fire. Schooner started running along the shore, tossing sticks to see if the small dog would fetch. Carin and I rolled a large log toward the fire, as Ratchet blew small sparks from below, trying to get the flames to ignite. Once the fire was going, Ratchet started skipping rocks with Schooner, using his one good arm, and Carin curled up on the log beside me, watching the flames as they climbed into the fall air. I put my arm around her shoulders, pulling her in closer to kiss her gently on the forehead. She didn't look up; she just leaned her head against me.

I remembered sitting on the side of the river with Ratchet when he told me her story. I knew it had happened in the bushes directly behind us, but she didn't look back at them. As I snuggled against her, knowing Schooner was home and we were all together, things felt good. I wondered if she had the same feeling.

We hung out all afternoon and into the evening. None of us had a reason to go home. After all, we weren't going to school anymore. The sky darkened as we roasted hotdogs. Schooner was finally still and quiet, holding the roasting stick with one hand, carefully turning his hotdog. His movements were calm, different than usual. The little pup was curled tightly between his boots, sleeping. His other hand stroked the puppy, who was safely tucked below him. Ratchet was quiet, not saying much all night.

Schooner rested the roasting stick against the log and reached into his pocket, pulling out a small silver chain. It had a clip on one end and a loop on the other. He threaded the one end through the loop, forming a circle, and placed it around the pup's neck. "Ha, fits him. Look little boy, ya got yourself a collar now."

"Where did you get that thing?" I asked.

"He's pretty small for a collar like that, Schoon," Carin added. "It might get caught on something."

"Just had it in my pocket. Boss gave it to me; figured it was mine, since they found it in the rail yard. I just kept it; been carrying it around. Thought it might come in handy," Schooner said.

Ratchet sat up, leaning forward, looking across the fire toward the pup's new collar. "Where did you say you got that thing?" he asked Schooner.

"Rail yard. I don't know; boss just gave it to me. Figured I dropped it there or something."

"It wasn't yours, though? You never wore a chain like that, right?" Ratchet asked. He stood up.

"Who cares, Ratch, it's a stupid chain. Leave it," Carin said.

"How did you get to be called Schooner?" I asked, changing the subject, since Ratchet was looking intense. "If your name is Dallas Prairie." I figured this was a safe enough question.

"Ha," Schooner shrugged, giving a quick laugh. "It's kind of a long story. Well, when I moved in with my grandparents ..."

Schooner had never talked about his past. We were hanging on his every word, surprised that he was sharing anything about his life at all.

"... when I was eleven, that's when I moved to Breton to live with them," he continued. "My grandpa told me he grew up in Saskatchewan. When he was a boy, he'd walk with his grandfather through the long grass and climb the hill across the field. They'd sit there, and his grandfather would tell him the story of the land. He remembered arriving on a ship, and waiting for hours at immigration. Finally, they received their homestead papers and were sent on their way."

Schooner was speaking so clearly.

He continued. "The immigrants rode in covered wagons, pulled by a team of oxen. You know the kind of wagon, with the white canvas tops?"

Schooner demonstrated with his hand.

"His grandfather would tell my grandpa to imagine the parade of wagons moving along together. I guess the white tops made the wagons look like the sails of ships on the sea. A ship was a schooner, so these covered wagons were called prairie schooners. Anyway, my grandpa had a tiny prairie schooner on his shelf that his grandfather made him. It was my favorite thing to look at. I'd always ask him to take it down for me."

Schooner paused, thinking.

"Grandpa would take it off the shelf so I could check it out." He chuckled quietly to himself. "One day, Grandpa took me to get an ice cream cone. The lady at the counter asked me my name. Instead of saying 'Dallas Prairie,' I said I was 'Prairie Schooner.' Grandpa laughed a lot. After that, he started calling me 'Schooner' and it stuck, I guess, even after he died. Can't think of the last time someone called me Dallas."

"But you made a tag with your real name?" I said.

"Ha! Yeah, I did. You saw that, hey? Ha!" Schooner replied, looking down at his pup. "That's how I got my name."

"So, you got that wagon back then? Is that what the guy was talking about in court? The guy who cleared your property? You found the little wagon?"

Schooner looked down. He nodded.

Ratchet moved toward the small pup. "Just wanna take a look. Wanna see this chain you got around him." He lifted it off the puppy's small neck. Below the loop was a black skull. You could see the trinket dangling off the first link of the chain.

"That's a great story, Schooner. I love that," Carin said, smiling.

"I sat at one of your old desks, back in Fairburn," I said. "Saw your DALLAS tag carved into that, too."

"Ha!" Schooner replied, thinking. But he didn't say any more.

Ratchet sat back on the log, threading the silver chain through his fingers, staring at it. He seemed preoccupied. He didn't listen to Schooner's story at all.

Schooner gently lifted the puppy up, to rub its pink belly against his cheeks. "You are so soft. Don't worry, little guy," he whispered in his ear, "you're safe with me. I'll take great care of you."

All we could hear was the crackle of the fire, and the water lapping gently beside us.

"So, this chain, the guy just found it in the rail yard?" Ratchet interrupted again.

"Why are you so obsessed with this stupid chain, Ratchet? Who cares? So, the guy found a chain and gave it to Schooner. Why you making it into such a big deal?" Carin almost shouted.

"I'm gonna call him 'Prairie.'" Schooner ignored Ratchet. He turned to all of us, "You get it? You know,

Prairie and Schooner, ha-ha. Prairie Schooner."

"That's an awesome name, Schoon," Carin said. "And he's the color of the prairies, too. It's perfect.

"Who was the guy, Schoon? What's your boss's name? The dude who gave you the chain?" Ratchet interrupted again.

"Murray ... guy's name is Murray, my supervisor. Don't know his last name. Guess I shouldn't have kept the chain. I don't need more trouble, Ratch. I could give it back, tell him it's not mine." Schooner started looking anxious.

"It's just a chain. Who cares, Schoon, you didn't do anything wrong," I said. "Don't worry about it."

"Schoon, I gotta borrow it," Ratchet said. "I need it for something. I'll get you a better collar for your pup."

The night was clear as we sat by the fire. Schooner looked up and pointed to Venus. "There's your star, Creigh."

He was right. There was my planet, Venus. But I didn't have that feeling of longing like I did before. I hadn't thought of Mom in days.

Our night at the river was a long one. Schooner was onto his fifth hotdog.

"Schoon buddy, I've never seen you eat so much," I said.

"I don't know what's up. I just feel so hungry tonight," he replied, as he squeezed the wiener off the stick with his bun.

Carin and I took a walk, alone. The air was cool, so I took off my plaid shirt and placed it over Carin's shoulders. There was a beach, behind the bushes, and large rocks among the cottonwood trees, hidden from the rest of the world. The small patch of beach sand became ours. We sat down and leaned our backs against the large rock.

"I wonder if your mom is staring at Venus, too," Carin said quietly.

"I don't know. Funny how it doesn't even matter now."

I leaned over, held her head in my hands, and kissed her. She kissed me back. She didn't stop.

"You okay?" I mumbled.

"Aha," she said in between breaths.

We slid our bodies down onto the sand.

I had imagined this moment many times, never thinking it would be at the river, the place she said she would never go. I didn't push her. I didn't plan on things going so far, but they did.

CHAPTER 26

"Schoon," I said, shaking him with my foot. "Didn't you say you had to be at the police station by eleven?" He groaned, rolled over, and covered his head with the sleeping bag.

It was October 18, the day after Schooner was cleared of his charges, the day after our night at the river, and Schooner was still asleep on my bedroom floor. I'd already taken Prairie out for a pee, and now there was a new puddle in the hallway. Prairie had dragged Schooner's boot into my bedroom. The lace was pulled tight. Now the pup was working on the sleeping bag strings. He stopped when I walked into the room, whimpered, and ran to my feet. I lifted the puppy up.

"Schooner!" I said again. "You gotta get up, buddy. I'm pretty sure you're supposed to be there in ten minutes.

Aren't you meeting the social worker to sign the court papers and stuff?"

Schooner scratched his head.

"What's the time? What's the time?" he said, looking around the room. He stood up, turned in circles, standing in his boxer shorts. He grabbed Prairie from my arms, kissed the pup's head. His eyes searched for his shirt and jeans, which were heaped on the bathroom floor.

"Your stuff's in the bathroom," I said. "Just give me the dog; I'll watch him. Get going."

"Crap!" Schooner replied. "I can't be late."

"You'll make it. Take my bike. Police station isn't far," I said.

Schooner ran down the hallway, trying to get one leg into his jeans, tripping as he went. He stepped in the puddle of pee.

"Crap!" he said again. "I didn't even take him outside yet." He wiped his wet foot with the dangling pant leg. He slipped on one boot and scrambled around looking for the other one. I tossed him the boot Prairie had dragged into the bedroom. It wouldn't slip on. The lace was pulled tightly together from Prairie's tugging.

"I didn't feed him, either. I can't believe I slept so long.

I never sleep like this."

"It's all good, Schoon, I got it covered," I said.

I put Prairie down on the grass as Schooner rode off on my bike. I didn't tell him he had missed a buttonhole. His hair was sticking up all over.

Carin was walking toward the house. She saw me on the grass with Prairie. I lifted the puppy up and walked toward her, holding his paw to wave. She was smiling.

"Creigh," she said kissing me.

We held each other longer than usual, Prairie in between us.

I threw some paper towels over the puddle on the hallway floor, as we walked toward my bedroom. I turned some music on, and Carin pulled me down beside her on my bed. We sat, watching Prairie attack a ball of socks, over and over again.

"You okay this morning?" I asked.

"Hmm," she sighed, smiling. "Yeah, I'm good, I think. A little freaked, though, since we didn't use anything."

"Pretty dumb of us. I hadn't planned ..."

Carin stopped me with her hand. "Don't! Just leave it. I can't think about that right now."

"What? Are you okay? Are you upset with me?" I asked.

"No!" Carin replied. She seemed annoyed. "I just can't deal with thinking about things like that right now."

"Well, is there other stuff going on?"

"Just Mom. You know. She's getting sicker. I knew the cancer was back, but it's not getting better this time. I just gotta focus on that, figure things out. It's not you, Creighton. She was really bad this morning. I figured it would go into remission, like it did before. I have to get some extra shifts at the restaurant. She can't do cleaning jobs, with her treatments and everything."

"Well, I can help you."

"She never tells me what the doctors actually say. I can't tell if she lies to protect me, or if she's in total denial herself."

Prairie sniffed around the bedroom. Carin leapt up.

"We need to take him outside," she said. She lifted Prairie and ran to the bedroom door.

I followed Carin to the backyard. She grabbed Dad's plaid jacket that hung off the back of his porch chair, and put it on as we walked outside. We sat on the step next to the barbecue. Prairie was sniffing the grass, exploring, when Schooner hollered from inside the house. He must have come through the front door, looking for me.

"Outside, Schoon," I yelled. "In the back."

He pushed open the porch door. He was out of breath. His hair was still sticking up. He looked more of a mess than when he'd left an hour earlier.

"You gotta come!" he yelled. "We gotta go to the police station. Ratch is there. He won't get out of his truck."

"Why is Ratch at the police station?" I asked.

Schooner ran to the bottom of the stairs. He picked Prairie up off the lawn.

"My boy," he said, squeezing Prairie in toward his neck. "I missed you, little fella." His voice was gentle when he spoke to the puppy. "It was a rough night for Ratchet," he continued, shaking his head. Schooner's voice got loud again. "He got stopped on the way home from the river. After he dropped us off last night," Schooner said. "Cops pulled him over 'cause of that one broken headlight."

"So, why do they have him at the police station for that?" Carin asked. "Why didn't they just give him a ticket?"

"Oh, they didn't take him in. Ratch took himself in. He's parked his truck out front, in the parking lot, and won't move it. He says he won't get out till they arrest Carcass. Come on, guys!" Schooner said. "We gotta go see him."

Ratchet's truck was parked at the main entrance of the police station. He was sitting in the driver's seat with his head back and eyes closed.

Schooner banged on the window, startling Ratchet.

"What the hell?" Ratchet said, rolling down the window. He rubbed his eyes, trying to wake himself up.

"What are you doing here?" I said.

"I ain't movin' from this spot, man. I told the cops that. Frick, they tried to give me a ticket last night 'cause of that broken headlight," Ratchet said. "So, I looked that dude right in the face and I said, 'You know, officer, you got way more important things in this town to worry about than a headlight that ain't workin'. How 'bout that baby that got stolen? You solve that crime yet? You wanna know who took that little Camille? Ha! Maybe ya better go have a word with that Carlos Gromson kid, instead of takin' in an innocent guy who wouldn't hurt a flea. Carlos is your man.'"

Ratchet was swinging his hands around. I could picture him leaning into the police officer's face.

"Then I got this idea. I told the guy, 'I'll drive myself to the station right now. I'll park my truck, with its BROKEN headlight right in your parking lot till you arrest Carlos. 'Cause I'm gonna be real honest with you, sir, I'm kinda afraid of what I might do if someone don't lock that kid up real soon.'"

"But they aren't going to bring Carcass in without some sort of evidence, Ratchet. You'll be sitting here forever," I said.

"Oh, they got evidence, all right." Ratchet grabbed a crinkled photo off the dash of his truck. "Check this out? The picture Ms. Hay gave us."

Schooner grabbed the photo. Carin and I were looking over his shoulder, trying to see. It was my fifteenth birthday. I was blowing out the candles, sitting at a desk in the classroom.

"You still have this picture in your truck? It's been in here forever." Carin laughed. "What's Creigh's birthday gotta do with this whole thing?"

"Look closer. Check out Carcass standing in the back."

Carin grabbed the photo from Schooner.

"I don't get it, Ratchet. What do you see? The whole class is behind Creighton. Carcass is just standing there like everyone else," Carin said.

"Give me that!" Ratch said. He pointed to Carcass's pants. "Check these out."

There, very blurred, was a silver chain attached to the belt loop of Carcass's jeans. He always wore a chain on his pants, probably with his knife clipped to the end.

"No way, Ratch," Carin said, pulling the picture into her face. "You can see the skull, too."

"Yup, there ain't gonna be too many of those chains kicking around. So, I gave it to the police last night, told them to talk to that Murray dude from the rail yard, who gave it to you, Schoon. They even took a picture of this photo, so they got a copy of that, too. Bet they're figuring it all out now. It's gonna come nicely together."

"Ha-ha!" Schooner laughed. "I didn't think of this, Ratch. You're the man! Boss said it was hooked on the gate. He found the chain hangin' there and figured it was mine, since that's the way I come in with my bike. Carcass must have climbed the gate."

"Stupid ass, losing his chain in the rail yard. I mean, he has no business there. People can't get in that part of the rail yard unless they work there," Ratchet said. "Right, Schoon?"

"How would he get over that gate with a car seat?" Carin asked.

"It's not that heavy, Carin. Even Ms. Hay was carrying it with one hand," I said.

"The fence is only about four or five feet," Schoon said. "You could get over the fence with that car seat, easy."

Ratchet had been in his parked truck for twelve hours, since his drive home from the river at 2 AM.

"I watched them guys. They got Carlos in there now. They took him in this morning, 'bout nine o'clock," Ratchet said. "They actually listened, if you can believe it. If they let him free, I'll totally go ballistic! I'm sitting right here until I see them take him away, to the same place they took you, Schooner."

Schooner clapped his hands, loving that Ratchet was defending him.

Two police officers walked toward us.

"Could we ask you kids to leave the property? You can go to the sidewalk, but we can't have you all gathered here by the main entrance," one of the officers said.

I grabbed Carin's hand and started to back up. Schooner followed.

"I ain't going nowhere," Ratchet said firmly. "I'm not causing any harm, sitting here in my truck."

"Thanks, guys," the officer said to us, as we walked about twenty feet away from Ratchet's truck to stand on the sidewalk.

We figured we should wait. We sat on the small patch of grass that divided the sidewalk and the station, ensuring we were off the property. The two policemen ignored Ratchet and walked back into the building.

We blocked Prairie between the three of us, so he couldn't run out onto the busy road. After about forty-five minutes, Schooner leapt up. He was looking toward the back of the police station, where the reserve cars were parked.

"See that white van pulling in? It's the same kind of van they took me in. You can see the bars inside. It's a Juvy van," Schooner yelled, as he leaned in to get a better look.

A man got out of the van. He wasn't in uniform.

"If they do take Carcass, they'll never take him out the front doors, especially if Ratchet is sitting right there in his truck," Carin said.

"You're right," I agreed. "They'll take him out the back door, for sure."

Schooner signaled to Ratchet. "Come! Get over here."

Ratchet got out of the truck and came to the side of the building, where the three of us were standing.

"The Juvy van just got here. They're gonna take him. They're gonna bring Carcass out, just like they did to me." Schooner talked in a whisper. "They'll handcuff him and put him in that van. Watch, guys! Just wait; you'll see," Schooner said.

Another hour passed. Prairie was restless. Schooner ran him back and forth down the sidewalk. We were all getting bored. Would they actually take Carcass away? I doubted it. He talked himself out of everything. I'm sure his mother was in there, too, making her boy sound like a preacher's kid or something. But it didn't seem right to leave Ratchet.

"Guys, guys," Carin said, tapping my shoulder. "Look! The door just opened at the back. Someone's coming out."

We turned to look at the back of the building. Schooner picked Prairie up. Ratchet ran closer. He wanted to have a perfect view. He didn't care if the cops noticed him or not. An officer looked toward us, saw us watching. He circled the back parking lot, looked around, checked on things, and then stood beside the van and waited. The same guy who drove the van into the back parking lot earlier came out, opened the double doors at the back of the van, and stood there, to the side, waiting. The back door of the police station opened for a third time. We could see another officer. He poked his head out, looking around. The cop who stood beside the van signaled to the officer at the back door, nodding his head.

And then it happened ...

Carlos Gromson, handcuffed, was escorted out of the building by two officers, one on either side of him, to ensure he walked directly to the white van. He ducked as the policemen helped him into the back, through the opened double doors. One officer climbed in with Carcass. The second officer opened the passenger door to sit in the front seat. The driver locked the back doors, once Carlos and the officer were seated. He walked to the front and climbed into the driver's seat. He turned the engine on.

Ratchet was still. Quiet. We were all still.

The van reversed. Ratchet ran toward it. We moved closer to the curb. The officer who was left standing outside—probably to ensure we did not approach Carcass as he exited the building—ran toward Ratchet. Ratchet tried to catch up to the van, as it slowly inched its way out of the parking lot toward the main road. When it stopped at the intersection, and signaled a left turn, Ratchet banged on the back window. He held up his middle finger against the glass, still pounding with his free hand, and shouted, "It's about time, asshole! It's about time you paid for all you did!"

"Move away!" The officer caught up to Ratchet. "Move away now."

The van turned down the busy road, away from the police station.

"Sorry," Ratchet said to the policeman. "Sorry, I just really needed to see that guy get out of this town."

"Okay, you've done your part," the officer said to Ratchet. "You be on your way and there won't be any trouble."

"Thank you, sir," Ratchet said. He backed away, turning toward us. Schooner jumped up and down, clapping, Prairie flopping in the air with each bounce. Schooner howled. Carin and I laughed, shaking our heads. I put up my hand and Ratch gave me a high five.

Carcass was gone.

That night, I thought about all of Ms. Hay's efforts, how hard she'd tried to make Carcass feel part of the class. I could see her in my mind, standing at the front of the room, showing Ratchet Carlos's skateboard. I thought of how she'd stood her ground so many times when he hurt other people. Even when he went to the extreme and spread mice guts all around her vehicle, she persevered. She refused to be afraid of him. Carcass could not push her away. I could see his face on the last day, when Ms. Hay told us she would not be back. He reached in for a hug, and then pulled away. "You're just like the rest of them," he said, walking out the door.

I thought about the birthday card Ms. Hay had given me. I got up, flipped on the lamp, and opened the drawer beside my bed. I pulled out the card that was tucked under my velvet necklace box. I read it again.

"If you gently touch a nettle, it'll sting you for your pains; grasp it like a lad of mettle, an' as soft as silk remains."

Sanskrit Proverb

I understood the words now. They made sense. Ms. Hay took all of us on like that. If she loved us hard enough, we'd soften. That's what she thought. It worked with Schooner and Carin. It worked with the rest of us. But was she wrong about Carcass? Or did she just need more time? Why did he go to such extremes? What did he want all those times when he tested Ms. Hay? Was he really evil, through and through, like his great-uncle Rigsby? Carcass had found someone who cared. And then she'd let him down, like all the rest, just as he'd said to Ms. Hay on her last day. The way Carcass's mom talked in Restorative Justice, defending him, making him seem like a perfect child, it didn't sound real to me. It was a show. What was his story? What had really happened in Carcass's life?

I turned off the lamp and climbed back into bed. The streetlight was shining in my room. I thought of Ratchet at peace. I imagined Schooner, with Prairie tucked under his arm beneath the covers. I laughed to myself when I thought of Schooner eating so many hotdogs at the river. I'd known Schooner for over a year, and he didn't eat much at all. Now that he was home, feeling settled, maybe, he was making up for lost time. I could see Carin. I knew she'd feel some peace, too, even though she was worried about her mom. Our night at the river had erased a bit of her terrible memory.

Over the next couple of weeks, news spread quickly that Carlos Gromson was in the Youth Custody Center in Valemont, a city about eight hours away from Breton, the same place Schooner was sent. We heard that Carcass pleaded not guilty at his first court appearance, so there'd be a trial. It was the same process Schooner had been through. If Carcass was found guilty at his trial, he'd serve at least sixteen months there, maybe more.

No matter how hard I tried to fall asleep, I couldn't stop thinking of Carcass in one of those yellow suits, sitting in a jail cell—alone.

CHAPTER 27

It was the middle of December, and Carin and I sat on the edge of my bathtub, anxiously waiting.

"I can't look. You look first," Carin said. She held the pregnancy test in her hand and we both stared, waiting to see if the little plus sign turned pink.

Carin pushed the test into my hand as she turned away. I waited. "Is it pink?" she said. "Did it turn pink?"

I nodded, handing her the stick so she could see for herself. "Don't think it could be any brighter," I said quietly.

"Oh, my God, Creigh." She stood up, her fingers twisting her lip. She turned away, paced around the tiny bathroom. "What do we do?" she said with watery eyes.

"What were the odds?" I replied, reaching for the pregnancy test she had placed on the edge of the sink.

"The odds were good, Creigh—we didn't use anything," she snapped.

She turned away again. She held onto the bathroom sink, staring into the mirror. "I'm only sixteen."

"You're seventeen in less than a month," I replied.

I twisted the test in my hand, still sitting on the edge of the tub, turning it around and around in my fingers, staring at the result, hoping the pink would start to fade.

"And you?" she said turning toward me. "You'll only be sixteen by the time we have this baby. Who has a kid at sixteen?"

"Your mom," I said, looking up at her. "Your mom had you at sixteen. She did okay," I said, smiling. I got up and wrapped my hands around her waist, pulling her close. I kissed her forehead. "Your mom did a damn good job, I'll say."

Carin pulled away. "Frick! Frick, Creigh," she said as she punched the sink. "I can't tell my mom. Not now. I don't want her to stress anymore. She's already scared she's leaving me."

I nodded, sitting back down on the edge of the tub. I pulled her onto my lap, holding my arms around her waist. She kept shaking her head.

"We can do this," I said. "We'll figure things out."

"Mom's not even going to be here when it's born," she said, starting to cry. Her hands were flailing. "She's in hospital more than she's home. How can I do this without her? I can't afford a baby."

"You have me, Carin. We'll be doing it together. And really, what's our option?" I asked. "You said you would never have an abortion. We can't give our kid away. So, what other choice is there? We'll do this!" I said.

"Our plans. I didn't want to be like Mom, having a kid so young, being trapped in Breton, cleaning houses like her," Carin said. "I figured I would do something. I don't want to work at a diner the rest of my life, either."

"What's so bad about Breton?" I asked.

"Nothing, nothing really. It's just nice to have the option, the freedom to get out and see the world."

"Trust me, Carin, I traveled all over this country, back and forth for twelve years. Breton is a pretty good place."

"I want to wait a few weeks before I go to the doctor, just to make sure." Carin said.

"You'll be seventeen by then," I replied.

"Exactly! Something about that seems better."

And that's what we did. We kept the news of the

pregnancy to ourselves until Carin's seventeenth birthday, on January 2, when the doctor confirmed she was eleven weeks pregnant, and we were having a baby in mid-July.

The walk home from the clinic was quiet that morning. Carin didn't say a word. I held her hand and gave it a squeeze every now and then. The crispy leaves, frozen to the sidewalk, crunched with each step. Her hand was cold. I could see her breath.

"Do you think I should go see Ms. Hay?" Carin finally spoke.

I didn't reply right away.

"Well, up to you. I don't know how she'd be with that. You know, since we haven't heard from her too much. We barely see her around, not like we used to, anyway."

"Yeah, I know. I'm sure it's tough to be walking around Breton after all that happened with Camille. I just wish I could talk to her," Carin said. "Maybe I'll wait a bit."

Carin was quiet as we walked.

"Somehow, we have to tell your dad."

"I know." I sighed.

"I feel like he'll be disappointed in me," she said.

"No, he'll be disappointed in me, Carin. Guess we should tell Ratch and Schooner, too. Maybe you can drive us out to the farm later, since you'll be a hotshot driver by this afternoon," I laughed.

"Ha! That's if I pass the test, Creigh."

Carin had scheduled her road test for that afternoon. Getting rid of her "L," so she no longer needed an adult in the car, was a big deal, since her mom was no longer well enough to drive. I'd gone into the motor vehicle office the day before to secretly pay for the test, since money was tight for Carin. Her mom was no longer working at all, constantly in and out of the hospital, and Carin had been picking up extra shifts at the diner, in order to pay their rent. She was also working hard on her homeschool program, mostly at the hospital, hoping to complete Grade 11 and 12 in one year. I didn't know how she could handle so much.

We walked to the motor vehicle office early. Carin had got special permission to take the paperwork to the hospital and have her mom sign, since a legal guardian had to give consent for the road test. Luckily, Breton was a small town, and most people understood the situation.

During her test, I walked down the road to the florist and stared at the large cooler filled with flowers.

"Can I get something for you?" the lady asked.

"A rose. Can I get a rose, please?"

The lady reached in to pull a red rose from the bucket.

"Actually, could I have a yellow one?"

A red rose didn't seem right. I wanted something different for Carin, since she wasn't an average girl.

As the lady wrapped the rose, along with some greenery, she said I could choose a small card.

I also stopped and got a cake from the grocery store. Figured we could take it along to the farm that evening, try to fit some sort of birthday celebration into Carin's full day.

When Carin walked back into the waiting room of the office, she had a huge smile on her face. I never doubted she'd pass, since there was no one more determined than Carin.

"I knew you'd be fine!"

I put the cake and rose on the chair beside me, as I stood up to hold her.

"Creigh, you bought a cake?" she said, looking over my shoulder.

"Yeah, I figured we could get your mom's car, go out to the farm and see the guys, try and have a bit of a birthday before you go to the hospital."

I handed Carin the rose as we left the office. She opened the small envelope and read my card. "Always by your side, Love Creigh." It didn't say much at all but, for some reason, the words made her cry.

"Why are you crying?" I asked.

"You do so much for me. You came with me today. You even paid for my test, Creigh."

"I don't do enough for you, really."

Carin cried quietly all the way home.

Schooner had also moved out to the dairy farm. Ratchet got him work a couple of weeks after he was acquitted. The two of them had fixed up an old travel trailer, built a wooden roof over top to stop the leaks, so Schooner had a place to stay.

The dairy farm was just outside of Breton, about twenty minutes away. Once we turned off the highway, we followed the dirt road to the end, and passed the large farmhouse, until we got to the barn. Ratchet's place was right next door. We pulled into the short driveway at the front of his shack. Prairie came running to the car, barking, as we got out. I could smell the farm, the manure. It was the odor Ratchet carried with him everywhere he went.

"Hey, buddy," I said, ruffling Prairie's head a bit. "Where's the boys?"

We climbed up the three front steps to Ratchet's shack, and Carin knocked as we opened the door.

"Ratch?" I called, realizing no one was home.

We turned around and walked back down the steps.

"Must be at Schoon's," Carin said.

We walked around back, through the long, frozen grass, toward Schooner's trailer in the distance. He had things set up really nice. The wooden roof overhung in the front, and they had built a small deck. Prairie followed us, and immediately grabbed a tennis ball off the pile of blankets that were bunched in the corner. He held the ball in his mouth, while rolling around in the bedding that obviously belonged to him. His two large dog dishes were spread about the deck. You could see where Prairie had chewed the edges. There was a broken red broom that Prairie also must have destroyed. I kicked a large dog bone off to the side, so Carin wouldn't step on it, just as Schooner opened the door.

"Wow," he said, with a big grin. "A cake! Ratch should be done here soon. Come in."

"Yeah, Carin's birthday today."

We had only been in his trailer once, when he first moved out to the farm, just to check it out. He seemed so settled now. There was a double bed built into one end. It was unmade. The navy-blue comforter that was bunched at the bottom was covered in Prairie's hair. There was a pile of clothes on the floor beside it. Schooner's pair of jeans still had his buckled-up belt looped through them. You could tell he never undid the belt at all. He could step right into them and pull them up over his narrow hips, in the same way he slid them off. On the table, attached to the front of the trailer, was a pile of National Geographic magazines. I knew Schooner couldn't read too well, but Ms. Hay had done her best to get him interested in something. Obviously, it had worked. Above the tiny propane stove was a shelf. Piled high were neatly stacked packages of noodle soup, a bottle of ketchup, and a giant box of cereal. Crookedly attached to the wall, in between the tiny bathroom and the bed, was a framed picture. The glass was dirty, and the corner of the wooden frame was chipped. It must have fallen as the bathroom door closed. Not surprisingly, in the frame was a photo of Prairie that Carin had given him.

"Looks great in here, Schoon," Carin said, looking around. "You fixed things up really nice since we were here last."

The trailer was old. I knew Carin didn't actually think it was nice. The interior was orange and brown, probably from the early seventies. But you could tell it was home to Schooner, just him and his dog.

"Hey!" Ratchet said, walking in. "Wondered where you guys were. Saw the car. Looks great in here, hey?" He probably felt good, having gotten Schooner so set up with a place and a dog. He noticed the cake on the table.

"Oh, yeah, January 2. It's your birthday, isn't it?" Ratch said to Carin.

The three of us squeezed onto the padded bench seats that surrounded the small table. As Schooner grabbed the few dishes for the cake, he talked a lot, mostly about his job at the farm. He seemed to be doing well.

Schooner said he was in charge of the feed, making sure the cows had bedding and plenty of food and water.

"Aren't you scared of cows, though, Schoon?" Carin asked.

"He's doing real good," Ratchet interrupted, as he passed around the cake. "It's almost been a couple months now, since October, hey Schoon?" Ratchet said, looking at Schooner. "You aren't scared of them anymore, right?"

"Not when I got a dog walking around the place beside me," Schooner replied.

"Hey!" Ratchet said. "Happy Birthday, Carin!" he shouted, before taking a bite of cake. "How's your mom doing?" he continued.

"Not too well. That's why we can't stay long. I should probably get to the hospital, hey, Creigh? But we got some news for you guys. Thought we better come tell you before you hear it somewhere else. You wanna say it, Creigh?"

I smiled. "You go ahead."

"Well, Creigh and I are having a baby. July. We are having a baby in July."

I was surprised. Carin sounded good when she told them. She was smiling.

"What the ..." Ratchet said, standing up as he pounded the table.

Schooner jumped up onto the seat. He gave a howl, like he did whenever he was excited. He hit the roof with his hand as he jumped to the floor, pushing Ratchet out of the way at the same time.

"Well, holy crap!" Ratchet said. "A baby! Jeez, man, I can barely take care of myself. But a baby?"

Ratchet could totally take care of himself, and Schooner, too, for that matter. Ratchet had been taking care of himself since the day he was born.

"Yup," I said. "Guess we're going to be parents, hey, Carin?" I grabbed her hand and held it on the table, squeezing it tightly, smiling at her. I lifted it up and kissed her fingers. She smiled back. It was real.

"So, what'll that make us? Uncles, I guess, hey, Ratch?" Schooner said.

Driving back from the farm, Carin was quiet. The January sky had darkened early. We passed the barren fields, where remnants of an early snowfall remained. We could see the lights of Breton in the distance.

"You okay?" I asked, as she pulled into my driveway.

She nodded.

I leaned over and kissed her. "Call me when you get home. Happy Birthday."

She was heading to the hospital after she dropped me off. She'd probably stay there overnight.

I knew she was trying to be okay, even though she wasn't.

Dad was sitting in his recliner when I walked into the living room.

"Dad," I said quietly.

"Oh, hi, son—didn't hear you come in. Carin with you?" he asked, looking behind me.

"No, she went to the hospital. Just dropped me off. She got her license today. She's pretty happy about that."

"Ah!" Dad sighed. "Good, that's really good. I'm sure she's relieved, with her mom not driving and all."

"I have to tell you something, Dad."

It seemed there was no better time. I had thought about waiting until Carin was with me, but I wanted to get it over with.

"Carin's pregnant. She's due in July."

He didn't say anything. He kept staring at the TV. And then he sat up, pulling the recliner in with his feet.

"Ha! This is your baby, Creighton? You're the dad of this child?" he said, still facing forward, sitting on the edge of his chair as if he was ready to get up and make his exit.

"Yeah," I said, laughing, surprised he would even ask that question.

"Ha!" he said again, turning toward me in the doorway. "Sit down for a minute."

I walked over to the couch and sat on the arm rest. I grabbed a cushion and held it on my lap.

"What were you thinking?" Dad said, looking at me.

I didn't say anything.

"I guess you weren't thinking, Creighton, were you?" he

replied, shaking his head. And Dad was silent again.

I was used to his long pauses, though, used to waiting for some sort of response. Never sure if there would even be one.

"She's a girl with a lot on her plate right now. Trying to finish school, losing her mom here soon. And all that happened to her, Creighton?" He shook his head again. "Wasn't expecting this, son. Figured she'd go somewhere in life, once she got through everything."

"Just because she's having a baby doesn't mean she can't go somewhere, Dad. Doesn't mean her life is ruined."

"No, it doesn't. But it's not gonna be an easy road. You got lots to think about, son. Wish you'd done some of that thinking before ... before you got her pregnant, Creighton."

And he left the room.

I could never predict how Dad would react to things. Sometimes he brushed stuff off like it wasn't important at all. Or maybe it didn't matter to him. He almost seemed angry about Carin's pregnancy, disappointed in me for being irresponsible, just as I expected. Like most important conversations I had with Dad, that was the end of it. He just got up and walked to his room, avoiding any further discussion. And I was happy not to talk about it again.

CHAPTER 28

On January 5, three days after her seventeenth birthday, Carin's mom moved into palliative care. Carin stayed put, at her mother's side, refusing to take any sort of break. I'd bring her dinner and sit with them, when I wasn't working, till Carin fell asleep on the cot the nurses had wheeled in for her. Each time I stopped by, I didn't know where to look. I didn't want to tell Carin, but being in there, beside her mom, who was shriveling smaller and smaller each day, terrified me. The image of Schooner's dead grandmother, lying on the bed, flashed through my head. I didn't know how Carin did it. She acted so strong. She reassured her mom, over and over again, that she'd be okay. Inside, I don't know if Carin was so sure about that, especially with a baby on the way.

In the early morning of January 8, 2000, Carin called me to come to the hospital. Her mom was moving in and out of consciousness. Carin said her breathing was changing. She felt it was near the end. I pulled a chair up next to Carin, put my hand on her knee, and gave it a squeeze. Carin turned to me with a small smile. She looked tired. She had no makeup on, and I could see the tiny freckles on her face. Her dread knots seemed unraveled in places, her eyes dark from days without sleep. I leaned in and kissed her cheek. Carin's mom noticed me. She turned her head in my direction, with such effort.

"You ... will look after ... my girl?" she said, wheezing breathlessly.

I nodded. I stood up, moving in toward her and took her hand in mine. I nodded some more.

Carin leaned in close to her mom's face, and sat on the edge of the hospital bed. She took her mother's hand from mine and placed her cold fingers against her belly. "I won't be alone, Momma," Carin whispered.

Her mom's eyes were closed.

That evening, at 8:17 PM, Mrs. Reiner took her final breath. Carin kept her mom's hand firmly against her stomach as she waited for the stillness to come. I stood behind Carin, tired from sitting, rubbing her shoulders. We could hear the sound of the intravenous, dripping rhythmically into her lifeless body.

When the nurse entered, Carin nodded at her. The nurse tilted her head to the side and gave a small smile. "I'm sorry, sweetie," she said. She put two fingers on Mrs. Reiner's neck, checking her pulse. And then she nodded at Carin, as if confirming the death. "There's no rush. You two stay here as long as you need."

Carin swallowed. And then she swallowed again.

We sat in the hospital room for a long time. I stayed quiet. Eventually, Carin released her mother's hand, allowing her shirt to drop back over her pregnant tummy as she stood up. It was the closest her mom would ever be to our baby. She gently moved her mother's arms against the side of her body and pulled the blanket up to her chest, tucking her mom in, as if she were saying goodnight. She kissed her forehead. "Thank you, Momma."

I stood up and pulled Carin tightly against me. She still didn't cry. "You'll come to my house tonight," I said.

Carin nodded.

We pulled into the driveway next to Dad's truck. I was

surprised to see the kitchen lights on, since Dad was usually in bed by nine. Carin's headlights were still shining as we climbed out of her car. I noticed something leaning against our small garage, something unfamiliar, that hadn't been there when I'd walked to the hospital earlier that morning.

"What the heck?" I said, closing the passenger door. I walked closer to the garage and, leaning on its side, was my single-bed mattress and box spring. "Why is my bed outside?" I asked Carin.

Dad was standing in the kitchen as we walked through the front door. He seemed agitated, maybe nervous.

"Hi, kids," he said. His shirt was unbuttoned, hanging loosely over his jeans. His wet hair was not neatly slicked to the side, as it usually was. It looked as if he had just got out of the shower, and quickly slipped some clothes on when he saw the car pull in. His bare feet kicked a few shoes to the side in the small mudroom, making room for us to enter. He looked at me, waiting for some sort of signal, unsure what to say, since he knew Carin had called me to the hospital early that morning. Dad and I had both known what that phone call meant, that Carin's mom was reaching the end. He hadn't heard from me since I'd raced out the door.

"She passed away about two hours ago," I said to Dad. He wasn't sure how to ask. I could feel the awkwardness in his silence.

He nodded.

Dad reached for Carin's hand. He put his other one on top, holding her small fingers firmly between his. He nodded some more. "Well, come. Come." He released her hand and walked down the hallway toward my room. We followed behind. He stood at the entrance, waving at us to come through. We both stood there, staring, shocked.

"I ... I got things set up for you kids. I hope that's okay," he said, turning to Carin. His voice was hesitant, unsure.

There was a double bed where my single bed once sat. It was covered with a new floral comforter, with many, many small decorative pillows resting at the top. There was a used wooden dresser, with an oval mirror that attached behind. On top was a small plant in a pink pot. The carpet was vacuumed. I hadn't done that in months. My laundry was no longer scattered on the floor. The dirty bowl, which I'd rushed to eat cereal from so I could get to the hospital, was gone. I could see the lines on my bedside table, where Dad must have dusted around my lamp and clock radio.

"You'll stay here now," Dad said, nodding as he looked

at Carin. "With the baby coming and all. Just thought I'd try and get the room ready. But you kids change things around or do what you like."

I heard Carin sigh. She was quiet, her eyes still scanning the room. She lifted her fingers to her lip, twisted it a little. She nodded. I could see the water in her eyes. She moved her finger up from her lip, discreetly giving her wet cheek a wipe. And then she turned to Dad, nodding some more, with a tiny smile on one side.

"I know you women like your pillows," Dad said, rubbing his chin. "But ... but you feel free to change anything, like I said. Toss the pillows out if you don't like them. Or, you know, we can pick out some other colors. We can go get your things tomorrow. We can take the truck and load up whatever you need from your place. I talked to the boys. Ratchet and Schooner said they'd come, whenever we need to move things out from your mom's."

Dad was rambling.

"But," he said, shaking his head, "when you're ready for that, Carin." He held out his hand toward her as if he were saying "STOP." I think he was trying to slow himself down, realizing maybe he had said too much, too soon.

"I'll leave you two," he said backing up toward the door.

"Give you some time. But let me know what you need," Dad said.

Carin walked toward my dad, who was still standing at the door, and lifted her arms toward him. He was facing me. His hands were by his side as she reached around his neck. Slowly, he lifted his arms, too, and wrapped them around Carin. I could see his grip tighten. Dad looked at me as he held her. His lip quivered. His nose got red. He turned away from me, closed his eyes.

"It's great, Dad," I said, breaking the silence. "Everything looks really good in here. You worked hard, getting all this ready for us."

He pulled away from Carin, keeping one hand on her shoulder. He gave her a pat while looking away, trying to hide his eyes. "Yup, it's gonna be okay," he said to her, nodding. "Things will work out." He gave her one last tap on the shoulder and left the room.

Carin sat on the edge of the bed, smiling at me. "Your dad's a good man," she said. "Like you."

Dad had come around, I guess. It had been six days since I'd told him Carin was pregnant. Each time she came by the house, he'd do little things to show he cared, even though he didn't mention a word about her pregnancy.

Throughout the remaining days of January, we all helped to box up Carin's condo. Her mom had gathered a lot of stuff over the years, and whenever we had spare time, we'd do a little more. Carin had to be out by the thirty-first—she'd paid the rent till then. We took boxes to the Thrift Shop, and Dad and Ratchet filled their trucks, several times, with loads to the dump. Sometimes, as we placed something in a box, Carin would grab it.

"I can't give this away," she'd say, reaching for a small broken elephant. "Mom loved this."

Some days were harder than others for Carin. She'd just start crying, right out of the blue. We could be sitting there, eating dinner, the three of us at the kitchen table, and I'd hear her sniffle, trying to swallow the lump in her throat that seemed to form without warning. Occasionally, we'd still eat in the living room, while watching TV, but mostly, Dad went out of his way to make Carin feel at home. He'd set the table, sometimes even folding three pieces of paper towel neatly into napkins for each place setting. He'd bring home groceries after work, and there was always fruit and vegetables in the bags. She didn't know that Dad had rarely bought fresh produce before she started living with us. Sometimes, out of the blue, he'd say, "Would you kids like a cup of tea?" Lots of things were different now. Dad even got on my case for leaving the toilet seat up.

"Come on, Creigh, you gotta put the seat back down with Carin here now. Women don't like that, guys leaving the seat up. Be considerate!" he said.

I'd watch Dad organize the cushions on the sofa. He even lined up the remote controls on the coffee table, as if that was something that would matter to Carin. He smiled when he came in after work. If he saw Carin doing her schoolwork at the kitchen table, he'd stop to take a look.

"So, watcha workin' on today?" he'd ask, staring down at her textbook. He'd shake his head and say, "You are one smart girl! Isn't she, Creigh?"

Dad and I didn't always pay attention to the small details of our lives but, one night, it occurred to me, he wasn't carrying a pack of smokes in his front pocket. I walked out to the enclosed porch, where Dad sat every single morning and evening to have a few cigarettes. The overflowing ashtray, which had rested in the middle of the old table for as long as I could remember, was not there. I went back into the kitchen, where Dad was standing at the counter, cutting an onion for his new favorite recipe, Pedro's Special. He had music on, humming as he worked.

"Dad," I said. "You aren't smoking anymore?"

He stopped cutting briefly, wiped his eyes with his sleeve. "You just noticed?" he said, laughing. "I figured I needed to stop, since we got a little baby growing in this house." He turned back to the onion, squinting as he continued to make the final few chops.

That evening, after supper, as the three of us were cleaning up the dishes, the song played. It was the Willie Nelson song Dad had repeated over and over that day Mom left. Since that August morning when I was five, it had come on the radio the odd time. Dad always shut it off. This was the first time since that horrible day that he let it play.

"It's good having you around, Carin," Dad suddenly said, as he loaded the dishwasher.

Carin looked at me and smiled. "It's good to be here," she replied.

And the music continued.

We carried on in the kitchen, tidying up together, like we had every day since Carin had moved in. Dad even sang a few of the words, in the same way he did with other songs that played. It seemed, with Carin around, he was more alive. And although this was the first time he'd mentioned that a baby was coming, I realized he had accepted it. Like Schooner, he needed time to process things, I guess.

I'm not sure if it was the fact that Carin was pregnant, or maybe it was something to do with her mom being gone, but Carin worked even harder in everything she did. I didn't think a person could be so driven. Aside from waitressing fulltime, she was bound and determined to finish two full school years, so she could graduate by June, a year earlier than she would have done. I barely worked on the Distance Ed. program at all. I didn't have the same kind of focus when it came to school. Maybe Mrs. Fitzgerald had been right about me. I just felt I had to earn money because of the baby coming along—that's what I figured was important.

On my sixteenth birthday, February 24, there was a knock on our front door, just as we were finishing the cake Carin had made me. Dad went to answer.

"She is, she is," we heard Dad say. "Would you like to come in?"

"Well, I can't stay long, but I do have something to drop off," the familiar voice said.

Carin put down the dish she was washing, wiping her hands on her leggings as she looked at me. I put down the dishtowel and we both headed to the door.

"Happy Birthday, Creighton," Ms. Hay said with a smile. "I hope I'm not intruding. I'm glad I'm not interrupting a big celebration or something. I heard I could find Carin here. And I wanted to wish you a happy birthday as well, of course."

Carin gave Ms. Hay a huge hug. "Yes, I'm here," Carin said.

"I've wanted to come for a while. I planned on going to your mom's service, but then I found out there wasn't going to be one," she said.

"No, Mom didn't want anything. She didn't want me to have to worry about that."

"Come in, Ms. Hay," I interrupted.

"Yes, come in," Dad said, leading her to the kitchen. She took off her black ankle boots and lined them up nicely against the wall, ensuring they were on the plastic mat, so the snow wouldn't melt onto the floor. "Come, sit down!" Dad said. "Can I get you something?" he asked. "Tea, a soft drink maybe?"

I pulled out a chair for her. Ms. Hay sat down. Carin sat next to her.

Dad looked flustered with a teacher in the house. He scrambled around. We had never really had visitors in our home before.

"Water? What can I bring you? Maybe you'd like a piece of Creighton's cake," he continued, as he took her long black coat from her hand.

"I'm fine, actually," Ms. Hay said. "I just had dinner."

I noticed Ms. Hay glance quickly at Carin's small belly.

Ms. Hayworth looked different. Her long hair, which she always tossed loosely into a bun, was cut short. She was wearing jeans and a gray sweatshirt.

"I've been carrying something around, Carin," she said, digging through her black purse. "I wanted to give it to you after I heard about your mom. I just wasn't sure when would be the best time." She handed Carin a small, wrapped box with a card attached. Carin opened it to read. Her eyes watered, like they often did since her mom died. She passed the card to me as she opened the small box. It said:

Carin, the butterfly has great endurance, even though it may seem fragile at times. It represents change, hope, and life. It signals a time of transformation, and its movement reflects the need to transition from where we are now to a new phase of being. Will made you the butterfly for a reason. Please take care. You are stronger than you know. I have no doubt you will do great things,

my girl. Thank you for giving so much to everyone else.
Ms. Hay

I passed the card to Dad. He held it in front of him for a long time. He moved it further away from his eyes, probably thinking, with distance, it would make more sense. He slowly put it down.

"Wow!" Carin said as she pulled a small leather band out of the box.

"It's a bracelet," Ms. Hay said.

In the center of the brown leather band was a silver butterfly.

"It's beautiful," Carin said. "It's very special, Ms. Hay."

"I know it's your birthday, Creighton, but I've carried that little box around for over a month. When I woke up this morning, I remembered the celebration last year, the party Carin gave you. I just decided, this is the day I'm going to make the delivery," Ms. Hay said.

"It's good to see you," I replied. "Are you doing okay?"

"It's been a long road, Creighton. Challenging some-times, in a small town the size of Breton, although there are many good, kind people, so many people wanting to help. I've definitely been a little terrified to let Camille out of my sight, but I'm getting better, as you can see. She's visiting her dad right now, just for an hour."

I knew Carin was wondering the same thing. Ms. Hay said Camille was "visiting" her dad. She must have left the guy in the end.

Carin and Ms. Hay chatted for over an hour in the kitchen, before we met them at the front door to say goodbye. I'd figured they wanted some time alone.

"Carin told me your news," Ms. Hay said, smiling. "I know it will be a challenge, but if there are any two young people who can do this, it's you and Carin."

She also left a bag for us to give to Schooner.

"I know he's the kind of guy who'd wish he'd said goodbye to me," Ms. Hay said. "The last few weeks of school were tough on him. I don't want him living with regret, wishing he'd come in that day to see Camille and me. So just give him this package. That way he knows I'm not upset."

Just as Ms. Hay got to the bottom of the front steps, I called out to her, "Thanks for everything, Ms. Hay. Thanks for all you did."

That night, as Carin and I lay in bed, I wondered whether Ms. Hay talked about Carcass. "Did she say anything about the kidnapping?" I asked.

"No, she didn't," Carin replied. "She just said, 'Everyone is searching for the same thing, Carin. Some just go about finding it in the wrong way.' I knew she was talking about Carcass."

"She told me that once, too, trying to make me feel better about my mom."

I could hear her breathing start to deepen. Carin was asleep.

I got out of bed to grab a drink of water. I could see the lamp on in the living room. Dad was in his recliner, watching TV. I noticed the plastic bag on the kitchen table, the bag Ms. Hay asked us to give to Schooner. I took a sip of water, and then looked inside. It was a dog collar. I could see the name PRAIRIE stamped into the leather. She knew about Schooner's dog. She knew his name. I put the collar back in the bag and left it on the table.

I stood at the doorway of the living room, took another sip of water.

"Creighton," Dad said. "You're still up?"

"Yeah, can't get to sleep," I replied. "Just grabbed some water."

I took another sip, shuffled my feet. Swallowed.

"Dad?" I said, still standing in the doorway. "Why do

you think Mom left? She didn't even say a word."

Dad turned away from me. He used his legs to pull the footrest of his old chair back into the upright position, as if he was done for the night. Leaning forward, his hands still on the armrests, his feet firmly planted on the ground, he paused before replying.

"Creighton," he said, turning toward me, "I've asked myself the same question for eleven years. Guess she needed more, searching for something I couldn't give her, son."

Dad got up, turned off the lamp beside his chair, and then walked toward me. He patted my shoulder.

"I just don't know, son. But I've missed her every day." He continued out the door, down the hallway to his room.

CHAPTER 29

It was only June 30, three weeks before the baby was due, when Carin arrived home from work unexpectedly. She was scheduled to close the diner that night, but felt sick, crampy. When she walked into the house, Dad was at the kitchen table, scratching a lottery ticket. I had just arrived home from the butcher shop, and was emptying the small cooler bag I used to carry my lunch.

"Carin?" I heard Dad say, as I rinsed my container from leftovers in the sink. "You're early."

I dropped the container on the counter, wiped my hands on my jeans, and walked toward her. "You okay?" I asked, kissing her forehead.

"Just not feeling great," she replied, rubbing her back.

Dad was already pulling a chair out for her. "Here, sit

down," he said. "I could make you some tea. Would you like tea?"

Making tea for Carin had become Dad's thing. He asked her often and she had grown to like it.

"Sure," she said. "I don't know, maybe I ate something," Carin turned toward me. "I had a salad at work earlier. It's not sitting right. I feel kinda nauseous."

I was standing behind the chair, rubbing her lower back. She leaned forward, making it easier for me. Dad plugged in the kettle, got the small teapot out, and dropped a teabag into the pot, turning back to watch Carin, keeping an eye on her. I noticed her grab onto the table with one hand.

"Nope! Nope," Dad said, pulling out the plug of the kettle. "We gotta get you to the hospital, my girl. I don't think this has anything to do with a salad you ate."

Dad walked around the table a couple of times, rubbing his hand through his hair, straightening the already straight kitchen chairs.

"You think this is labor?" I asked Carin.

"Yup," Dad said, clapping his hands together as he took a deep, deep breath. "Get her stuff, Creigh—does she have a bag?" Dad's voice was flustered. He spoke fast. His eyes darted all over the kitchen. He rubbed his hands together, and then on his jeans. I squeezed Carin's shoulders. And then I felt her take a deep, deep breath. She held it. She was still.

"Carin?" I said, tilting my head around to look at her. "You okay?"

She finally breathed out. "I don't know. Maybe your dad is right," she said, looking up at me. Her eyes were wide. "I have to stand up."

Carin held onto the table as she lifted her body. "Oh, my God," she said, breathing in deeply, again. "Yeah, I think this might be it."

"Yup! Yup!" Dad said. "We gotta get her to the hospital. Come on, Creigh, get her outside."

Dad ran out to start the truck.

He pulled his pickup forward, maybe three more feet, and left it running. I held her waist and walked Carin through the porch. Dad met us, held open the screen door, and got on the other side of Carin. We both supported her down the cement steps. When we got to the bottom, she stopped moving and stared at her legs.

"Ohhh ..." Carin said. "My water broke, I think."

"It's okay, keep going. We gotta get you to the truck. Keep moving, girl. Keep walking." Dad was pushing her.

"It's okay," I kept telling her. "Just breathe, like the nurse told you."

I was starting to shiver. I hated that every single time I needed courage, I would shake. I could feel the sweat pooling on my lower back. My heart was racing. We weren't ready for this. She had talked about packing a bag, but it was still three weeks away, we hadn't got to any of that yet. We had a bassinet in the bedroom; Ms. Hay had lent it to Carin—that's all we'd picked up so far. We had no car seat, no stroller. We'd planned to take a trip to Fairburn to buy a bunch of baby stuff, but we hadn't—I was still saving. And Carin was so close to finishing her Grade 12 year. She'd worked so hard, using every single bit of free time to complete schoolwork. But she wasn't quite done.

Dad tried to lift her into the truck.

"I can climb in," she said, smiling at him.

I had barely closed my door when Dad started reversing madly out the driveway. The tires spun as he put the truck in gear to go forward. The quiet evening on our small street was disrupted. The hospital was only a few blocks away. Dad sped around each corner, as I held onto Carin.

"Dad," I shouted. "Slow down!" I could hardly keep my

balance while holding onto her. He looked at Carin more than he watched the road.

He pulled right up to the emergency doors, slammed on his brakes, and climbed out of the truck, almost all in the same motion. He ran to the passenger side as I was opening the door.

"Come on, Creigh! We gotta get her in there."

Carin didn't seem to be in as much pain—she even looked at me and laughed a little. I shook my head. Neither of us could believe how fast Dad was moving around.

As I helped Carin out of the truck, he ran to the entrance, grabbed a wheelchair, and ran back toward us, pushing it at full speed. "Here, here," he said, still about ten feet away from us. "Put her in this."

As Carin sat down in the wheelchair, she cramped up again, bending forward, holding her belly. Dad quickly pushed the chair inside.

"We got a girl in labor here," he announced loudly, as we entered the waiting room. "Where should we take her?" he asked the nurse who stood behind the counter, interrupting the conversation she was having with another patient.

"Just have a seat, sir. I'll be right with you," the nurse said calmly.

Dad did a few more circles, rubbing his hands through his hair, occasionally wiping them on his jeans. I massaged Carin's shoulders.

"Okay," Carin said. "I gotta go," she yelped in pain as she tried to straighten her body out in the chair. She was lifting her tummy up, her head back. "I gotta get out of this chair."

The nurse noticed.

"Come on, lady," Dad said sharply. "Get her to the delivery room."

The nurse ignored him, but took hold of the wheelchair handles. She pushed Carin through the glass doors. Dad and I followed. We both stood in the small glass enclosure as the nurse admitted Carin.

"What's your name, dear?" the nurse asked Carin as she took her blood pressure.

"Carin. Carin Reiner," she replied, spelling it out. "It's Car-in," she emphasized.

"Is this your father?" the nurse said, pointing to my dad.

"Kind of," Carin said, smiling. She looked calm again. She didn't seem to be having the same intense pain.

"And your brother?" the nurse asked.

"No, he's the father. The baby's dad," Carin replied, looking at me.

The nurse was writing down some information, when Carin swung her head back in pain again.

"It's okay, darling—take a big, slow breath. I want you to breathe through that pain. We'll get you to a room now. Just b..r..e..a..t..h..e ..." the nurse said in a soothing voice, her hand on Carin's forehead.

"Her water already broke," Dad interrupted.

"Yes, I see that, sir. It's okay, the doctor will be here shortly."

We followed her down the long hallway to the delivery room. Outside the door were three chairs and some vending machines. I held onto Carin's hand as she was pushed inside. I didn't let go.

"Sir," the nurse said, turning back to Dad, who was standing at the door watching us. "You can have a seat on one of the chairs in the waiting area. I will come and chat with you shortly, after I get things organized." Dad nodded, straining his neck around the nurse, trying to get a final glimpse of me and Carin. The nurse walked back toward him and closed the door.

I could see a cart filled with instruments. Gloves, latex gloves. She handed me a blue gown.

"Put this on—it ties at the back. And slip these boots

over your shoes," the nurse said. I watched how she fastened the paper booties over her white running shoes and did the same to mine. She pulled a pair of gloves from the box and tossed them to me, before squeezing her hands into another set. She handed me a mask. She put hers on. I watched how she pinched it at the top of her nose. I did the same. She took the silver loop off Carin's eyebrow and placed it on a tray. She removed the stud from her nose.

It all seemed like a blur after this. Maybe I was in shock, watching the pain Carin went through. I could see Carin's belly. It looked like an alien. The baby was flipping, poking, stretching its way out of that tiny space. The skin of Carin's stomach rolled around in ways I didn't think were possible. She screamed, many times. I'm pretty sure I was ghost white ... sweating ... shaking ... scared to death. The doctor arrived, rushing to suit up, just before the baby poked its little head into the world.

It was 12:15 AM, July 1, when the doctor placed the crying baby on Carin's chest.

"Congratulations," she said. "You have a little girl."

I was stunned, exhausted just from watching. Amazed that such a small being was inside Carin's body for almost nine months.

I leaned in toward the baby, kneeling beside Carin.

"Oh, my," Carin said, smiling. "Look at her, Creigh. Look at her little hands," she said, holding onto her fingers.

The baby was trying to open one eye. The lights were bright. Her screaming slowed down. She was covered in blood, her brown hair wet, sticky. With my fingers, I brushed Carin's sweaty dread knots away from her face and kissed her cheek.

"She's so beautiful," Carin said.

"You did it!" I sighed. "I can't believe how hard that was."

The baby was staring at Carin, its little eyes squinting. The nurse covered the two of them with a fresh sheet.

"I'll clean her up shortly—just let her be on your chest for a while," the nurse said.

"You are so brave," I told Carin.

"And it's July 1," Carin replied weakly. "Things happen for a reason, I guess. She came early for me so she could be born on July 1. Thank you, my little girl," Carin said, nuzzling her face into the baby's cheek.

I nodded. "You'll never think of Canada Day the same way again."

We both stroked her little hands, touching each one of her slender fingers. Her tiny white hospital band around her small wrist said:

"NBF: REINER, Carin (MOTHER)—July 1, 2000 @ 12:15 AM—6lbs.7oz—Breton, BC."

"NBF?" I asked.

"New Born Female, maybe? So, what do you figure we should call her? We had so many boys' names picked out. I can't believe we had a girl," Carin said.

"I know, we were both so sure," I replied. "There was a name I kept thinking of—for a boy, though. But maybe it could still work."

Carin continued to stare at the baby, stroking each part of her face with her finger. She traced her little nose, moved her finger gently around the baby's small lips.

"Maybe Dallas. We could call our little girl Dallas."

Carin looked up.

She nodded. "Dallas," she said. "Hmm. I actually don't mind that. Dallas," she repeated. "It is a boy's name, I guess, but maybe she'll grow up to be a strong and fierce woman."

"Like her mom," I added.

I could see the carved word on my desk in Fairburn. DALLAS. I imagined Schooner carving his name. Maybe he was in Grade 6. He probably got news the family didn't want him anymore, that he'd be sent away to Breton. Was this his final mark? The last time he'd write his real name? It seemed ironic that I was given the same small desk in Grade 7. A sign. The beginning ...

"I was thinking, if you wanted her to have your last name, I'd understand. You know, since you are the last Reiner and all," I said.

Carin shook her head as she moved her finger gently around Dallas's face, tracing her tiny lips. "Maybe a middle name. Although Dallas Reiner doesn't sound very good."

Carin stared at her some more, stroking all of her small parts, thinking.

"Dallas Rein. Dallas Rein Fischer," Carin whispered.

"That's really pretty. Yeah! That's a good name," I said.

"Creigh?" she whispered.

"What's the matter?" I asked.

Just then, the nurse walked back into the delivery room, interrupting Carin's thought. "I'm going to take your baby girl for just a moment," the nurse said. "I'll clean her up and bring her right back."

Carin handed our baby to the nurse, who held open a blanket. She wrapped it around our little girl and left the delivery room.

"There's this tiny part of me that's freaking out right now," Carin continued.

"Being a mom?" I asked.

"I'm not afraid of being a mom. The *strong and fierce* part is what scares me. I wanted to be that woman. Please don't let me become a cleaning lady, like my mom. I used to figure I'd make her really proud. I'd come back to this little town and take care of her, be someone. Funny how everything changes."

"I know," I said. "I knew you had big dreams. You were never meant to stay in Breton."

"She's so beautiful, so sweet—history just repeats, it seems. Even when I figured I'd do it all differently," Carin said.

Dallas was cleaned up and brought back, swaddled tightly in a white blanket. She had a pink knitted toque on her small head. The nurse placed her in my arms. She was fragile. I was afraid to move, break her with my awkwardness.

"Dallas Rein," I said, kissing my baby's cheek. Carin smiled.

"You should get your dad, Creigh—he's probably really anxious out there."

I had been checking on Dad throughout the night, and the nurse gave him the news we'd had a girl. But it was 1:30 AM, and we knew Dad wouldn't go home till he'd seen us all.

I handed Dallas to Carin, relieved. I had no idea how to hold her.

"Well, would you look at that," Dad said, as he walked toward the bed. His chin was quivering, just as it had the night Carin lost her mom. He was trying not to cry, fighting his tears. He laughed and shook his head.

Carin held Dallas toward him. He didn't hesitate, unlike me. He seemed more confident taking a baby into his arms.

"So, this is my little granddaughter," he said, shaking his head. "She looks just like her momma, doesn't she?"

"She does," I said. Now that Dallas was cleaned up, her puffy mop of brown hair wasn't stuck against her head. "Except for her blue eyes," I added.

"Yup, she has your eyes, Creighton, your mother's eyes."

That was the first time Dad had ever talked about Mom that way, like I had a mom.

"They could turn brown," he said. "Babies always have blue eyes—your mom told me that when you were born.

But yours never changed, Creighton. They stayed blue, always looked like your mom's."

After a few minutes, the nurse came in.

"Well, Carin, your room is ready. I'd like to take you down there, try and get the baby feeding soon. Maybe you could both come back in the morning," the nurse said, turning to Dad and me.

"You give us a call, let us know what you need, or if there's something we should pick up," Dad said to Carin, as he handed baby Dallas to the nurse.

"You'll be okay?" I said to Carin, afraid to leave her side. I held onto her hand, kissed it.

"Yes, try and get some sleep. You look a wreck," she laughed.

Lying in bed alone that night, something I hadn't done in six months, a thousand thoughts kept me awake. I tried to imagine Dallas beside our bed, tucked into the bassinet Ms. Hay had loaned us. I thought of Carin, sitting at the kitchen table, rocking the baby with one arm, as she tried to do her schoolwork, getting Grade 12 out of the way, like she desperately wanted to do. What would happen after she graduated? After all, we lived in Breton. I'd basically finished Grade 8. And really, in all my years of schooling,

I had done nothing. I didn't feel like I needed school. Yet, to Carin, it seemed to be everything. I didn't know what pushed her so hard. Maybe, losing her mom, she felt she needed an education, to be independent, able to take care of herself. Or was it her pregnancy, knowing a baby was on its way, that made her determined to get somewhere in life, just like Dad figured she would? I worked at a butcher shop. And that seemed to be enough for me. I didn't need more than that. Carin wasn't supposed to be a Lane Oslo kid. She wasn't like the rest of us.

I got up. I took her card off the dresser and re-read Ms. Hay's words:

Carin, the butterfly has great endurance, even though it may seem fragile at times. It represents change, hope, and life. It signals a time of transformation, and its movement reflects the need to transition from where we are now to a new phase of being. Will made you the butterfly for a reason. Please take care. You are stronger than you know. I have no doubt you will do great things, my girl. Thank you for giving so much to everyone else. Ms. Hay

"You will do great things, my girl," I said to myself.

What did it mean, our baby being born on July 1, the day Carin had hated since she was thirteen? What was the reason?

I thought about Mom, her leaving, what Dad had said: *"Guess she needed more, searching for something I couldn't give her."* I repeated his words over again, in my mind, *"Guess she needed more, searching for something I couldn't give her."*

I could not sleep. It was 6 AM now. Before Dad woke up, I walked to the hospital. I passed the nurses' station.

"Early today?" one of the ladies said. "You must be an excited daddy."

"I am," I replied, continuing to Carin's room.

I quietly pulled a chair close to her bed. She was asleep. I sat beside her, wanting to touch her face, to kiss her, but I knew she would wake up. I waited patiently. Dallas was in the nursery, the lady had said. So that Carin could rest.

It was 7:30 when Carin rolled to her side, peeking with one eye open, obviously feeling my presence.

"You came early," she said, stretching.

"How you feeling?" I asked, taking her hand.

"Not too bad."

"We don't have to do this, Carin." I couldn't wait any longer. I needed to talk to her.

"Do what?" she said, sitting up. I adjusted her pillow.

She looked at me. And then she turned away.

"Can you raise the top of the bed?" she said, pointing to the button on the side.

As the bed was tilting, so she could be in an upright position, I stood up, leaning into her.

"Raise our baby," I said quietly.

"What are you talking about?" she said, rubbing her eyes and yawning again. "What do you mean, raise our baby?"

"I don't want you to feel trapped, like my mom. I don't want you to be stuck in Breton when you're meant to do big things, like Ms. Hay told you."

"Creigh," she said, grabbing my hand. "Stop talking. You're making no sense," she laughed, shaking her head.

The nurse heard us talking. "You're awake? Well, so is your baby. I'll bring her in."

"Just leave it, Creigh—we said we would do this together and we will."

The nurse brought Dallas in. She was tightly wrapped again in a white blanket.

"See how she latches this time—you did well in the night," she said to Carin.

Carin pulled her gown to the side. Dallas's mouth was wide open, searching, like a hungry baby bird. She teased the baby, as the nurse told her to do, touching her nipple against Dallas's small lips.

"Great," the nurse said. "Now in, push it in far."

Dallas attached. The nurse seemed happy. "You've got this. You're a natural," the nurse added.

She left the room. Just the three of us, alone.

"What will you do in Breton when you graduate, Carin? What is there in Breton for you?" I asked.

Carin didn't say anything. She looked down at Dallas, who was contently nursing. She stroked her brown hair to the side.

"You've worked so hard," I continued. "You're almost done, Carin. I don't want you to be unhappy, like Mom. You told me you were scared yesterday."

"Stop!" Carin shouted, starting to cry. "Just stop, Creighton. I'm not going to leave you like your mother did. I would never leave you and Dallas."

I stopped talking for a bit.

"That's exactly my fear. You won't leave. You'll just

be unhappy, thinking about the big things you could have done in this world."

"What about you, Creigh? Why are you so worried about me? Is that what this is about? You're scared, scared to give up your freedom?"

"I don't care about some things the way you do, Carin. I don't need school. I'm good to go to work and come home at the end of the day. I'm not looking for big things."

I finally stopped talking. I'd upset her. I went to the waiting room, paced around. I took a walk outside. It was a beautiful July day. The sun was coming up over the mountains. I decided to go back home. Wait for a bit. Cool off.

When I walked into the kitchen, Dad was pouring his coffee. "Jeez, Creighton, I didn't even realize you were gone. Thought you were still asleep, getting some rest after the night."

"No." I shook my head.

"What's up, son? Everything okay? Were you at the hospital already? Carin okay?" Dad looked worried. He was holding his mug of coffee. His hand was on my shoulder.

"I don't know, Dad," I said, sitting down at the table. He sat across from me. "I'm just wondering if this is the right thing to do. Just thinking of Mom, what you said about her, that she needed more, how she was searching for something you couldn't give her. Just worrying about Carin, that's all. I know she wants more in life."

Dad took a sip of coffee. He got up, nodded. He put his mug on the table, walked down the hallway to his room. I figured it was one of those times; he'd ended the conversation, like he often did, giving me nothing. Instead, he came back with a folded piece of white paper. It was soft, worn, the creases firmly pressed from years of being touched and re-read.

"This is what your mother left when she disappeared early that morning." Dad dropped the note on the table in front of me. He sat back down, sipped his coffee, and held the mug with two hands, looking away as I read the message:

Hey, Babe, I gotta go. It's not you, never think it was you. It's just me. I got so much to figure out, I don't even know where to start. Please love that precious boy of ours. I can't be around him anymore. His constant smile, he's so happy, such a good little guy. I can't give him what he needs. I don't want to make him sad like me. I don't want to keep hurting you. Both of you deserve so much more. Be happy, please be happy. Don't come looking, just let things be. Gracie xoxo

I closed the letter. It almost folded on its own, it had been opened and closed so many times.

Dad looked at me, waiting. Maybe for a conversation he had dreaded since the day she left. But I didn't need to say anything. I had nothing more to ask.

"Carin is a smart girl, Creighton. I mean, that stuff she's learning about, those books she reads ..." Dad said, shaking his head. "She's a good, good girl, Creighton. She's got a solid head on her shoulders, that's for sure. It's a shame this baby came along before she got to use it."

I arrived back at the hospital at 11:30. I was surprised to see Ms. Hayworth sitting in a chair beside Carin's bed. She was holding Dallas, rocking her gently. Carin's face was red, blotchy from crying.

"Ms. Hay."

"I wanted to see this baby of yours," Ms. Hay said. "She's beautiful, Creighton. I love the name. Schooner will be so excited when he hears."

"You okay?" I asked, lifting Carin's hand off the bed.

Carin nodded.

"Lots of different emotions when you have a baby," Ms. Hay said, looking up from Dallas. "Makes you think of things you never considered before, doesn't it?"

"Yeah, that's for sure," I replied.

"Carin and I were talking, Creighton. She told me what you said this morning. You're right, though. You two don't have to do this. It's a big job; I can speak firsthand about that. It's a big decision you two have to make. You have to trust that your little girl will be loved," Ms. Hay continued. "There are so many people looking to love a little girl like Dallas."

I nodded, squeezing Carin's hand.

Carin's eyes watered. I kissed her forehead.

"Only you two will know what's best," Ms. Hay said. "I know you can do it. You would both be responsible parents. But you are so young."

"And Carin is meant to do big things," I said, patting her hand.

Ms. Hay nodded. She gently placed Dallas back in Carin's arms. "I'll leave you two, give you some time. I'm around when you need me. Should get back to Camille—I'm not great about leaving her with a sitter."

As Ms. Hayworth left the room, Carin pulled Dallas close to her face. She sniffled, kissing the baby in between her sobs. I rubbed Carin's leg. I didn't know what else to do.

There was nothing more to say.

CHAPTER 30

I tossed a flat stone into the river. It skipped perfectly ... five rings. Carin threw one after me. "One, two, three ..." she said, sitting down. She looked up at me, her brown eyes filled with sadness.

It was July 4. The evening sun was hot, not a single cloud in the sky. We'd found our own spot, away from the groups of people who gathered close to the bridge. She didn't want to be around anyone, to be recognized and have to make small talk. Behind us was the soft patch of sand, hidden by the cottonwood trees, tucked between the large rocks, the special place it all began, where Dallas came to be.

I crouched down behind Carin, rubbed her back.

"I don't know if I can survive this, Creighton. What did we just do?" she whispered, holding her fingers against her lips.

"I know," I said. I could feel the lump in my throat, my chin quivering, just liked Dad's did when he tried not to cry. "I know."

"What if she ends up with horrible people? What if it's like Schooner and they give her away, decide they can't keep her?" Carin said.

"They'll check all that out. You know they'll be good people. The social worker said they have some great couples who've been waiting for years."

"I feel sick. Maybe it would have been easier if I never saw her at all, if they'd just whisked her away after the birth."

"No." I shook my head. "I'm glad we met her."

I stood up, tossed some more pebbles, the smooth ones from the pile I'd gathered.

Carin put her head between her knees, her bare feet soaking in the cool water. I heard her sniff loudly. She wiped her nose with the bottom of my T-shirt, the blue one she liked to wear. They'd been her maternity clothes for the last two months. I sat down beside her, threw the last few pebbles in. I watched them sink into the deep green water, one after another.

"She'll be crying now, wanting me to feed her. I can see her tiny mouth, searching, turning to the side."

"Don't torture yourself. You know they transitioned her to a bottle before they gave you that shot. They made sure she was feeding well. They were more worried about you, making sure your milk dried up before we left."

"And why? What am I going to do with my life, anyway? What's so important that I couldn't be a mom?" Carin cried harder. She grabbed the sand with her hands and threw it away. "It's so selfish, Creigh. I'm so selfish. Mom was sixteen. She survived. She managed to raise me, somehow."

"Carin! That's what you didn't want, to be your mom, to repeat things."

"Why did we screw that up? Why did we go and mess all that up? I felt like I was finally dealing with things," she shouted, pointing toward the bushes far in the distance. "Since that asshole grandpa of yours ruined me!"

"Okay, don't go there. Don't call him my grandpa ... don't do that," I said.

"Yeah, well, it sucks, Creigh. Things were finally looking up. And then Mom." She grabbed a handful of sand and tossed it. "Now this. And if I go to school, then I leave you, too."

"Carin, look at our class. Why do you think we all ended up in a school like Lane Oslo? Do you want that life for Dallas?"

I stopped talking. Carin's sobs grew louder, uncontrollable.

"And doesn't it bring you any peace, knowing Dallas will have two parents loving her, raising her together?" I asked.

"Jesus, Creigh," Carin shouted. "We *were* two parents. We did love her. I feel like we made a huge mistake. Why didn't you stop me, damn it!" Carin stood up. She grabbed a huge rock with her hands and heaved it into the river.

I reached my arms out to grab her shoulders. "Stop!" I said. "Calm down. You're going to hurt yourself."

Carin pulled away, turning to grab another large rock.

"Don't tell me what to do," she screamed, as she struggled to maneuver the small boulder off the ground. "Argh," she grunted as she pushed it, only a few feet from the shoreline. "You'll never get it. You don't know what it's like—giving birth, then having your baby taken from you."

Carin grabbed at pieces of driftwood, throwing what she could, kicking stones with her bare feet.

"Dallas was my baby, too!" I yelled. "You're going to hurt yourself."

She turned away, picked up an old beer bottle, partially buried in the sand. She held it in her hands, above her head, preparing to throw it with force. Her head was staring up to the sky and she screeched loudly, as if yelling would give her strength.

I grabbed her from behind, pulled her hands down. "STOP!" I said. "Just drop it. You just had a baby, Carin. You can't be doing this right now."

"I know I just had a baby," she said, crumbling to the ground by my feet. "That's the problem, Creighton." Her voice was weak. She had grown tired from her rage. "That's exactly it," she said, almost in a whisper. "And here I am at the river without her."

I crouched down, holding her exhausted body between my legs. She leaned her head on my knee and held onto it tightly. "It's okay," I said, burying my head in her hair. "It's okay."

Carin's voice softened. She cried quietly. I laid her down in the sand, my body cradling hers. I was scared to say anything. Uncomfortably, my hand rested underneath her head. I felt Carin's breathing deepen, like it did when she fell asleep. I could feel the jagged rocks underneath me, poking into my hip. I did not move. I didn't dare disturb the calm. She slept, the shade from the large trees protecting her from the heat of the evening sun. The voices of children in the distance faded. I knew what it looked like by the bridge, because Schooner and I were always the last to go home. The remaining cars, parked along the busy highway, would be leaving now, the crows claiming the remnants of food left behind. I could hear the river, the sound of the current meandering along the shoreline.

I held Carin tightly. My arm was numb.

I thought about Schooner and me walking along the edge of the water, the day we threw rocks, trying to hit the small island in the middle of the river. I remembered his story about the grizzlies he and his friends had seen, neither of which existed.

I remembered my first time hanging out with Ratchet at the river, a cold October afternoon. I could see him lighting his smoke, inhaling that first puff deeply. I could remember him telling me Carin's story.

I re-read Mom's note in my mind, unfolding the softened paper that Dad had worn down with his longing. Why did she have such sadness? A sadness so deep, she had to leave her family behind. I could see her singing in Strasville, her glassy blue eyes, still in pain. I watched her throw back her head, drinking down the small glass of brandy, as the man groped her body. She was still unhealed, broken, allowing a man to treat her badly, probably like her father did ... and her brothers. It's what she was used to."

I thought of Dad, how his eyes were alive with Carin around. I didn't know they had lost their spark until he smiled again. He had lived eleven years thinking about Mom, wondering what he could have done, how he could have made things different, to keep her around.

Carin was waking. Her leg stretched. "Ouch," she said, adjusting herself. "This isn't very comfortable," she mumbled, rolling onto her back.

I leaned over, stroked her hair, pulling it away from her face. The loose strands were stuck, glued to her dried teardrops.

"I love you," I whispered.

"I know you do," she said, staring up at me. "I love you, too. I'm sorry."

"Shh!" I whispered.

"I'm sorry I can't be what you wanted, Creigh," she said with a weakened voice, exhausted from her anger.

"You'll finish up Grade 12, go to university. That's what you're going to do," I said.

We lay quietly, neither of us moving.

"You have that money coming, Carin, that survivor benefit you told me about. I've got some cash saved, too."

"That money is for your truck, Creigh. I'm not taking any money from you," Carin said. "Thinking I should talk to my dad. I know I've only met him a few times. Maybe I could stay there, finish school. There's a university ..."

She turned her body in toward me. I wrapped my arm around her tightly, pulling her close. I couldn't imagine Carin being away from me, a life without her. It's not what I imagined. She was crying. The sobs muffled against my chest. I pulled her off me, gently. Sat up. Unfastened the clasp behind my neck.

"Here," I said, passing her my VENUS necklace from Mom. "You keep this on and when ..."

Carin sat up, too. She interrupted.

"... I look up at Venus, I'll know we're under the same sky. And I will feel close to you," she said, finishing my sentence. Her deep brown eyes stared at me.

"Yeah," I said smiling.

"You're really going to give me your necklace? You said you would never take it off. That's what you told me once."

I shrugged. "I didn't know I would have you to give it to."

I stood in the doorway of my bedroom, staring at the double bed Dad had given me and Carin. Everything looked so bare. The top of her wooden dresser was empty. The piles of textbooks and binders were not in the corner of the room. Beside the bed was her glass, just a small bit of water left. I sat on the edge of the bed, picked it up, turned it around in my fingers. I could see the smudge where her lips had touched it.

I could hear my mom's voice in Strasville, before her last song, "This next one is kinda special to me, so I saved it for the end. It's one of my own. It sorta reminds me of ... well ... my life. It's about searchin' for something. Trying to find some light when darkness keeps following ya around. And regrets of sorts, and not really knowin' how to fix 'em. I guess we're all looking for something. A soft place of some kind, just a soft place to fall, I guess."

I could hear Ms. Hay's voice. "Creighton, we're all searching for the same thing, you know. I guarantee, a day has not gone by without your mom remembering what she left behind. But it's hard to give to others what you haven't received yourself."

We had all been searching for the same thing. Ms. Hay was right. She had taught us what it looked like. She gave us a taste of what it could be.

Carin leaving was different than losing Mom, maybe

because I understood this time. There was something calming about it, like I was freeing her from a pain that one day would have suffocated her. The image of my mom on a rainy day, wrapped tightly in her covers, whimpering quietly, flashed through my head. Carin was doing what she needed to do, knowing I was there, waiting. And Dallas was safe. I could have kept her, raised my little girl alone. The thought had crossed my mind. But then she would have wondered her whole life why her momma left.

I knew there would be emptiness in my life without Carin, but it was a different kind of loneliness, because everything made sense this time.

TWELVE YEARS LATER

I wipe the steamed mirror with the side of my fist, clearing a small space large enough to see my face. I balance my phone on the edge of the porcelain sink. I dry my hand on the towel that is tied around my waist and swipe the screen again:

> "Hey Creigh it's Carin. Hope
> you don't mind me contacting
> you. Been a while hoping to talk,
> catch-up if u r ok to c me
> that is. Will be in Breton next
> week. how bout Barkley's
> July 1?? 7pm? c u then maybe?"

I've re-read her message a hundred times this week. I still feel sick to my stomach.

I lather my face with shaving cream and slide the razor faster than usual across my skin, leaving a nick on my chin. I tear a small corner of toilet paper off the roll and stick it on the blotch of blood, which is annoyingly visible. I step into my jeans and rummage through the drawer. I pull out my favorite T-shirt, hold it against me, then toss it on the bed. I grab the black one instead. I realize I'm shaking. I pull my shirt forward and spray some cologne, the kind she loved. I see her clearly in my mind, as I breathe in the familiar scent. I attempt to grab my brush, and realize how ridiculously sweaty my palms have become. I wipe them on the towel and throw it back on the floor. I haven't had this feeling in twelve years. As I stare into the mirror, I wonder what she will think.

I say it in my head, and then aloud, "Hey, Carin." "Carin! You look great." Nothing sounds right.

I climb into my old truck and realize I forgot my phone on the charger. I race back in, feeling frantic. 6:53. I open the red velvet box I keep in my bedside table. I take out the baby hospital bracelet, as I have done many, many times:

NBF: REINER, Carin (MOTHER)—July 1, 2000 @ 12:15 AM—

6lbs.7oz—Breton, BC.

I shove the tiny band in my pocket. I have imagined this moment over and over since she left. What made her come back now?

I struggle to cross the tightened seatbelt over my chest so the beeping will stop, just when "November Rain" ironically comes on the stereo. Pounding my hand rhythmically on the steering wheel, I see us dancing in Ratchet's shack.

I pull into the parking lot and wonder if she's watching me. I scan the cars, imagining what she drives. I try to walk casually, in case she's looking, but it's hard to look casual when I've thought of this moment for years.

I open the large wooden door of Barkley's Bar & Grill, squinting, as my eyes adjust to the lack of light. I scan the tables, but I don't see her.

"Creighton! Hey, bro, can I get you a beer?" The familiar voice of Marcus breaks my focus, as I wait for my pint of Kokanee and a side of Clam. He slides it over the counter toward me. Then ...

"Hey, you," she says, touching my shoulder from behind. "Oh, my God!" she says, smiling.

"Carin," I say, leaning against the bar, trying to make my shaking less obvious.

I stare at her gentle brown eyes and remember their softness. Her dread knots are gone, and her dark hair flows in waves over her shoulders. She wears dark-rimmed glasses. I can see the small freckles on her fair skin. They aren't hidden anymore. She looks smart, successful; maybe it's the glasses. My eyes move toward her red sundress. There it is, resting on her chest, my charm—Venus.

"You look great, Carin." My voice cracks. "The same. I mean, you look like you always did. Pretty good for twenty-nine!" I say, awkwardly.

"It's so good to see you, Creigh," she says, pulling me in for a hug. "You have no idea!"

I set my beer back on the counter, and hesitantly place my arms around her waist.

"I am finally here," she sighs.

We take the table by the window, where it seems a little more private. I signal to Marcus, and he sends a server our way.

"A Corona, please," I say to the waitress, while turning to Carin. "You still like Corona, right?

"Ha! Corona and lime, still my favorite." She looks around the bar. "So, this is what Barkley's looks like. It's funny how we couldn't wait to get in this place when we were kids. And I never got here till now."

"It's the same, really. Don't think anything's changed since I turned nineteen," I say.

"I guess nothing really changes much in Breton," Carin whispers softly.

There is a silence, but it's not awkward. We look at each other and stop smiling. She twists her lip with her fingers, as she always did. The scars, the repetitive cuts line her wrist.

They are healed now.

I dig for the small hospital band in my pocket, and place it on the table in front of her.

NBF: REINER, Carin (MOTHER)—July 1, 2000 @ 12:15 AM— 6lbs.7oz—Breton, BC.

Carin lifts it to read the fine print. "New Born Female," she whispers. "You kept it."

I hold up my beer, and Carin brings her bottle toward it. "Cheers!" I say, tapping her Corona. "Happy twelfth to our baby girl!"

"Happy birthday, Dallas Rein, wherever you are," Carin says.

"You came back, like you said you would," I say quietly.

"Yes!" she sighs.

I want to ask if she is staying, what her plans are.

"Creighton ..." She pauses, swallows. "Thank you for helping me. Thank you for coming into my life when you did."

I look down at my beer, unsure what to say.

"I wouldn't be okay if it weren't for you. It's taken me twelve years to figure things out, but I understand now," she continues.

I shake my head. "Carin, you'd have been fine, with or without me. There wouldn't have been a baby to complicate things."

"There aren't too many sixteen-year-olds who'd give up everything for someone. I know you wanted our little family. You'd have been so good to us. You gave that up for me. You always said I was the strong one. But it was you, Creighton."

I shake my head, smiling. "So, it was the right thing in the end? We did the right thing?"

"It was the right thing for me, Creighton. I'm a high school counselor now. Sometimes, when these young girls talk to me about their lives, I think, 'I wish they had a Creighton, like I did, to guide them quietly from behind.'"

"I knew you'd do something like that in your life. I didn't doubt you'd get there," I say, shaking my head.

"I have something else to tell you," Carin says.

Waves of butterflies flush through me. I feel a sudden nervousness, worry.

"There's this principal here in Breton, who asked me to come work, said she has a perfect job." Carin laughs.

"Ms. Hay's hiring you?" I say, taking another sip.

I feel myself shivering. Nervous excitement. I cross my legs under the table, making it less noticeable. I want it to be real. Carin, being in my life again, is all I've imagined, what I've hoped for since she left twelve years ago.

"That's great. Ratchet says she's turned the school around. There were a few other principals at the high school after Roland retired ... heard nothing good about any of them. It's a middle school now, Grade 6 to 9."

"Ratchet?" Carin asks. "He's still around?"

"Yeah, his oldest starts Grade 6 there, this September. He's got three now."

"Oh, my God, that's amazing. What about Schooner? Where's he at?"

"Where do you think Schooner's at?" I ask. "Ratch runs the farm now. Schooner's always been his number one guy. Ratchet makes sure of that, you know."

"I've missed this place," Carin says.

I signal to the server for two more beers.

"No regrets?" I ask. "You did okay after we gave her up, I mean?"

"You know, Creigh, there were some bad times. I can't tell you how often I wanted to drop everything and find her, come back to you. But it was something you said. Something Ms. Hay told you, how we're all searching for the same thing."

Carin stops talking. She puts her fingers to her lips, thinking. She looks down at her drink, fiddles with the coaster under her beer.

"And then, it suddenly occurred to me." She looks up. "It's what we gave our little Dallas. She'll never be a lost soul like the rest of us, because she is safe, loved—she is part of something. She belongs to a family."

I turn my glass around and around, pour in some more Clam, wipe the drips with the edge of the small white napkin.

"Ah," I say, looking up at Carin.

"And now, when all these lost kids come see me, wanting help, I understand. It's like Ms. Hay. She knew exactly what we needed, what we were searching for."

I nod my head. "You're as wise as you ever were," I say.

"Sometimes, it's crappy things in life that make us wiser, I guess."

"Yeah. Wonder how Ms. Hay got there?"

"Funny … I've always wondered the same thing," Carin says.

She looks down at her beer. She is quiet for a moment.

"Creigh, I'm sorry I didn't keep in touch." She looks up at me. "I wanted to … I … but I couldn't. I just couldn't figure out how to have both."

"What do you mean, have both?"

"Carrying my past *and* making a change. I didn't know how to do that."

Carin takes a sip of her Corona.

"I had to leave Breton behind in order to move forward. My mom, the assault, our baby …. If you were in my life, it would all have followed me. I don't expect you to understand. I didn't expect you to wait."

"Stop!" I say, shaking my head. "I don't need an explanation, Carin."

"Your mom, Creigh. It all makes sense," she interrupts.

I nod.

"So, you're here now? You're really in Breton to stay?" I change the subject.

"Yeah, I got here last night. I'm renting one of those apartments on Purcell Street. Just kind of dumped my stuff in, set up a mattress on the floor for now. Lots of unpacking to do."

"You know, you were right about Ms. Hay and Carcass. Guess who took him on when he was released from Juvy?"

"No way? She didn't?" Carin says, laughing.

"Yeah, he had to do community service for eight months after his release. Ms. Hay supervised his hours. Carcass had to spend time with Camille. Ms. Hay dragged him to a bunch of baby programs, you know—the library, swimming lessons, a bunch of different activities. Guess she was determined to find the good in him. She wasn't like the others, after all."

"Wow! That's amazing. She is seriously a saint," Carin says.

I look around the bar. It's the same orange and brown carpet. The stonework around the fireplace has been there, probably, since Barkley's opened in the seventies. I remember Mom telling me, when she found out she was pregnant, that she emptied her bottle full of tips to join the parade of trailers at the carnival with Dad. I can see her serving these tables with a phony smile, a deep sadness in her eyes, searching for a way out of Breton, a chance to leave the abuse behind, to get far away from her dad and brothers. She put in her time at Barkley's, like so many Breton girls. Traveling from town to town with the carnival must have seemed like a dream, a ticket out of town. Freedom.

"Should I bring another round?" the young woman asks with a smile.

I look at her eyes. It could have been Carin. This could be her, bringing rounds of drinks, day after day, in the little town of Breton, in the darkness of the bar, with the same clock that hasn't stopped ticking.

"No ... no, thank you, I think we're good," I say.

I leave a large tip on top of the bill.

I open the heavy wooden door and hold it for Carin. It's after nine now, but the light of the summer sky still feels bright in comparison to Barkley's. I place my hand on Carin's hip and guide her through.

She stops. She looks out at the parking lot. We can see the road ahead, lined with large chestnut trees, the same trees that towered over us twelve years ago. She takes a big breath.

"I love the smell of Breton," she says. "Let's walk. I need to make another stop, before I go home."

Dad is sitting in the porch, in the same spot he's sat

in since he bought the house, at the old table resting on the green indoor-outdoor carpet. There are no flats of empty beer cans piled underneath. There's no ashtray, overflowing with old cigarettes. Reading glasses rest on the tip of his nose, as he looks down at the newspaper. His music is playing—Kenny Rogers's "The Gambler."

Carin swings open the door.

"Hey!" she says as Dad looks up.

He tosses his glasses on the table and drops the newspaper, staring. She hesitates, briefly, and then wraps her arms around his neck.

"I'm home!" she says, smiling. "I finally made it."

I stand inside the porch, watching them. I can't help but smile. Dad is shocked. His eyes light up.

"My girl!" he says, laughing. "My girl is back."

"I did what you told me to do. I got out of Breton to become something." He pulls another chair out from under the table.

"Sit," Dad says to Carin. He looks at me, smiling. "Did you know she was coming?"

I shake my head.

I sit on the edge of the built-in bench. I lean my arms on my knees. It doesn't feel real.

"Thank you," Carin says to Dad. "Thanks for helping me so much. With everything."

Dad nods. I wonder what she means. Taking her in, maybe? After her mom died.

"So?" Dad asks. "What did you do with yourself all these years?"

"I'm a high school counselor now," Carin says. "It takes a long time to get there. Took most of my life, actually, learning how to do this job well." She laughs.

"I'll be darned," Dad says. "I knew you'd figure things out on your own."

"It was never on my own."

"Tea?" Dad interrupts. "Can I get you some tea?" He leans on the table and pulls himself up from his chair.

I'm pretty sure Dad had not taken the teapot out of from the back of the cupboard, since the morning Carin left. But he still had it. Waiting, I guess.

The three of us talk in the porch for a while.

"You still make the best tea I've ever tasted," Carin says, pushing back her chair. "It's after eleven. I should go. I have a lot to do tomorrow."

I walk Carin to the front of her apartment building. It's down the hill, just a few blocks away.

"I love Breton in July and August," she says.

"Yeah, we had some good times, didn't we?" I reply.

We stop talking. We stand on the sidewalk in front of the Purcell Street Apartments.

"So, how did you do it?" I ask. "Did you end up living with your dad? Did he help you out with school?"

"No," Carin says. She shakes her head. "He never answered me."

She starts walking toward the front step as she speaks. I follow.

"There was a bit in that survivor benefit. And I did a lot of waitressing."

She stops walking and sits down on the step. She kicks off her flip-flops.

"And I had a guardian angel." She smiles. "Someone who felt I needed saving, I guess."

"Hmm?" I say. "No, someone who got a second chance to do things right, maybe."

"Well," Carin says, picking up her flip-flops. "I gotta get some sleep." She stands up and turns toward me.

"Glad you're back," I say. "Let me know if you need help moving anything. Guess you have my number now. I can drive you to Barkley's to grab your car tomorrow, if you like."

I reach out, touch her shoulder.

"I'll let you know, Creigh." She takes my hand. "I'll be in touch soon," she says, squeezing it.

She turns toward the entrance of the apartment building. She holds her flip-flops in one hand; her small black purse is crossed over her chest. She swings her dark brown hair behind her shoulder and turns back toward me, smiling.

I walk to Barkley's to pick up my truck. I drive to the river. It's 11:30 now, almost midnight.

Sitting on a log at the edge of the water, I toss a smooth stone and listen for the sound of ripples. One ... two ... three ...

It's July 1. The leaves of the cottonwoods are rustling in the breeze behind me. The sound of the river, its calm current meandering through our small town, is peaceful. It's the same night Carin was attacked, back when she was thirteen, in the bushes down the way. It's the same night she gave birth to our baby girl four years later. It's the place I've come every July 1 for twelve years since Carin left.

Each time, I sit on this log. I toss pebble after pebble, searching for the smooth ones, counting the rings. Each time, I wonder if she's thinking about me. Is she looking up at the sky, searching for our Venus? Not my mom. I decided not to worry about her long ago.

I think about Carin.

I reach down to the pile of flat stones I've gathered beside me. I pick up a few—actually, five.

I toss the first one. Schooner. One, two, three. I imagine him asleep in the shack on Ratchet's farm, his dogs probably on his bed beside him.

I throw another for Ratchet. He's in the farmhouse, next to his wife. He's making sure those three kids are safe. He'll look out for them, keep things fair, protect them, treat his wife well.

The third one is for Dad. I toss the stone and listen for the sound of ripples. I imagine him stuffing some cash into an envelope, month after month, year after year, the small bit he can afford. He licks the seal and presses it firmly shut. On his way to work, he pulls up to the red mailbox near the end of our street. He opens the slot and drops it in. He smiles. He is proud.

Ms. Hay was right. We're all searching for the same thing.

Carin is safe, asleep on the mattress that lies on the floor of the Purcell Street Apartments in the little town of Breton. She is home. It doesn't matter anymore if I find

Venus or not. I don't have to wonder whether she'll be back, if she's okay.

Her stone skips. Four rings ...

I hold the last smooth stone. It's mine. I don't know what will happen with me and Carin. After all, I'm just a butcher, working in the same shop since I was fifteen.

I toss it. I'm okay. No more questions. No more wondering and waiting. There's nothing more to figure out. I guess this is it. It's what Mom's still searching for—a soft place to fall.

"Out of suffering have emerged the strongest souls;
the most massive characters are seared with scars."

~ *Kahlil Gibran*

ACKNOWLEDGMENTS

Before Trauma Informed Practice was recognized in education, an energetic and extremely passionate principal hired me. You could never find this man in his office, because he was always with students, somewhere, making them feel valued and important. It was all about *relationship*. Thank you, Rod Giles, for throwing me into challenge after challenge, believing I could do it. It's these early experiences that shaped me as a teacher and counselor. You were the master at creating a sense of belonging for our students.

Thanks to the former James Ross Memorial Pool in Creston, BC. My many years lifeguarding and teaching swimming lessons at this outdoor facility taught me the importance of *relationship*. This was the place many children gravitated to, because they felt cared for by the lifeguards. Rain or shine, there were the dedicated regulars who spent their days at the pool—not because they loved to swim—but because they felt a *sense of belonging*.

Peter Carver of Red Deer Press, I viewed your thoughtful rejection letter as hope. You took the time to provide valuable feedback and I followed it. Thank you for taking a second read (after several rewrites), rather than tossing my manuscript aside, into the pile. You gave me a chance and made sure my story got published, despite the many hurdles caused by a worldwide pandemic. I feel honored that I had the opportunity to work with the most renowned children's editor, in my opinion, before your well-deserved retirement. I am forever grateful.

Penny Hozy, copy editor for Red Deer Press, I appreciate your keen eye for detail. You skillfully reviewed my manuscript while respecting my intent.

Beverley Brenna, I have no doubt you will become the "Godmother" at Red Deer Press over time. I am glad it was you who stepped into Peter's large boots, a final set of sharp eyes to take me across the finish line. I loved that you reviewed my novel through a "teaching" lens.

Luanne Armstrong, a mentor to many. Thanks for

taking me under your wing. The many edits, texts, e-mails, coffees in King Fisher Books, and the constant reassurance throughout this writing journey have been essential in making this book happen.

I appreciate those of you who were available for conversations, questions, advice, and/or early reads of various drafts: Tesse Poznikoff, Josie Fullarton, Danielle Sonntag, Elaine Poznikoff, Charmaine Shortt, Darryl Adams, Haley Hurford, Lori Simpson, and Shelley Livingstone. A special thanks to Michele Jack and Sandra Cheverie, for the many pages of notes to help with edits, and to Hayley Fitzgerald for all of your help with the courtroom scene. Cindy Healey, I'm grateful it was you who read my first draft (how embarrassing). Thanks for always being one step behind, picking up the pieces throughout my career.

My family ...

Mom, for encouraging me to fly high, and for instilling a love of the "lost boys." Thanks for the sixty-five billion reads of this novel, the 5 AM texts, and for never doubting it would happen.

Dad, for giving me drive and determination, and for your wise and insightful feedback.

My children, Kieran and Tess, and stepchildren, Rylee,

Jenna, and Brendan—you've all grown up to be hardworking adults. But most importantly, thank you for being kind.

Tesse Rae, I'm excited you chose teaching as a career, and for loving these kids, too. I have no doubt you will always take care of your crew, making sure they feel connected and loved.

JenQ, my daughter-in-law, thanks for venturing all over town with me, in order to capture the ideal "author shot." Also to Dayle Wiens and *Mackenzie Tori Photography* for the professional support in photo re-formatting.

And finally, to Brad, my husband—every human being needs a safe haven, a soft place to fall. You have always pushed me to be my best. And in all my busyness, you're there at the end of my day, taking care of me, supporting what I do, and loving me.

To all of my former students, especially those of you who offered me a challenge: You kept me on my toes, adding extra gray hairs and wrinkles, but also giving my career such purpose.

Take strength from life's challenges, allowing yourself to become wiser, more empathetic, and kind.

Thank you for this story, Ms. P.

© *Jenna Quyn Photography*

INTERVIEW WITH
TANYA CHRISTENSON

What made you want to tell this story?

I wrote this book because I want kids to understand that, even if you've had little control of your past, you can control your future. You can choose to push through life's obstacles and get to a place you want to be. Negative experiences don't have to ruin you. They aren't a sentence for doom. That pain can help you grow stronger, wiser, more empathetic, if you make the effort to choose a healthy path.

I also want others to see the bigger picture, have greater empathy, take some time to show more care, reach out a little more, even when it seems you are being pushed away. Most kids are so accepting of differences now, but when it comes to challenging behavior, there is much less tolerance.

I know firsthand how frustrating it is to be a student or teacher or EA in a class, when the negative behavior never seems to stop. A lot of students will avoid these kids, sometimes out of fear. It's tough to notice anything else about the student, other than what you see on the outside. Try and look a little more deeply, though. What is the behavior all about? It's communicating something to us, but we have to make the effort to understand it.

The most important characters are young people who have not had anything like a "normal" family life. To what extent do you think that's what has led their going to Lane Oslo?

It's the fact that none of these students were "connected," they had nowhere to "belong," that led to their going to Lane Oslo. Disconnection and lack of relationship is a lonely feeling.

Through their behaviors, (whether it be aggression, violence, impulsivity, lack of self-regulation, detachment, avoidance, need for control, self-harm, lack of motivation, rudeness, etc.), they were communicating their pain. Fortunately, they were sent to Ms. Hay, an empathetic and kind teacher, who understood that there was much more to them than what is seen on the outside. She didn't focus on the behavior; instead, she focused on what was underneath.

Despite being deprived of one parent since he was a five-year-old, Creighton has managed to grow up as a sensitive and aware individual. Why do you think that has happened?

Creighton's own pain has helped him become more sensitive and aware. The fact that he was always trying to figure out his own life, why his mom left, has helped him to be observant. While growing up, his dad didn't talk to him much. He had to process things on his own and make sense of them. He did this by watching others and learning from them.

I also believe Creighton is very much like his dad. Creighton's dad does not initially appear to share these sensitive qualities, until much later in the story, when he begins to heal himself. We eventually learn that he is also an empathetic and aware individual, underneath his hardened exterior. What appeared to be disinterest and a lack of care for Creighton was much more about his own pain from losing Gracie, a woman he loved deeply. Luckily,

Creighton's dad got a second chance to be the man he wanted to be, when Carin moved into their home.

Creighton was also fortunate to be taught by Ms. Hay. Having such a positive and caring role model significantly impacted him. He learned a lot about people and life from Ms. Hay, who brought out the best in him.

On the other hand, Carlos is an unpredictable individual who resists all Ms. Hay's efforts to reach his better nature. Why did you want to include this character in your story?

Carlos is a hugely important character, because he is an example of how easily we dismiss some people. Even the students at Lane Oslo make no effort to understand him, because he makes himself unlikeable right from the start. It isn't until Carlos is taken into Youth Custody, when Creighton reflects and recognizes that he knew nothing about Carlos. He never made an effort to learn. At this point, he feels some empathy, recognizing that Carlos might feel lonely in prison, and he wonders what might have caused him to be so horrible in life. He regrets not looking more deeply.

The second reason that Carlos is such an important

character is to emphasize Ms. Hay's dedication as a teacher. The reality is, regardless of how much one gives, some students will be harder to reach than others. Even though Ms. Hay tries everything, Carlos continues to reject her. However, she is willing to persevere, to learn about what's underneath, what's unseen. I like to believe that, even in her short time with him, Ms. Hay was the one and only person who remained loyal in his life. And even though he did the most horrific thing, taking her baby, Ms. Hay was able to process and understand (with time) what that action was about. He didn't hurt the baby, but he did let Ms. Hay know just how important she was in his life, by taking the very thing that took her away from him.

Finally, Carlos is important because his character shows us the extremes some kids go to, in order to be heard. If Ms. Hay hadn't gone on a maternity leave, she would have had more time to connect with Carlos, and understand what the negative behaviors were all about. We reach the end of the novel, and we still do not know Carlos's story, why he did the things he did. This lack of information was intentional, because a year with Ms. Hay was not enough for this young man; his pain was too great. He is a reminder that if we don't take the time and effort to learn about someone like Carlos, the behaviors will continue.

Carin experiences a lot of challenges in her life: having a father she never sees, a sexual assault at the age of thirteen, the death of her mother, the birth of a child at the age of seventeen, and finally, the decision to give up her baby. How is it that Carin ends up successful, despite the many traumatic events she endures?

Carin is an example of resilience. She is an important character because she proves that, with effort, you can choose to rise above pain and be a survivor. When trauma after trauma hit, Carin took control in a healthy way. She became more determined to succeed, and managed her life so she could get there. Yes, she had some setbacks, like a pregnancy at a young age, but she battled through it all and came out on top. She had a caring adult as her role model, Ms. Hay, someone who believed in her, who never doubted she would make something of her life. She also had Creighton, a steady sense of security, who was always behind her. These gentle supports helped her discover her own strength.

If a stranger walked into Ms. Hay's classroom, it would seem like chaos, not an educational setting. Why would this not be a correct impression?

A stranger observing this classroom would need to do so for a long time, in order to understand the profound and positive impact Ms. Hay was having on her students. For kids who have experienced trauma, it takes time and effort to make them feel safe and secure. Ms. Hay was "the calm" for her students when they arrived, somewhat dysregulated, anxious, angry, etc., as a result of their chaotic lives. She always focused on the students first, not their actions, and she did so peacefully, creating a sense of safety for all of them.

Over time, an observer would learn that there is no quick fix for challenging behaviors. It's about perseverance and truly believing that forming a relationship with a student, and creating a sense of belonging for them, will eventually result in positive change. Ms. Hay wasn't afraid to put in this time, even though on a day-to-day basis, the room may have appeared chaotic.

I created the final chapter (twelve years later), for this purpose, to show that in the end, these kids are all okay. They broke the cycle of trauma in their lives, but it didn't happen overnight. Their time with Ms. Hay, one adult who took the time to connect with them, was a key factor in their long-term survival and success, I'm sure.

Why do you think Creighton decides not to speak to his mom when he has the chance in the Strasville pub?

I think Creighton had imagined meeting his mom many, many times throughout his life. But the fear of rejection was too powerful in the moment. When he saw his mother being groped by a strange man, and the way she poured a glass of brandy down her throat, he sensed that she was still unhealed, dealing with her own pain. This realization was frustrating, since she'd been gone so long. Perhaps, if he didn't have Carin in his life, he would have taken the risk to speak to her. But Carin's presence in his world already made him less insecure and needy for his mother.

Gracie is important in the book, because she doesn't overcome her past experiences and continues to hurt, as far as Creighton can see. He recognizes this. I think he feels some anger when he sees her, too. The fact she is allowing a man to touch her in such a demeaning way bothers him.

You have chosen to use fictitious names for the communities where the story takes place —Fairburn and Breton. Why was that?

I chose fictitious names because this story is everywhere; every community has a Carlos, Carin, Ratchet, Schooner, and Creighton. It's a reminder that these kids are in your class. You may only see the challenging behaviors and be exhausted from them. You may think the student is unlikeable, unfixable. But ... you could be that friend or principal or teacher or educational assistant who makes an effort to look a little deeper. You can give that person your time, and the long-term impact could be life-changing for them.

This is your first novel. What were the challenges you faced as you thought about, and then created, such an ambitious project?

Time has been my greatest challenge. I work fulltime and have a busy life, with a lot of responsibilities. My family is very important to me, and so is my job—I love being a teacher and counselor. So, finding the time to balance everything was always a challenge. These characters became a part of my life for many, many years. They were continually on my mind. Every minute of the day, I thought about them, worried about them, and wondered how they would respond to certain situations. New ideas would suddenly pop into my head, and I would get excited, but I couldn't just stop my life and write when I had one of these brainwaves. I had to be patient and wait until I had an hour or two, and then I would immerse myself in my book. I looked forward to this time every single day.

Another challenge was the fear of working so hard, never to find a publisher. I've always believed that if you want something badly enough, and you put in the effort, you will make it happen. I've taught my own children and students the same thing—to put your mind to something and make it real. So, deep down, I knew I would never give up, and I would get this book published, but many times, I had to be stronger than my own fear. I had to work hard at maintaining hope.

Thank you, Tanya, for your many thoughtful insights into your characters and their story—and into the writing process.